# Influence:

## *Death on the Beach*

*An Influence Novel*

# Influence:
## *Death on the Beach*

*An Influence Novel*

*Carl Weber*

*www.urbanbooks.net*

Urban Books, LLC
300 Farmingdale Road, NY-Route 109
Farmingdale, NY 11735

Influence: Death on the Beach; An Influence Novel

ISBN 13: 978-1-64556-019-7
ISBN 10: 1-64556-019-8

First Hardcover Printing May 2020
Printed in the United States of America

10 9 8 7 6 5 4 3 2 1

Distributed by Kensington Publishing Corp.
Submit orders to:
Customer Service
400 Hahn Road
Westminster, MD 21157-4627
Phone: 1-800-733-3000
Fax: 1-800-659-2436

# Prologue

*Life is good.*

It was the perfect cliché to fit the beautiful view of the sunset on the ocean waves and the feeling of sand between her toes; but then the stirring of her body and the slow fading of the scenery led to the realization that this wasn't real. She drifted between the land of the living and the realm of the dreamers for a few more moments before coming into full consciousness. Still, her eyes remained closed, her body soaking in the peacefulness of a warm bed, cherishing the precious moment of tranquility.

Being Savannah Kirby, an award-winning, platinum-selling music artist, meant that opportunities for peace and serenity were rare. She was determined to enjoy the feeling for as long as possible before total consciousness took over and it was time for her to get up and out of bed. She opened her eyes slowly in an effort to prepare herself for the whopping headache she suspected would arrive at any moment, a result of the heavy drinking she'd indulged in the night before.

"Yesss," she quietly cheered, realizing the absence of the pain in her head and a narrowly escaped hangover. Sitting up in the bed, she stretched her arms as wide as the yawn that came from her mouth as she looked around the spacious master bedroom that she shared with her husband, Academy Award-winning film star and rapper Kyle Kirby. Everything in the room was custom designed and extravagant, from the large chest that held her collection of jewelry to the hand-chiseled headboard, the 70-inch television mounted on the wall, or even the gigantic closet her husband had built just for her. Her favorite things in their room, maybe even the entire home, were the collection of ceramic angels that lined the wall that faced their bed. They were the first thing she'd focus on when she woke up each day. Despite the fact that she wasn't very religious, Savannah knew that being a mega star was a blessing, and she thanked God daily for the amazing life she lived. The angels were, in a way, her own personal altar.

As usual, Kyle remained motionless in bed beside her, still knocked out under the covers. He was such a deep sleeper. It didn't matter what time she went to sleep the night before; she was always awake before he was. Last night, she'd come home drunk and wanting sex, but he hated to be woken up, so she went to sleep frustrated. Now, she thought about playfully hopping onto him, forcing him to wake up, but opted to take a softer approach.

Reaching under the covers, she gently rubbed his back. "You want some breakfast, baby?" she asked, leaning into his ear.

Normally, he would grumble and push her hand away when she tried to wake him, but today he gave her no response.

"Kyle?" Savannah called his name again, this time louder, and nudged his shoulder. Still nothing. She slipped her hand under his T-shirt, and her face folded into a grimace. Her husband would sweat in his sleep at times, especially after a long night in the studio, but the cold dampness of this skin this morning was different. Something was wrong. Very wrong.

"Kyle, what the—"

She pulled her hand back from under the covers and stopped mid-sentence, horror-stricken as she stared at her fingers. What she initially thought was sweat, wasn't that at all. It was blood. Unable to move the lower half of her body, Savannah gripped the covers, slowly pulling them away from Kyle. A high-pitched scream that originated in the pit of her stomach slowly crept upward and made its way through her lips. Her husband's body was completely covered in blood, and now so was Savannah's ivory satin nightgown.

"Kyle, w—what's going on?" she asked. "Is this some sort of a joke? Kyle? Kyle!"

She grabbed his shoulder, struggling as she turned him from his stomach to his side. Her eyes fell on the deep gashes in his back, and her screams filled the room again as she fearfully pushed herself away from Kyle's lifeless body. Her movement was so fast that she fell from the bed with a thud. As she tried to regain her footing, she spotted something on the floor beside her: a bloody knife. Her entire body was shaking, and tears poured from her eyes as she stumbled into the far wall and took in the bloody scene before her.

*Dead*. Kyle was dead. This couldn't be happening. *When? Who? Why?* Savannah willed the events from the night before to come back into her head. She'd gone to a movie premier with her manager, and even though she'd had quite a few drinks, there were no blackout moments. But she must have been more drunk than she thought, or else how could this have happened? She couldn't make sense of it. Was he already dead when she climbed into bed last night? Or, what if it had happened while they were sleeping next to each other?

Her eyes darted around the room. Could someone still be there? Was she in danger?

"Oh my God," Savannah said, the confusion and fear making her queasy. "Think, Savannah, think."

She closed her eyes and tried to focus her thoughts. She'd seen enough movies to know that calling the police wasn't the smartest thing to do first, especially as a black woman. As soon as they arrived, they'd take one look around and assume that she was the killer. There was no way they'd believe that she found him that way when she woke up. The thought of being hand-cuffed and locked away for a crime she didn't commit was just as frightening as the fact that her husband had been murdered in the first place. She wasn't built for prison.

Savannah finally regained as much of her wits as she could and made a move to the nightstand, picking up the red Celine bag she'd carried the night before. She reached inside and pulled out her cell phone, staring at it for a few moments before she scrolled to the contact she was looking for and made a call.

"H–hello?" she croaked out when the call connected. "Please. I–I need your help. *Now*."

# 1

## *Bradley*

"Now, *that's* how you take care of business!"

My daughter Desiree gleefully sang my praises as we stepped triumphantly through the doors of a high-rise building in Manhattan. We bumped fists, the gold Rolex on my wrist sparkling in the sunlight.

We were leaving the offices of a rival law firm. We'd just finished a pre-trial negotiation on behalf of our client, Lisa Randelle. She had been the picture-perfect trophy wife to her high school sweetheart turned millionaire broker and husband. She'd been a full-time mother to their four kids and never worked—his choice, not hers. When her husband told her that he was leaving her for a much younger woman after ten years of marriage, Lisa was blindsided. The divorce papers he tossed in front of her and demanded that she sign were even more of a gut punch. He was offering her a minimal amount of child support and no other assets. Lisa had contacted the Hudson firm, and now she thanked God daily that she did. Not only would she be walking away with their house, but since she hadn't signed a pre-nup, she was entitled to up to fifty percent of everything her husband owned, in addition to his pension, child support, and the alimony that he would be required to pay. Those revelations were enough to prompt him and his attorney to place a generous offer on the table that Lisa was happy with.

"Did you see her soon-to-be ex-husband's face?" Desiree asked.

"I did." I grinned as we headed in the direction of the Rolls Royce parked in front of the building. "He looked like he was gonna shit when he had to add all those zeros. I'm sure he'll be in a better mood when we draw up all the paperwork and it can all be truly over."

"Yeah," Desiree scoffed. "And he can finally be completely with his mistress."

"No. Men like Trevor Randelle will never be able to give themselves to anyone but their own selfish needs. His mistress will be one of many," I said and nodded to my driver, an older man named Freddy, as he opened the back door to the Rolls Royce. "You can count on that."

"And you know this how?" Desiree raised an eyebrow at me.

"Because I'm a man, and I know how men think," I replied matter-of-factly.

My answer was good enough to satisfy Desiree's curiosity. If nothing else, my daughter understood that I was faithful, and I'd never given her or anyone a reason to think otherwise. Still, she seemed relieved by the response to her question.

"Oh, true. I'm glad we were able to help Lisa, though. I couldn't imagine being a single mother of four small children, with no work experience or source of income. How was he expecting her to survive if he didn't provide for his family?"

"I don't think he was considering any of that. Like I said, men like him are selfish. He used her for what he needed, and when he was done, neither she nor his children were his concern. But I agree. I'm glad we were able to help that poor woman. And here I thought this was going to be another one of your charity clients."

I couldn't resist teasing her. I never missed the opportunity to comment about the pro-bono cases my bleeding-heart daughter constantly pursued. Granted, I understand that all law firms, including the one I own, are expected to work a certain number of cases for which there would be no compensation. Not only was it an opportunity to serve the community, but it was also great PR for the firm. The problem was that my daughter oftentimes made such cases a higher priority than big-wig clients that paid for our legal expertise.

She gave me half a smile as we climbed into the back of the car. "Yes, you were wrong, and that selfish bastard even agreed to pay the whopping attorney's fees we'll be sending the bill for. So, way to go, Desiree." She pretended to pat herself on the back.

"Good job," I relented and reached for the phone that vibrated in my pocket. It was a text from my wife, Carla. At the same time, Desiree was pulling her phone from her purse.

"911?" She read the message aloud.

I'd gotten the same message. We looked at one another, our faces mirroring the same look of alarm.

I immediately hit the number and pressed the phone to my ear. My wife answered after one ring.

"Where are you?" Carla asked. "We have a situation."

"I'm just finishing up my meeting downtown. What's going on?"

"I can't talk about it over the phone, but you need to get to the office. We've got a problem that I don't know how to handle."

"Okay, I'm on my way," I told her.

"Everything okay?" Desiree asked.

I was too wrapped up in my own thoughts to respond. Carla not being able to handle a problem was cause enough for me to know that whatever was going on was major. Handling situations was her specialty, and she did so with the precision and tenacity of Olivia Pope on *Scandal*. Her intelligence was matched by her wit, and those traits, along with her charming personality and nurturing spirit were the reasons I not only fell in love with her, but why I stayed in love. Then there was also the fact that she was gorgeous. It helped a little.

"Dad," Desiree repeated, looking concerned. "Is everything okay?"

"I don't know. That's the first time I think I've ever heard Carla say that she can't handle something." I leaned forward. "Hey, Freddy, step on it, will you? We need to get to the office fast."

Freddy nodded back at me through the rearview mirror as he accelerated. The car weaved through heavy traffic so fast that every building we passed seemed to mesh together. My anxiety increased with each passing minute, and although I tried to remain calm for the sake of my blood pressure, it was useless. There was only one thing that would help ease my mind, and that was to get to the office to find out what had my wife so alarmed.

# 2

## *Lamont*

"Goddamn!" The blissful whimper of a woman experiencing a world full of pleasure filled the air.

Teresa moaned as I squeezed her round bottom and pushed deeper inside of her. She opened her mouth to call out again, but my lips on hers prevented any words from escaping. Our tongues intertwined as I rhythmically thrust in and out of her womanhood the way she'd begged me to moments before. Her walls throbbed around my shaft, a clear indication that she was on the verge of climaxing again. On cue, I brought one hand up to her breast and pinched her nipple as hard as I could while continuously stroking her G-spot. Teresa snatched her lips away and buried her head into my neck as she trembled from the power of her orgasm.

"Shhhiiit!" she shouted, following through with more erotic cries.

As I arrived at my own climax soon after, it felt as if my soul left my body right along with the load I shot into the condom. My breathing was shallow as my softening manhood eased from inside of her. Even after I rolled onto my back, it took a few moments for me to recuperate enough to finally be able to sit up. Slipping the condom off, I discreetly checked it for any leaks before tossing it in the trash next to the bed, then returned to Teresa's side.

The sticky perspiration that covered our bodies didn't stop us from cuddling up to each other. I turned to her with a smile and saw that she looked just as content. Her beauty was undeniable. The way her thick black hair sat slightly disheveled over the smooth, golden brown skin of her shoulder did something to me.

The light peeking through the window hit her eyes in a way that made the brown in them brighter and her cheekbones higher. I reached with one finger and stroked her cheek gently.

"You okay?" I asked.

"Yeah," Teresa answered, still slightly breathless. "I'm better than okay, actually. That was really good."

"Good?" Her comment amused me.

Teresa shifted onto her side and placed her hand on my chest. "Yeah, it was good. I had an orgasm. To me, that's good. Way better than expected."

"You weren't expecting to have an orgasm?" I asked, now wondering if I should be insulted. I always took pride in being a skillful and gratifying partner, even more so with Teresa. "Better than expected" was a bit surprising. We'd had sex plenty of times before, and it had always been spectacular. Based on the intensity and number of orgasms she had, I could tell she enjoyed our time together just as much as I did. Why she thought today would've been any different, I wasn't sure.

"I was hopeful, but not confident. But I'm happy to say that you surpassed my expectations. I actually had more than one," Teresa told me.

"You're bullshitting me." I stared at her for a moment, until finally, the corners of her mouth turned up, and the laugh she'd been suppressing escaped. Yeah, she was messing with me.

"Calm down, man. It's always good when we get it in. I don't even know why you go through this whole discussion every time." She sighed.

"Hey, I'm just trying to make sure my partner enjoyed it as much as I did. That's all." I pulled her supple body closer to mine, enjoying the warmth it provided.

"Let me find out you're one of these dudes who needs to hear how good they are in bed in order to feel accomplished. Fine, I'll say it. Yes, Lamont Hudson, it was the best dick I've ever had, and I came more times than I can count. Is that enough ego stroking for you?" Teresa raised an eyebrow.

"Don't act like you weren't enjoying being stroked yourself a few minutes ago," I said, playfully smacking her ass. "So, I take it we're going to be doing this again soon?"

Teresa leaned over and kissed me softly. "Why put off for tomorrow what you can do today? I'm not due back in the office for another two hours."

Her words made my smile broader, and my manhood jumped slightly. *Thank God I brought plenty of condoms*, I thought.

Just as I was about to retrieve one, the loud ringing of a cell phone caused me to pause.

"That's my work phone," Teresa announced as she reached for the iPhone on the nightstand beside her. She glanced at the caller ID before answering the call.

Her tone was pleasant. "This is Teresa."

I waited patiently, noticing the sudden change in her demeanor as she listened. I went to say something to her, but she held up one finger to silence me and shook her head.

"Holy shit! Are you serious? I'll be there as soon as I can," she exclaimed, swinging her legs around and standing up in one swift movement. It was clear that the plans we'd just made were changing and our afternoon of pleasure was over.

"What's up?" I asked.

"Something big just came up at work . I'm going to have to take a rain check on round two."

"Shit happens." I shrugged, curious about what was causing her to rush off, but choosing not to ask anything more about it.

Like me, Teresa was an attorney, but she worked on the other side of the system as a prosecutor for the state. In a sense, I was sleeping with the enemy.

I was determined for her to make good on her rain check offer, so I made a suggestion of my own. "How about we get together Saturday night? I'll cook."

"You cook?" Teresa asked, obviously surprised.

"Like Chef Boyardee. Bring your appetite and condoms."

We shared a laugh before Teresa kissed me again on the lips, and I lustfully watched her stroll across the room to the bathroom. There was something about that woman that just put me in a good mood. I wasn't in the market for a serious relationship, but if I was, Teresa would undoubtedly be a front-runner.

A loud vibration snapped me out of my thoughts, and I realized it was my phone. I located my pants on the floor near the bed and reached into the pocket to take out my cell. There was a message from Carla, the office manager of the firm and my father's wife.

"Shit." I clenched my jaw when I saw that the text simply said 911.

The distress call meant I needed to get to the office as soon as possible. There was no time to waste as I gathered the rest of my clothes and headed in the same direction Teresa had gone. Whether she wanted company or not, I would be joining her in the shower.

It didn't take too long for me to reach the office in my silver 2019 Porsche 911. That vehicle was built for speed, and I loved to push it to its limits. I stepped out of the vehicle and smoothed the wrinkles in my fitted, tailored suit. My timing was perfect, because my father and sister pulled up in the Rolls Royce just as I arrived at the front of the building. I waited for them to catch up.

"Did Carla text you?" I asked Dad.

"Yeah," he answered. "But she didn't want to discuss what was going on over the phone."

"Me either," I said. "This should be fun. Hey, Dez."

"Hey, Lamont. Nice suit." Desiree smirked as she looked me up and down.

"What's wrong with my suit?" I admired my reflection in the nearby window.

"Nothing. Just, why the hell is it so tight?"

"It's not tight. It's fitted. And what's it to you, anyway?"

"You just look more like an Instagram model than a lawyer."

"I could say the same for you," I shot back. "What are you trying to do, seduce men into plea deals?"

"Jerk."

"Stupid."

"You two cut it out, now," Dad commanded while shooting a no-nonsense look at my sister and me as if we were toddlers. "We have things to attend to, remember?"

"Sorry, Daddy," Desiree said.

"She started it," I said with a small smile. I opened the door and motioned dramatically with the other hand. "After you two."

The three of us headed into the building where we were greeted by Keisha, the firm's receptionist, who looked stressed.

"Mr. Hudson, Carla is waiting for you in her office. I'll page her and let her know that you all have arrived."

Dad nodded. "Thank you, Keisha."

We continued past the reception area, then past half a dozen cubicles until we reached the executive wing where my father's office was located. The door was standing open. Inside, Carla sat on the edge of his mahogany desk, staring at a TV on the wall. She was so engrossed by whatever she was watching that she didn't even realize we'd entered until my dad spoke.

"Honey, what's going on?" Dad asked.

Instead of answering, Carla pointed to the screen. We turned our attention to the Asian female news reporter holding a microphone. Behind her was a humongous beach house with police cars and crime scene vehicles parked in front.

"We've been told that the victim was found in his bedroom, here in the home he shared with his wife," the reporter announced.

My eyes went to the bottom of the screen to read the words that scrolled past.

*Breaking News: Actor and rapper Kyle Kirby found murdered in his beachside home.*

"Damn," I said and shook my head. "Kyle Kirby, that's crazy. He was a real talented dude."

"And fine, too," Desiree chimed in. "Real fine."

Dad turned to Carla. "This is sad. But we need to talk about this 911 text that was sent to everyone."

"*This* is why." She motioned toward the TV.

"What do you mean?" Dad frowned.

"She's talking about Kyle being dead." A voice came from behind, and we all turned around.

I instantly tensed at the sight of Billy King, a former client, standing in the doorway. I'd never liked Billy for several reasons. Not only was he a narcissistic know-it-all who didn't know how to shut his mouth and an all-around asshole, but he still hadn't paid the money he owed us for defending his ass a few years ago. The way Billy sauntered in the room let me know that nothing had changed since our last meeting.

"Please tell me this has nothing to do with the 911 text," Dad murmured.

"Good to see you too, Bradley." Billy spoke as if he and Dad were old friends, which they weren't. "How's the best lawyer money can buy? I hope you're ready for a new challenge, because I damn sure got one for you."

"I'm sure." The look on Dad's face showed that he wasn't any happier to see Billy than I was.

"The only challenge you need to be worried about is paying your fucking bill, you deadbeat piece of shit!" I took a few steps toward Billy.

"'Aight, 'aight," Billy said, taking two steps back. "I may owe y'all a few dollars, but you ain't gotta call a brother a deadbeat! Have a little respect."

"You want some respect? Then pay your goddamn bill. We busted our asses to keep your sorry ass out of jail," I snapped.

"Lamont." Desiree put her hand on my shoulder.

"Billy, unless you're here on legitimate business, I suggest you leave," Dad interjected.

"Oh, this is definitely legitimate business, Bradley, and believe me, you don't want me to leave. I done brought y'all a new client who's going to make you more famous than F. Lee Bailey, Johnnie Cochran, and Cellino and Barnes combined," Billy said, then turned to Carla. "Ain't that right, Carla?"

We waited for Carla to confirm whether Billy's claim held any truth. Her only response was the troubled expression she offered along with a simple shrug, giving legitimacy to his words.

"Is he for real?" My brows furrowed.

"Maybe," she finally answered.

"What is he talking about?" The tone of Dad's voice indicated that he'd lost the small amount of patience he was holding onto. I knew if someone didn't give an explanation soon, all hell was going to break loose, and no one wanted that to happen.

Instead of answering his question, Carla walked over to the door that led to the conference room connected to Dad's office and opened it. Dad followed and peeped past her. His eyes widened at whatever he was staring at, but he didn't say anything.

"I told you," Billy bragged with a smug smile.

Making my way over to see for myself, I blinked and slowly sucked in air at the sight before me. Sitting in one of the conference chairs was a woman as familiar as the man's face on the TV behind them. She shivered in the blood-stained nightgown hanging from under her coat. Tears streamed down her face, and it looked as if she'd been through hell and back.

"Dad, what is it?" Desiree asked.

I answered before he got the chance. "It's Savannah. Kyle Kirby's wife."

# 3

## *Bradley*

I was stunned, unable to move while I processed the fact that Savannah was sitting in my conference room, wearing clothing covered in what I presumed was her husband's blood. There was no longer any question about why Carla had texted 911 and also why she hadn't wanted to discuss this over the phone.

The initial shock wore off, and I rushed into the conference room, now in full crisis mode.

"Oh my God, are you all right? Is any of this your blood?" I asked Savannah. I gently grabbed her arms, extending them as I examined them. Savannah shook her head, barely making eye contact. Her eyes quickly shifted from me back down to the floor.

"Okay, that's good," I said, then turned to Desiree and Carla. "Do either of you have any clothes in your offices that will fit her?"

"I think I may have a dress in mine," Desiree spoke up.

"That'll do for now. Take her down to your office and get her cleaned up and changed. Put the clothes she's wearing in a bag, then bring her to my office."

"Got it." Desiree put her arm around Savannah to guide her. "Come on. Right this way."

I turned to my wife and son, who were anxiously waiting for my instruction, and began spitting orders like tobacco into a cup.

"Carla, I want one of your people monitoring the news feed and the internet on this thing twenty-four seven. I don't need anything to sneak up on us. And get Perk down to the crime scene."

"On it. What about him?" Carla motioned toward Billy, who was facing the TV in my office.

"Yeah, what about me?" He grinned. "You know, the guy who brought you the big case."

"Lamont, I need you to put the past in the past where it belongs and take Billy down to your office so you can interview him. I want to know everything he knows about what happened today. Can you do that without breaking his neck?"

"I can try," Lamont grumbled.

"I need you to do more than try," I told him. "Now isn't the time to deal with anything other than the obvious. You understand?"

"I got you, Dad." The nod he gave me was as reassuring as the look on his face.

"Good. I'm holding you to that," I told him.

He walked out of the office with Billy close on his heels, and I collapsed into my executive chair, my jaw clenched tight and the veins in my temple throbbing. I'd been ambushed with possibly the biggest case I'd ever taken on. And I'd handled some big ones.

"Breathe," Carla said as she walked back into the room. I could see the worry on her face as she rubbed my arm, and I knew she was worried about my blood pressure.

"I'm breathing." I exhaled loudly. "I'm just thinking."

"Okay, penny for your thoughts?" Carla faced me.

"Save your money," I replied. "Because the words have yet to find me. Ask me again when we get more information about what's happened."

# 4

## *Detective Steven Barnes*

Before I even arrived at the Kirby house, I was greeted by chaos and commotion. The yellow tape that roped around the outside did nothing to stop the crowd of onlookers with their phones and cameras out, along with the mass media, all hoping to get a glimpse of something they could put on the six o'clock news. I finally found a place to park and climbed out of my car, shaking my head.

"Makes me sick," I said out loud as I slammed my door.

"What? The type of crime scene we're about to investigate?" CSU Investigator Alexis Ransom asked as she got out of the passenger's side.

"That and the fact that these people have no respect for the dead."

"Well, it's not every day that your favorite artist gets murdered in his own home," Ransom stated, sounding a little too fan-girlish for my taste. "Come on. We have a job to do."

We made our way past the officers outside and walked inside the impressive home. I watched Ransom's eyes get big as she looked around. The floor to ceiling windows allowed so much natural sunlight that there wasn't a need to use any light fixtures.

"Damn," she said. "What I would give to live in a place like this. I can't believe I'm in Kyle Kirby's house. *The* Kyle Kirby."

"*Dead* Kyle Kirby," I reminded her. Unlike Ransom, who was looking forward to being assigned the murder case of a celebrity, I wasn't. This case was about to be a huge pain in the ass, and the micromanagement was going to come from everywhere: higher ups, politicians, and any other influencer who felt the need and had the power. And if there was anything I hated, it was being micromanaged. I did my job, and did my job well, and I wasn't looking forward to having every move questioned or dictated.

"Officers!" Debbie, Ransom's assistant, called from the end of the hall when she saw us round the corner. "In here!"

She was standing outside, pointing into what turned out to be the master bedroom. Ransom walked ahead of me and entered first, heading straight for the victim, whose body was lying face down on the bed. The crime scene seemed to be confined to the bed. Dark blood spread out in a pool around the body, but the lack of a splatter pattern indicated that the victim hadn't put up much of a fight.

*Jeez,* I thought. *Poor dude must've been asleep. Was probably dead before he even had a chance to react. I hope he went quick.*

There was a pungent odor in the room, a sign that he'd been dead for several hours. If the body wasn't removed soon, the whole house would be engulfed in funk.

"Debbie, get some pictures, will you?" Ransom instructed as she slowly moved around the bed without taking her eyes off Kyle Kirby. Given her earlier demeanor, I'd expected her to be a little more star struck, but she seemed to no longer care that it was the famous music mogul lying in the pool of blood. She was a true professional.

"Right away, ma'am," Debbie answered and did as she was instructed.

"Whatcha got?" I asked.

"Well, it's obvious that whoever did this climbed on top of him. Probably straddled him to keep him from moving while they plunged the knife into his back." Ransom got closer, removing a pair of gloves from her back pocket and slipping them on. She pulled back the covers on the unoccupied side of the bed.

I could tell by the dip that was still in the sheets and indentation on the pillow that somebody had been sleeping next to him. Probably the wife, who hadn't been located yet. My eyes went to the blood streaks on the comforter and the sheets, and I followed them to the edge of the bed.

"Interesting." Ransom said the words that I was thinking as I stared at the bedside floor.

There were faint bloodstains on the carpet that were barely visible. Then, I spotted it at the same time Ransom did: a bloodied knife.

"Make sure she gets a photo of that before you collect it," I said. "And we need prints off it."

"What you got, Ransom?" A man's voice boomed as he entered the room. "I've got five news vans out there, and the deputy director's up my ass, so it's only a matter of time before the mayor crawls over here too."

"Seven stab wounds of varying depth," Ransom answered Walter Garner, the chief of police. "Most likely done with this." She turned and pointed to the knife on the floor. Next to it, she had placed a folded yellow crime scene card.

"I want prints off of that knife ASAP!" Garner said, and Ransom nodded.

*Here they go with the micromanaging.* I cut my eyes at my boss but didn't say anything.

Garner turned to me. "Do we have an approximate time of death?"

"I'd say sometime between ten and two last night. He was probably sleeping when he was attacked. If I were to guess, I'd say a crime of passion," I answered.

"I want to be updated on everything you find out. This case is a top priority and will remain so until the perpetrator is found. I need a list of suspects on my desk before the end of the day, Barnes. You're the best detective in the department, so I'm counting on you to get this done. Treat this like your life depends on it."

"Hey, that's how I treat all my cases," I told him, hoping he understood that I didn't need a babysitter while I did my job.

"That's why I assigned it to you. I'll be waiting on your call to update me within the hour." Chief Garner turned and walked out.

A couple of other CSU investigators entered the room with a gurney, and Ransom stepped out of the way so that they could get to the bed. With gloved hands, they gently lifted Kyle's body onto the stretcher.

"You know, growing up I had the biggest crush on him. Me and my sorority sisters used to joke about him being our baby daddy. Shit, I still thought he was a fine chunk of man," Ransom said nostalgically.

"I didn't know he was a singer, but I liked him in that *Batman* movie," I said.

"He wasn't a singer," Ransom corrected me. "He was a rapper. Some say the best of all time."

"If you say so. I'm not much for that rap crap. I'm more of a rock 'n roll kind of guy."

"I'm sure you are," she retorted.

I walked over to the shelf on the far wall facing the bed. I held up one of the dozens of ceramic angels. "What's with all the angels? Are these people religious freaks?"

"No, those are collectibles. A lot of black people collect angels. It's a cultural thing. Some even think they bring you luck," Ransom explained.

"Yeah, luck," I scoffed and glanced at Kyle Kirby's dead body being wheeled out of the room.

Glancing out the nearby window, I saw a large man ducking under the crime scene tape. "Well, I'll be damned."

Ransom came up behind me and looked outside. "Who is that?"

I watched as the man placed his sunglasses over his eyes and shook hands with the officers on the scene like he was some sort of celebrity. He was tall, dark, and resembled an action movie star. I didn't know why he was there, but I knew him well enough to know he wasn't there to gawk like the celebrity-watchers in the crowd outside the property.

"You don't know Mr. Perk Simmons?"

"No, but I'd like to. He's fine," Ransom answered with no shame.

"Perk's kind of a local celebrity. He went to school in the city, played a couple years in the NFL until he blew out his knee, then surprisingly, he became a cop." I stepped away from the window.

"He's a cop?" Ransom asked.

"He was. Damn good cop, too, until Bradley Hudson hired him away from the force."

"The lawyer?"

"Yep. Now Perk's a private dick working exclusively for Hudson."

Moments later, he was standing at the entrance to the master bedroom.

I walked up to the door, straightening my posture and puffing out my chest. "Perk Simmons, what are you doing at my crime scene?" I asked.

He glanced at Ransom and then gave the room a once over before motioning for me to walk with him. I excused myself from Ransom, who seemed to be entranced by Perk's presence. He and I stepped out of the room and into a private area overlooking the ocean.

Once we were out of earshot, I gave the young man a hard stare. "Now, I'm gonna ask again. What are you doing here?"

"Savannah Kirby, your victim's wife, is a friend to the firm. I'm just trying to get ahead of this just in case my services are needed," Perk explained.

"Well, if you have any idea on where we can find Mrs. Kirby, we'd like to speak to her. It sure would help in finding out who did this."

"Lieutenant, right hand to God, I've never laid eyes on the woman other than at a concert. I couldn't tell you where she is." Perk sounded sincere.

"Translation, your boss hasn't told you where she is so you wouldn't have to lie to me. But I bet he's seen her and knows exactly where she is."

I wasn't happy with Perk's answer, and I wanted to let him know I was all too aware of the game being played. There was a homicide on my hands. I didn't have time to waste. I wanted some answers, and quickly.

"If you're looking for Savannah, you will have to ask Mr. Hudson," Perk said with a shrug. "And you know Bradley."

"That I do. So cut the shit, Perk. Why are you really here?" My eyes bored into his.

"You wanna talk to Savannah; I wanna see your crime scene. If I arrange for Savannah to come in for an interview, you let me come in, take a few pictures, and look around your crime scene as you process it."

I rubbed my chin while mulling over Perk's offer. The last thing I wanted was Bradley Hudson's henchman to poke his nose around this investigation, but it almost felt like I didn't have a choice. Garner expected a list of suspects, and Savannah Kirby was at the top of my list. I needed to talk to her to get a clearer understanding of what had taken place in their bedroom.

"No promises on arrest," I finally answered. "If the evidence points to her, then she walks out in cuffs."

"I'd expect nothing less," Perk said with a smile then motioned back to the bedroom. "After you."

# 5

## *Lamont*

I'd promised my father that I wouldn't physically assault Billy, but it was a test proving to be harder than I ever imagined. We were in my office, and as he sat across from me at my desk, I wanted nothing more than to knock the cocky bastard's head from his shoulders. He couldn't pay his bill, yet he was sitting before me wearing a silk button up from Fendi's latest collection and had a Rolex on his wrist. Motherfucker had nerve.

As I stared at him, fighting the urge to put my hands on him, Billy looked around at the degrees, awards, sports memorabilia, and family photos hanging on the walls. When he was done scanning the room, he finally focused his attention back to me.

His smile was sly. "It's been a long time, Lamont. You still seeing that fine-ass—"

I slammed my hands down on the desk, unable to contain myself any longer. I'd had enough. The loud thud stopped Billy in mid-sentence but didn't remove the upward curve from his lips.

"Do me a favor while you're here. Let's not pretend that we're still friends, 'cause that ship sailed a long time ago," I warned.

"You're taking this kind of personal, aren't you?"

"Yeah, I'm taking it personal. Real personal. A hundred grand is a lot of money, especially since I'm the one who talked my old man into taking you on as a client in the first place."

Billy sighed. "I told you I was gonna pay you back once the loot starts rolling in from Savannah. I got some big plans for her."

"Looks to me like some of that loot already has started to roll in," I said, looking directly at Billy's watch.

"Oh, this? This was a gift."

"Save it, okay? We gave your trifling ass a payment plan, and you didn't make one payment. Now, we could sue you for the money and win, but that would just make us look petty. Besides, there's one thing that we know that you don't."

"And what's that?" Billy asked, his eyebrow raised curiously.

"You've made a nice life for yourself as a manager, Billy, but you're more street than Hollywood. I know that, and you know that. One day you're going to screw up and really need us. And on that day, you're going to wish you had paid us." I looked Billy straight in the eye, happy to see his smirk fade. "Now, what's your angle with Savannah? You screwing her?"

He sat back and folded his arms defensively. "Nah. She's my client. I'm doing my job, managing her career."

"I'm going to ask you again. Are you sleeping with Savannah?"

"No!" Billy had the nerve to act offended. "Savannah is—was a married woman. You may not think very highly of me, but not even I could do something like that. Too messy."

"You're not getting off that easily," I told him. "How are you involved in this case?"

"I'm not involved with nothing, man. Savannah called me up crying and told me Kyle was dead, so I scooped her up and brought her here. I didn't even go inside the house," he explained.

"So why bring her here?"

"Like you said, I'm more street than Hollywood, and so is Savannah. Everybody knows she's got anger issues after the way she slapped the shit outta Keisha Whitney at the Grammys last year. I'm just trying to protect my meal ticket. I didn't want the cops talking to her before she had a chance to talk to a lawyer, just in case she did it."

"Did she?" I pried.

"I don't know, and I didn't ask. Plausible deniability. Isn't that what y'all called it when you were handling my case?"

"You know what, Billy? For the first time in your life, you may have actually done something smart."

# 6

## *Bradley*

I sat at my desk, lost in thought and thankful to finally be alone. My office was completely quiet. I always did my best thinking in total silence. Flashes of Savannah in her blood-covered nightgown kept coming to the forefront of my mind.

The cell phone ringing in my lap interrupted my thoughts but didn't shock me. I'd been waiting for the call.

I answered the phone. "Talk to me."

"Good news and bad news, boss," Perk, the firm's private investigator, said.

"Hit me with the good news."

"I was able to check out the crime scene. Nothing too gory, but the murder weapon was still at the scene. A knife. Kyle was stabbed seven times in the back, and they say by the way he was laying in the bed, he had to have been 'sleep when it happened."

"Okay, and the bad news?"

"I had to strike a deal with the lieutenant investigating the scene. In exchange for me poking my nose around, the police want an interview with Savannah Kirby." Perk sighed.

"When?" I sat up, slamming my hands on the desk in surprise. I knew we would have to deal with the authorities soon, but not this soon. I'd hoped we'd have at least twenty-four hours.

"At five o'clock this evening. If I could have bought more time, I would have, but that's the best I could do."

I settled back in my chair and took a deep breath, reminding myself that I'd gotten clients out of all sorts of situations in the past. Perhaps not a celebrity murder, but I had proven resourceful time and time again—and this situation would be no different.

With confidence in my voice, I replied, "I understand, Perk. You do what you have to do there. We'll handle the rest from here. Good job."

"Thanks, boss."

The call ended, and when I spun around in my chair, I was met by a pair of awaiting eyes. Savannah stood in front of my desk, wearing a modest long-sleeved dress that Desiree had provided. It didn't fit quite right. The girls were different sizes, so the dress was baggy in some places, but anything was better than what Savannah had shown up in. Her expression was free of all emotion, but I could tell by her intense stare that she was worried.

"Savannah, I'm going to ask you a question, and I need you to answer honestly, no matter how scared you might be, okay?" I spoke slowly.

"If you're going to ask me if I killed my husband, the answer is no, I did not," she said, looking me square in the eyes without blinking. "Who was that on the phone?"

"That was my lead investigator," I said as I checked my watch for the time. "We have four hours to prep you for a police interview. I need you to tell me everything that happened. And don't leave out a thing, because your freedom is at stake."


It turned out that prepping Savannah for her police interrogation wasn't the hard part. Rather, it was getting her to leave my office and meet with the authorities. She was convinced that they were going to arrest her on the spot. It took a good hour before I was able to calm her down enough to get in the car.

Savannah and I rode side by side in the back of the Rolls Royce to get to the police station. The place was swarming with news reporters, cameramen, and paparazzi. Someone must have leaked the news that she would be arriving for questioning.

Savannah's nervousness was obvious from the way her fingers played with the bottom of the conservative dress that she'd changed into. Desiree had curled Savannah's hair and done her makeup to make her look presentable—and to hide all traces that Savannah had been disheveled and covered in her husband's blood earlier that day—but her solemn expression remained. Her head faced the tinted window, but she seemed to be looking at nothing at all behind her dark shades.

I placed a comforting hand on her arm to get her attention. She turned, and I gave her a single nod. "Now, when we get out of the car, I'll do all the talking," I instructed. "I've been doing this a long time, and the press can be your best friend or your worst enemy. It's my job to make them your friends."

Freddy opened the back door for us, and I stepped out first, followed by Savannah. Billy, who was in the front passenger seat, exited the car. Then, he and I did our best to shelter Savannah from the massive crowd of onlookers as we fought our way to the front doors of police headquarters. The flashes of light were blinding, and the barrage of questions would overwhelm even the strongest person.

"Savannah! Did you kill your husband?"

"Savannah, what led to you stabbing your husband to death?"

"Was he cheating?"

"Savannah! What do you have to say to your fans?"

After we'd made our way to the front of the building, I stepped in front of Savannah as if shielding her, tucking my dark sunglasses in the chest pocket of my jacket. I smiled at the reporters as they shouted a cacophony of questions at me. Only when the commotion died down did I begin to speak, making sure my tone was calm and pleasant.

"Ladies and gentlemen, as you can see, Mrs. Savannah Kirby is here during her moment of grief to help the police in any way possible to apprehend the person or persons responsible for her husband's death."

"Savannah, did you kill your husband?" a reporter asked, extending the microphone in her hand.

"Let me remind you, Mrs. Kirby is here of her own free will. She was not brought here in handcuffs, and no warrants have been issued for her arrest. She is here for one reason and one reason only: to help find her husband's killer. Thank you."

I placed an arm around Savannah and ushered her to the entrance. We made our way inside, and all the noise was instantly silenced. We were welcomed by two officers who were waiting to escort us to a designated location.

"It's okay," I assured Savannah, who wore a panicked look on her face.

We followed the officers to a cold interrogation room, and when we arrived, one of them opened the door while the other gestured for us to go inside. Savannah and I entered, while Billy agreed to wait in the lobby.

"Remember. Don't say anything to anyone. Just sit there and be quiet," I reminded him, realizing that I should've accepted Lamont's offer to come with us. He could've kept watch over Billy. The last thing I needed was for him to say anything that would jeopardize her defense.

The doors closed, and I sat beside Savannah at the long, wooden table across from a man and woman who were already seated. I took notice of the video camera pointed in the direction of the table just as I locked eyes with the man. Perk had failed to mention that the person investigating the scene was Lieutenant Barnes. He'd likely omitted it on purpose, not wanting to psych me out before the encounter. It was a well-known fact that Barnes and I had history, some of which wasn't good. Actually, most of it wasn't.

"We appreciate you coming down, Mrs. Kirby. I'm Lieutenant Steve Barnes, and this here is ADA Teresa Graham. She's the lead prosecutor for the Queens District Attorney's Office," Barnes started. "We're just trying to fill in some holes leading up to your husband's death. If you could tell us everything that happened last night, it would be really helpful in apprehending your husband's killer."

"Savannah's here to cooperate anyway that she can, Lieutenant," I said.

"That's great," Teresa said, speaking in a smooth tone. She was a beautiful woman, with a reputation among the local legal community as an independent and successful talent. Many men, from judges to paralegals, and even defendants, were entranced by her beauty. However, she could and would beat them in an intellectual argument and turn down their dinner date request in the same breath. Short story, she knew she was good.

Teresa gave Savannah a sly smile and asked, "Mrs. Kirby, would you like some water, or perhaps some coffee?"

"No, thank you." Savannah shook her head. "I'm fine."

"No problem." Teresa gave her a kind smile. "So, Mrs. Kirby, when was the last time that you saw your husband alive?"

Savannah looked at me, and I gave her another nod before she took off her sunglasses and placed them on the table. Her long eyelashes over her brown eyes commanded the attention of the room, and she looked from Teresa to the lieutenant. At least fifteen seconds passed by before she finally spoke.

"I left the house around seven-thirty last night. Billy K, my manager, and I went out to the premier of *Sister Girls*, the new Gregg Anderson movie, so I could walk the red carpet. . . ." Her voice was soft as she gave her account of the night before, and she stared into the distance as if she were remembering.

*Savannah grinned at her reflection after she put the finishing touches on her makeup. She was standing inside her huge closet in front of the tall mirror at the back, making sure she was on point for the night. She used to have a makeup artist, but after he messed up her look for an important photo shoot, Savannah had started beating her own face. After all, nobody knew how she wanted to look better than she did. That night, she opted for a nice smokey eye and a dark cherry lipstick to match the bottom of her Louboutins and the Celine bag she'd been dying to carry.*

*"Okay, let me hurry up before Billy kills me for taking so long," she said to herself and stepped out of the closet.*

*Before she left the bedroom, she approached a long dresser that she shared with her husband. They kept their favorite colognes, perfumes, and lotions on top. She closed her eyes to choose her scent for the night at random.*

*"Chanel," she said when she opened her eyes and saw the little glass bottle in her hand. "Somehow, I always seem to choose you."*

*She wasn't complaining. Chanel No. 5 was one of her favorite classic scents. She only sprayed her wrists and collar bone, not wanting to overdo it, and left the bedroom. As soon as she stepped into the hallway, she recognized that she wasn't the only one smelling good. The delicious aroma coming from the kitchen made her mouth water instantly and put a pep in her step.*

*"Mmm, mmm, mmm! Momma Kirby, don't nobody fry chicken like you!" Savannah said as she entered the dining room. Her mother-in-law, Cathy Kirby, had a special gift in the kitchen, and anything she cooked was like gold.*

*Savannah had come in just as Cathy was placing her son's plate on the table. Kyle was sitting at the dining room table alone, while Billy sat on the other side of the room, waiting for her. She sneaked up on Kyle and snagged a piece of the still hot fried chicken from his plate.*

*"Hey!" He playfully slapped at her hand.*

*"What?" she protested. "I just wanna put a little something in my stomach before we head out for the night." She took a big bite from the chicken and then put it back on Kyle's plate. It was still steaming hot on her tongue, but she didn't care. The delicious seasoning overpowered the heat, and her taste buds were in heaven. Cathy always put her foot in her soul food, and she knew it. Kyle knew it too, because he was digging into his food with a protective arm around the plate to prevent his wife from taking any more.*

*"You could learn if you'd slow your ass down long enough for me to teach you," Cathy said with a raised eyebrow. "Don't you think it's time that you learned to cook?"*

*"Your son didn't marry me for my cooking," Savannah said, leaning toward Kyle and kissing him on his lips.*

*Cathy shook her head before joining her son at the table.*

*"You ready, superstar?" Billy asked.*

*"Always ready," Savannah said and turned to her husband. "Wish me luck."*

*Billy stood to his feet and gave Kyle a fist bump before going for the front door. Savannah planted another kiss on Kyle's lips before following after Billy.*

"Do you usually go to these things without your husband?" Teresa asked, interrupting Savannah as she recalled the tale aloud.

"No," Savannah answered. "But Billy thought that if I went solo, I might have a chance to pitch myself to Gregg Anderson for his next project."

"So, you went to the premier and then came straight home?" Barnes asked.

"No, Billy and I went to the release party afterward. I told you, I was trying to pitch myself to Gregg."

"How did that work out for you?" Barnes asked.

"Good, actually. He offered me a starring role in his next film."

"Congratulations," Teresa said with a smile. "I'm sure you wanted to share that information with your husband. What time did you leave the party?"

"How the hell should I know?" Savannah said, making a face. "But I know what time I got home."

*The Mercedes-Benz G-wagon pulled back up to her beach-front home. Savannah swung the passenger door open and got out, trying to keep her footing. Balancing was proving to be very hard at that point, and there was no doubt that she was drunk. She swayed and sang to herself as she shut the door and waved one of her hands.*

*"Bye, Billy! I had a really great time," she said then made her way to the house.*

*"You good?" Billy called from the car.*

*"Yesss!" she called back with a giggle.*

*She unlocked the front door and waved one more time to Billy. As usual, he didn't pull off until the door was shut. Stumbling to the alarm system, she set it and saw that the time read 1:15 a.m.*

"So, now you're home?" The lieutenant interrupted her. "Did your husband come and greet you at the door? What did you do next?"

Savannah smacked her lips with a slight attitude before speaking again. "I was drunk, high, and horny. I was trying to decide whether I was going to finish the fried chicken and sweet potato pie in the refrigerator or go down the hall and get busy with my husband."

"So, what did you decide?" Teresa asked.

"I decided that getting some dick was gonna be way better than fried chicken and sweet potato pie."

Teresa nodded her head and wrote something down before looking back up at Savannah. "Please, continue."

*All the lights in the house were turned off, but the moon shone brightly enough so that Savannah could see her way around. She giggled to herself as she staggered into the master bedroom, where Kyle was sound asleep. Staring lustfully at the covered body in her bed, she whispered, "Oh, hell no. You're not sleeping tonight. And I know exactly how to wake you up."*

*She grinned wide as she went to a drawer and removed a silk nightgown before going into the adjoining bathroom. Savannah turned on the faucet of the deep bathtub. While the tub was filling, she stared at herself in the mirror as she slowly undressed. She had always loved seeing herself naked. Her curves were smooth, and her stomach was flat.*

*She smiled at herself and grabbed some makeup wipes from the sink to clean her oily face. Once she was back to her naturally beautiful self, she stepped into the hot water in the tub.*

"So, you took a bath? Then you made love to your husband?"

"Hell no," Savannah said, shaking her head. "My ass fell asleep in the tub."

"You fell asleep in the tub?" Barnes asked, visibly irritated.

"That's what I said, isn't it?"

I put a hand on her arm, trying to signal that she should tone down the attitude.

"That just doesn't make any sense," Barnes said, then glanced over at me as if he expected me to give an explanation, which I didn't.

Savannah took notice and snapped, "I wouldn't expect your old, dusty ass to understand anyway. You probably haven't taken a bath in years. But yeah, we women do that sometimes. There's nothing more relaxing than a hot bath." She turned to Teresa. "You're a woman. Tell him."

"Why don't we all just calm down here for a moment?" I suggested, passing Savannah one of the bottles of water in the middle of the table. Her emotions were getting the best of her, and I needed her to regroup.

She drank from it, her hostility still visible.

I leaned in and whispered, "You're doing fine. Take a few deep breaths and drink some more. There's no rush."

She took a few more gulps and inhaled deeply. After a few moments, she seemed calmer and more receptive to the conversation. The questioning continued.

"So, Mrs. Kirby, when you woke up and finished your bath, what did you do then?"


*Savannah jerked awake and realized her head was leaning on the side of the tub. She must have fallen asleep. For how long, she didn't know, but the steaming hot water was now only lukewarm, and her toes were wrinkled. She finished washing herself up and grabbed a towel so she could step out. She dried off, applied lotion to her body, and slipped into the cool nightgown. Before leaving the bathroom, she let the water in the tub drain out and turned off the light.*

*She walked quietly over to the bed and crawled in beside her husband with a smile on her lips. "Kyle, honey, wake up, baby. Momma's got something for you," she said softly.*

*She nudged his arm to get him to wake up, but he didn't budge. She nudged him again a bit harder, but he was sound asleep. She sighed and plopped down on her pillow, deciding to just call it a night. Maybe she'd get lucky in the morning.*


When Savannah was finally done talking, Teresa and Lieutenant Barnes looked at her with the same frustrated expression. They were silent for a few moments as if they were waiting for Savannah to add more to the story. When she didn't, Teresa cleared her throat.

"What happened to making love to your husband?" she asked.

"Nothing happened, literally. I had every intention of making love to him until I put my head on that pillow. Once I did that, I was out like a light."

"You know what, Mrs. Kirby? I don't believe a word you're saying," Barnes said in a disgusted tone.

"Screw you, then. I don't give a shit," Savannah fired back.

An awkward silence filled the room, and I was the one to speak next. "You didn't believe Matthew Wright either, did you, Lieutenant?"

Barnes jumped to his feet. "You know, I'm getting sick of you bringing that up every time I see you."

Not to be outdone, I hopped up and invaded his space, my face in his. The way we glowered at each other reflected just how much we disliked one another. Had we been in another setting, we might have gone at it.

"What am I supposed to do, forget it? You helped railroad an innocent young man into spending five and a half years of his life in prison," I spat.

"I didn't railroad anybody!" Barnes yelled. "I presented the facts as they were at the time, and you know it."

I stared intensely into his eyes without blinking. "What I know is that an innocent man spent time behind bars because of you!"

"Enough!" Teresa shouted. "You two can have a pissing contest another time. I'm trying to conduct an interview."

We took our seats, but that didn't stop the daggers that we shot at one another.

"Let's get to the point, Mrs. Kirby. When did you realize your husband was dead?" Teresa asked.

"The next morning. I tried to wake him up again, but I . . . I saw the blood. On him, on me. And I tried to turn him over, but he was like a dead weight. Because he was dead, I guess," Savannah replied.

"You gotta be kidding me," Barnes scoffed. "You want us to believe that you slept in the bed with your husband last night and didn't know he was dead?"

"I don't *want* you to believe a damn thing. It's the truth," Savannah insisted. "I was intoxicated. If I could go back and experience that night sober to figure out how this happened, I would."

He continued to berate her, not buying her excuse. "If what you're saying is the truth, why didn't you call the police?"

I leaned in to intervene, but I was too late to stop Savannah from speaking up.

"Because my husband was dead. I've watched enough TV to know that the first suspect is always the wife."

"Mrs. Kirby's manager is an old client," I jumped in. "I tell all of my clients that at the first sign of trouble, their initial act should be to contact me. In this case, Savannah's first call was to her manager, who brought her to me. Now, we've been here for almost two hours. My client has answered all of your questions. She's been as up front and helpful as she can be. If you are not going to charge her, I think it's time we leave."

"One last question, Mrs. Kirby," Teresa said, directing her attention to Savannah. "Did you kill your husband?"

"No. I didn't kill my husband," Savannah told her firmly.

"Okay, you may leave. But we might have more questions. Where can we find you if we're looking?"

"She'll be at her manager's house. But if you have any further questions, please contact me." I pulled out a few business cards and set them on the table before Savannah and I stood to our feet.

It was obvious that Barnes wasn't happy that Savannah was just walking out of there, but there was nothing he could do about it. I gave both him and Teresa a satisfied nod before leading Savannah out of the room. My client wasn't in the clear, but I'd kept my word and made sure she wasn't arrested.

# 7

## *Desiree*

"Girl, black twitter is on fire!" Keisha exclaimed. "Everybody and their brother is talking about Kyle Kirby's death. Did you see that shit Kyle's mom put out there?"

We were at a bar called Lucky's, not too far from the office, during happy hour. The place was buzzing with people chatting, dancing, and drinking. Keisha and I sat at a table off to the side, waiting for Perk to get back to the table with our drinks.

I took out my phone to see exactly what was being said about Kyle Kirby's death. Everybody online was an investigator suddenly, and everyone had a theory about what happened. Some of the things being said about Savannah weren't good, but Cathy Kirby took the cake. While the entire world mourned her son, she let it be known on each and every one of her social media platforms that she truly believed Savannah had killed Kyle. She accused Savannah of being a money hungry bitch and claimed that she was a hussy who had never loved Kyle in the first place.

"Accusing Savannah of killing her son? Yeah, I saw it," I said, shaking my head. "If you were his mother, you'd do the same. But it's definitely not helping Savannah's case."

It had been one of the most hectic days I'd experienced in a while, but there was no denying that it had given me a rush. The whole "who done it" aspect lingering in the air was invigorating, despite the unfortunate circumstances that had caused it. As a Hudson employee, I was trying to remain neutral in the midst of everything going on, but deep down, I knew that if I were in Cathy's shoes, I would have come to the same conclusion. Why else would Savannah have fled the scene of the crime if she wasn't guilty?

"Maybe." Keisha shrugged. "But it's really too early to tell, and too many stones are left unturned. What do you think?"

"Here you ladies are." Perk walked up, balancing two glasses of wine and a bottle of beer. Keisha and I took the wine, and he took a seat beside us.

"Thanks, Perk," Keisha said with a flirtatious stare.

"No problem." Perk turned to me. "So, guess what the hot topic of conversation is at the bar?"

"Let me guess." I pretended to be deep in thought. "Kyle Kirby's murder."

"Ding, ding, ding." He raised his glass.

"You think they're going to arrest Savannah?" Keisha asked, taking a sip of her wine.

"There is no doubt in my mind," Perk stated. "It's not if, but when."

Keisha posed another question. "Aren't you supposed to be innocent until proven guilty? How can they arrest her without evidence?"

"And how long you been black?" I asked with sarcasm.

Perk chuckled, and after taking a swig of his beer, he placed the bottle on the table and excused himself. "Hold tight. I'll be right back."

"Where's he going?" Keisha asked, not even attempting to be subtle as she watched him walk away.

"I don't know. Probably to get another beer."

"So, what's this I hear about him moving into a new place uptown? You two aren't roommates anymore? Or did you move in with him, you little slick bitch?" Keisha batted her eyes at me.

"What are you talking about?" I cringed. Her question had caught me off guard.

"I know you were screwing him while y'all were living together. I mean, how could you not? The man is so fine he's gotta be the definition of the word!" Keisha continued.

"Me and Perk are like brother and sister. We're not dating or having sex. Sleeping with him is like me sleeping with Lamont." I shook my head, hoping my response would dead the conversation about Perk. I'd rather go back to talking about Kyle Kirby.

"No offense, but that's not exactly a nightmare to me, because that's a sexy motherfucker too."

"I think I'm going to be sick."

"Girl, all I'm saying is that they can both get it. Both of them look like they can lay it *down*, okay? They look like they could just put a sister to sleep!" Keisha fell back into her chair and clutched her chest.

I couldn't help but laugh as I shoved her playfully.

"Seriously, though, if I get with him, you're not going to have a problem with it, are you?"

"No, not at all," I said as if it were no big deal.

Keisha giggled. "Are you really telling me you've never even *seen* it?"

"No!" I exclaimed. "And if I did, I wouldn't tell your thirsty ass how big it is."

"Hater," Keisha said, making a face and downing her wine. "I'm gonna go get another glass. You want one?"

"Yeah, please, just one more. Then I'm gonna head back to the office."

"Say no more," Keisha said and was gone.

I picked up my phone and scrolled through Twitter to check out what else the world was saying about the Kirby case. The comments were cringeworthy, and I made a mental note to make sure Savannah was advised to stay off social media until all of this was over. Knowing about her temper, Dad might want to take her phone away entirely. Celebrities are always tweeting reckless things, and Savannah seemed like the type to incriminate herself by responding to these online conspiracy theories. I continued to peruse the #KyleKirbyMurder hashtag, which had quickly become the number one trending topic.

Savannah knows she killed that man. She needs to just go ahead and answer for her sins.

She did it for the insurance money! I heard she hasn't been too booked and busy lately.

Off with Savannah Kirby's head! I hope that bitch gets what she deserves.

The comments went from bad to worse. Some people were making gruesome death threats to Savannah. Savannah's mentions were most likely blowing up with hate mail full of things that no one should have to read.

Before placing the phone back down on the table, I shot a text to my father: Make sure Savannah stays offline. These people are relentless.

"I come bearing gifts!" Keisha's voice rang out as she approached with two more wine glasses in her hand. "You aren't even done with your first one, so you'd better drink up, girl."

I looked down at the glass and noticed that it was still half full. Without hesitation, I threw it back and finished it with one gulp. The smooth and refreshing sensation it caused as it went down made my whole body warm.

"Happy now?" I grabbed my second glass of wine from Keisha's hand.

"Very." Keisha grinned and sat down. "Now, back to you and Perk."

# 8

## *Bradley*

When nightfall came, it seemed too soon—maybe because I wanted more time. After the police interview, Savannah was dropped off with Billy K at his home, and I went back to my office to go over my notes. To my surprise, no one in the press asked me the million-dollar question: did I think Savannah was innocent? I couldn't answer that truthfully even if I wanted to, considering I hadn't yet made up my mind. However, I had already prepared a generic answer that would avoid addressing the question: Savannah was my client, and I would do everything in my power to make sure she was represented correctly.

The office was dim, the only light in the room coming from a tall lamp in the corner. I stood at my desk and poured myself a much-needed glass of liquor. After the day I'd had, it certainly was well earned. Of course, as expected, the media was having a field day with the story, but so far, nothing had escalated, which was a good sign for the case. I strolled over to the window, drink in hand, and stared out at the Brooklyn skyline. The swig of Remy Martin I swallowed left a burning sensation as it made its way down my throat.

I hissed and took another gulp. "Ahhh!"

"Having Happy Hour without me?" Carla said, entering the room and shutting the door behind her.

I whipped around and saw her carrying an iPad, looking both worried and exhausted. The events from the day had taken their toll on more than just me. I looked down at the liquor in my hand and then back at her, shrugging slightly.

"Not at all. This is just something to take the edge off. Today was one of those days." No matter how many high-profile cases

I took on—most of which I'd won—it was always exhausting dealing with determined prosecutors and aggressive cops, all desperate to lock my clients up. It was worse when the client was a celebrity. That led to the general public turning into professional investigators, spewing their conspiracy theories all over the internet.

Carla sighed in agreement. "Tell me about it. We just had a girl covered in blood in our building. That's actually a first for us."

"I was just getting ready to come downstairs and check on you. You ready to go home?" I asked.

"Yeah. I'm just waiting on the girls to finish up their background report on Savannah. How'd the interview at the station go?"

I sighed. "Well, she wasn't arrested, so that's a good thing for now. They're saying she's just a witness, but you can bet your ass she's a suspect. They're holding back something. What did you find out?"

"Right now, public sentiment is mixed. Most people think Savannah did it but are confused about why, especially women. For all accounts and purposes, their relationship was perfect. There were never any cheating scandals, or even hints that Kyle was entertaining the models and video vixens that constantly flocked to him, hoping to catch a rich married celebrity. We can use the public's confusion about motive to our advantage, but if you're right and Savannah and Billy are holding back, I'd sure like to know it sooner than later."

"Yeah, so would I," I said, taking a sip of my drink. "You want one? You sure look like you could use it."

"No thanks," Carla answered and leaned against my desk.

I studied her as she removed one of her heels and massaged the bottom of her foot, cocking her head to the side.

"What's wrong?" I asked.

"These heels are killing me, and it feels as if I've been on my feet all day," Carla whined. "I can't wait to get home and into something more comfortable."

"Oh, I can't wait for you to slip into something more comfortable either," I said seductively with a devilish grin.

Carla shook her head and wagged a finger at me. "Oh, no you don't. Not tonight, baby. If my feet are aching, that means the rest of my body is aching too. Don't start getting any ideas, Bradley Hudson."

"The only idea racing through my head is to make my wife feel better. Come here."

I set my drink down and lifted Carla onto the edge of my massive desk so that she was perched comfortably. I slipped off her other heel, letting it fall to the ground before massaging her feet like a professional masseuse. Her soft feet seemed so tiny in my hands.

Carla closed her eyes as she savored the moment, purring as I applied pressure with my thumbs. "Damn, I almost forgot how good you were at this," she breathed.

"Woman, I am a man of many talents, especially when it comes to my wife. I guess I'll have to keep reminding you of that."

"No, you won't."

"Don't worry. I don't mind it." I grinned.

"Well, in that case, remind me, baby."

A soft moan escaped her lips when my hands made their way up her calves. She relaxed as my hands moved up farther, pushing her skirt up and revealing the top of her garter. I smiled, suddenly turned on. It was mind boggling how the simplest sight could be so sexy.

"How do you feel now?" I asked.

"Like we need to lock the door," she whispered.

I picked up the remote control that controlled many things in my office, including the lock on the door. I pressed a button, listening to the door latch with a faint clicking sound.

I tossed the device to the side, then looked lustfully at my wife. She was still the most beautiful woman I'd ever laid eyes on, and not a day went by that I didn't feel blessed to have her by my side.

She began to unbutton the top of her blouse, giving me a show before reaching and loosening my tie. "Take this off," she urged, her fingers fumbling with the buttons on my shirt.

I was still in great shape for a man my age and had the body to show for it. My shirt fell open, and I proudly flexed my muscles for her.

"Bradley Hudson, you are one sexy man." Carla wrapped her arms around my neck.

"Says the woman who didn't even want me to give her a foot rub," I reminded her.

"That was then, this is now. Living in the past is so overrated. Come here."

She pulled me to her, and our lips locked passionately as my hands roamed her body. Moaning into my mouth, Carla opened her legs wider, allowing me greater access to my final destination. She pulled away and gave me a sneaky smile as her hands pushed the back of my head down gently.

I didn't need to be told what she needed. I knew exactly what to do. Placing my hands on the back of her knees, I forced her down on the desk with her legs in the air. She squirmed under me in anticipation as I placed soft, sensual kisses on her inner thighs. Just as I was about to use my teeth to slide her panties to the side, there was a knock at the door.

"No! Don't stop," Carla begged when she felt me hesitate. "It can wait."

I was prepared to ignore whoever was on the opposite side of the door and go back to pleasing my wife, but a second knock came, more insistent this time. I sighed and stood to my feet while Carla sat up. Whoever it was had better have some seriously important information.

I buttoned my shirt as I walked over to the door, unlocking it and cracking it open. "This better be important!"

Perk stood in the doorway, a sheepish grin on his face. "Uh, sorry, boss. I didn't mean to interrupt, but we've got a problem."

"What kind of problem?" Carla said from behind me. She was already fully clothed and had even slid back into her uncomfortable heels.

I opened the door wider and stepped out of the way so that Perk could come into the room. I didn't much like the sound of his voice, and it sent an unsettling feeling down to my stomach.

"I just bumped into a new contact that works at the crime lab," Perk said. "While we were talking, he got a call verifying that Savannah's prints are all over the murder weapon."

"The knife?" I asked.

"Yeah."

"Damn it. You know what that means, don't you?" Carla said.

Before I could respond, my cell phone rang. I answered.

"Bradley!" Savannah sounded panicked. "Bradley! The police are outside! Th–they came out of nowhere."

I spoke in a fatherly tone. "I need you to calm down for a moment and listen to me, Savannah. What I'm about to say is very important. You are about to be arrested. Do you understand what I'm saying?"

"Arrested? I can't go to jail, Bradley. I don't want to go to jail! I did not kill my husband!"

"I know you don't want to go, but right now, you don't have a choice. We are going to get all of this ironed out. It will be okay, do you understand?"

"Yes."

"Do not say anything to anyone but me or one of my team. Not *one word*."

"Okay."

"Good. Now, my plan is to get you in front of a judge as soon as possible. Unfortunately, that probably won't be until tomorrow morning. In the meantime, do not resist. Do not put up a fight. I want you to completely comply. Do you understand?"

"Yes, but I'm scared," Savannah said tearfully.

"I know you are, but I still need you to comply. That's very important," I stressed.

"Okay," Savannah said sadly and then spoke to someone in the background. "You can let them in, Billy. Here. Take my phone."

I listened to the movement on the other end of the phone. After some rustling, I could faintly hear a different voice, most likely a cop, reading off Savannah's Miranda rights. I could only imagine the thoughts going on in her head, and I hoped she kept her cool.

After a few minutes had gone by, a man's voice spoke into the phone. "Bradley?"

"Billy?" I asked, recognizing the voice.

"Yeah. They have her. She's in the back of the squad car. She's too beautiful to look this miserable, man. This is not a good look for her career. Please tell me that you have a plan."

"We can't do anything right now but wait until the morning. Keep me posted on anything you may hear. Got it?"

"Got it," Billy said.

"And Billy . . ."

"Yeah?"

"Remember what I told you earlier. Do not say anything to anyone. *Nobody*." My tone was aggressive since I knew how foolish Billy could be. He needed this advice drilled into his head.

"I got it, Bradley. Damn," Billy huffed before ending the call.

The hammer had finally come down, and I knew exactly what the police had been holding back—the murder weapon. That asshole Barnes hadn't mentioned anything about it during the interrogation, and that had been a smart strategy. I felt blind-sided, and I would have to think quickly.

At least having Desiree keep the nightgown at the office had worked in our favor. If Savannah or Billy had turned it in to the police, there would have been no doubt in the public's or the police's minds that Savannah was responsible for her husband's death. I, on the other hand, still wasn't sold on it.

"So, what now?" Perk asked.

I turned and looked him in the eye. "Now that we're getting a better idea of what we're up against, we can start building a defense for our client."

# 9

## *Savannah*

*How the hell did I end up here? Yesterday, I was riding the wave of mega success, being offered the lead in a movie by the biggest producer in cinema. And now, my husband is dead, and here I am in the back of a police car facing murder charges.*

The handcuffs on my wrists were way too tight. I tried telling that to the arresting officer as she was putting them on me, but the bitch just smirked and put them tighter. It was true: the police didn't give a damn about money or fame. I swear, it seemed as if they were excited and getting some kind of sadistic pleasure as they forced me into the back seat of the nasty-ass cruiser. While I was horrified, those uniformed bastards were getting some kind of cheap thrill.

*Fuck the police.*

My reflection in the window mirrored exactly how I felt: sad, defeated, and embarrassed. I swallowed the big lump in the back of my throat as tears fell from my eyes. All I could think about was Kyle. He was the only person who always knew exactly what to say to make me feel better, no matter what was happening. I needed him now more than ever. But my husband was dead. The thought that he was never coming back made me cry harder. I'd lost the love of my life, and now I was being accused of killing him.

I hadn't even noticed we'd reached the jail until the car door opened and a hand reached inside to assist me out. I looked up and recognized that it was Lieutenant Barnes, the same asshole from the interrogation interview. He seemed as happy to see me as I was to see him. Neither one of us said anything; we just glared at each other.

The crowd of reporters and photographers that had greeted me the first time I was there seemed to be even bigger. As soon as they spotted me, they didn't hesitate to thrust their microphones in my face and bombard me with questions.

"Did you think you would get away with it, Savannah?"

"What will become of your career, Mrs. Kirby?"

I kept my head down as I was escorted into the building. My pride wouldn't allow me to look up at any of their flashing cameras, nor would I allow the world to see the tears on my face. The entire ordeal was humiliating. Thankfully, my long hair fell over my face enough to shield me until we were inside.

The next fifteen minutes of my life seemed to be straight out of an episode of *Law & Order*. I was fingerprinted, then given a mug shot card to hold up as they took my photo. So much for the image I had carefully crafted throughout my career. Within hours, my mugshot would be available for the whole world to see, and I knew the blogs were going to have a field day. I could see the headlines already: GLAMOROUS SAVANNAH KIRBY NOW DISHEVELED, TEARY-EYED, AND LOCKED BEHIND BARS. If the mugshot weren't bad enough, I was horrified when they strip-searched me and then issued an orange jumpsuit.

"Home sweet home, darling," a deputy said, pointing inside my new cell.

I opened my mouth to complain, but Bradley's voice rang in the back of my head, telling me to comply and not say a word. The loud clanging of the door closing behind me caused me to jump. I turned, my eyes locking with those of the deputy, who didn't say another word before retreating down the long corridor back to wherever he was going.

I glanced around the small cell. I don't know what was nastier: the toilet or the cot. Both looked as if they'd never been cleaned. I sucked in a breath and did the only thing I could think to do: I dropped to my knees and began to pray.

After an hour-long, tearful conversation with God, I scooted to a far wall in the cell and leaned against it. I was exhausted mentally, physically, and emotionally, and huddling in the corner of the tiny room felt more sanitary than anywhere else. I finally drifted off, but it felt like only a moment had passed when I heard my name being called.

"Mrs. Kirby?"

The deep voice sounded like a distant echo in what I thought was a nightmare. My eyes remained closed.

"Mrs. Kirby," the voice called again. I felt a hand on my shoulder, pushing gently.

I woke up, blinking repeatedly as I focused on someone standing in front of me. It wasn't a nightmare. I really was sitting in jail, and the person waking me was a deputy with his hand outstretched to me. I was hesitant at first, but after a few seconds, I allowed him to help me to my feet.

"It's time for court, Mrs. Kirby," he said and gestured for me to exit the cell.

I was still in shock and couldn't think clearly. There was no way I could go to court yet. My voice was hoarse from my night of crying, and more importantly, I hadn't spoken to Billy or my lawyer. Now I was expected to go and stand in front of a judge? How? Would the Hudsons be there?

"But . . . ?" I whispered as my wrists were cuffed and ankles were shackled. I'm not sure whether the deputy was ignoring me, or he just didn't hear me, but his only response was to guide me by the arm.

As we walked, Kyle's face popped in my mind. I bit back tears, caused by the ache of missing my husband and the fearful knowledge that my fate was now in the hands of the justice system. It was too much. I couldn't even mourn properly. Instead of being arrested, I should've been making sure Kyle had a proper funeral. His affairs needed to be handled, and as his wife, that was my job. It's what Kyle would've wanted. I had to get out of there, and I prayed that Bradley Hudson would make good on his promise to not let that happen. If he didn't, Kyle's life wouldn't be the only one that was over. Mine would be too.

# 10

## *Bradley*

Marvin Gaye's voice crooned softly in the background as the Rolls Royce moved through Brooklyn traffic. The morning had finally come, and I was hoping that Savannah had held up all right after spending the night in jail. If I'd had it my way, she wouldn't have ever seen the inside of a jail cell, but that wasn't the way the law worked.

The Rolls Royce came to a stop in front of a restaurant. I slowly smoothed down my tie and focused on the person sitting beside me, looking a bit nervous.

"I told you this from the beginning. Working for me is like pledging a prestigious fraternity," I explained. "You're going to have late nights, sometimes no sleep at all, and you'll spend most of your time in the library. By the time you get home every night, you'll feel as though you've been hazed."

The door opened, and Freddy stood out of the way so that we could step out.

Michael nodded. "That's not a problem for me, sir."

"You've been at the firm long enough to learn how I run things, but this case is going to be different—*way* different," I continued as we walked toward the diner. "High profile cases are a totally different beast, but not a beast that can't be conquered. Keep your eyes and ears open at all times."

"I'm up for the challenge," Mike reassured me.

"You'd better be. Now, let's put that Harvard education of yours to work."

I opened the door to the diner and walked through with Mike close behind me. The aroma of food on the griddle and coffee in the brewer made its way to my nostrils. I scanned the dining room, spotting the men I was looking for, and made my way over to their table.

Howie Goldstein, a Jewish man in his sixties, and Snow, a rough-looking musician, were sitting off to the side, enjoying their breakfast. Upon seeing me, the men stood up to greet me. After all introductions were out of the way, Michael and I sat and joined them.

"You two hungry?" Howie asked once we were all situated.

"No, we've just eaten," I said, declining the offer.

"No worries. I really appreciate you for taking on Savannah's case, Bradley," Howie said. "Maybe I'm just old and gullible, but I just really don't think she's capable of killing someone."

"That's good to hear, Howie. But for the record, I haven't completely come on board yet, and as her former manager and the man that ran her record label, I was hoping you could help me with that decision."

"Anything I can do to help, I will."

"Good, then let's not beat around the bush. Why is a five-time Grammy award-winning singer, married to a mega motion picture star, having trouble scraping up enough money to pay my retainer? What is it that I'm missing?"

Howie glanced over at Snow before leaning back in his seat. He adjusted his yarmulke with a look of concern on his face.

"Why is everybody acting like there's some big secret?" I asked. "Was Kyle abusive?"

"Hell no," Snow chimed in. "I'm the one who introduced them. If that was the case, I'd have killed him myself."

"So, then what's the problem?"

"Well, see . . ." Howie started, seeming to struggle with finding the right words. "Savannah has an addiction. A very serious addiction that we've been hiding for years."

Those words were the exact opposite of what I had hoped to hear. Savannah having an addiction would make her case even harder to defend and damn sure wouldn't help prove her innocence.

"Drugs? Or alcohol?" I asked.

They both hesitated for a moment, glancing at each other as if neither could even utter the words.

"Shoppin'," Snow finally answered when Howie didn't.

I smirked. "Shopping? If that's the case, my daughter has the same addiction." Hell, every woman in the world had a shopping addiction as far as I was concerned. "And so does my wife."

Snow shook his head. "Not like this, she don't."

"Bradley, Savannah has oniomania," Howie told him.

"Excuse my ignorance, but what the heck is that?"

Mike, the young Harvard-educated junior associate I'd recently taken under my wing, spoke up now. "Oniomania, or CBD as it's more commonly called, stands for Compulsive Buying Disorder. It's an addiction to shopping. CBD has been known to completely wipe out families financially."

"Smart young man you have here, Bradley," Howie said.

"Yes, he is." I nodded my approval and slowly began processing the information at hand. "So, if she has CBD, then why haven't I heard about it? She hasn't filed for bankruptcy or anything."

"Because she had me, then Kyle, to bail her out and cover it up. It's an insatiable obsession. People think it's bullshit, just an excuse used by bored housewives to justify their exorbitant credit card bills, but it ruins lives and relationships," Howie explained. "When they got married, Kyle had to pay off nearly two million in credit card debt. After that, he wouldn't let her anywhere near his finances. And she fired me for telling him about her disorder."

"Hence the dirtbag Billy K managing her career," Snow scoffed.

I stroked my chin as I contemplated the situation. "Mm-hmm. Now it's all starting to make sense."

# 11

## *Lamont*

Queens County Courthouse was swarming with news reporters and paparazzi. Carla held firmly onto my arm as we headed toward the entrance, ignoring all the questions being yelled in our direction. I opted for a black fitted suit for my courtroom attire, along with a pair of Louboutin dress shoes and the darkest shades that I owned. I knew I would be on camera, so I wanted to make sure I looked good.

"It's like a madhouse out here," Carla said incredulously.

"Just people trying to keep up with the current big story. Next week it will be something else," I told her and pointed to the stairs that led to the entrance. "Come on. We need to go this way."

We hadn't even taken two steps when Billy K stepped in front of us. He was clearly equally concerned with his on-camera appearance, because he was also dressed in a suit and looked as if he'd just stepped out of the barber shop.

"It's about damn time you showed up!" he said emphatically. "Where the hell is Bradley?"

"He has something important to handle this morning. He'll meet us after the arraignment," I answered.

"What the hell you mean, *more important*? You have an A-list celebrity about to go in front of a judge for murder, and your overpriced daddy has more important things to do?" Billy snapped.

I wanted to punch him dead in the mouth, but I was fully aware of the optics that would create for the news crews behind us.

"Don't worry about the arraignment, Billy. I got this." I moved past him and continued up the stairs with Carla, but Billy was right on our heels.

"*You* got this?" Billy asked, his voice a little louder than necessary. "You ain't got shit. We didn't pay for a wannabe. We paid for Bradley Hudson!"

I halted in my tracks, officially sick of hearing Billy's voice and his asshole comments. I inhaled deeply before turning around, but before I unleashed the cussing-out I'd formulated in my mind, Carla beat me to the punch.

"First of all," she said, her finger in Billy's face and her tone scathing with the same level of disgust that I felt, "you're not paying us for shit, because you're not the client. Secondly, you wanna talk about paying someone, pay us the hundred grand you owe us. Thirdly, Savannah didn't hire Bradley Hudson. She hired Hudson and Hudson, and our job is to put the right person in the right place. Now, do you want a press conference, or do you want to take your client home?"

The look on Billy's face indicated that he hadn't expected all that fire to come out of Carla. He cleared his throat and humbled himself in a matter of seconds.

"Take her home," he answered.

"Then shut the fuck up, and don't you ever again question his credentials, you worthless piece of shit," Carla berated him.

"A'ight, I get it. I was just asking a question. You ain't have to get all sensitive." Billy shrank back.

Satisfied that she had made her point, Carla whipped back around to me. I gave her an approving fist bump as we walked in the building to the designated courtroom.

Fifteen minutes later, the case was called. I took my place at the table to the right of the Honorable Betty Jackson and next to Savannah, who had just been brought out. I glanced to the left to see who had been assigned as opposing counsel and was shocked to see my competition was none other than Teresa. Because this case was so important, I had expected a more experienced ADA. Not that Teresa couldn't handle it.

Our eyes met, and for a brief moment, images of her naked body flashed in my mind. I broke our stare and shook my head in an effort to get my thoughts together.

"Mrs. Kirby, you've been charged with second degree murder. How do you plead?" Judge Jackson asked.

I leaned over to Savannah and whispered in her ear.

"Not guilty, Your Honor," Savannah repeated for the judge to hear.

"Due to the seriousness of the charge, the People request remand, Your Honor," Teresa said.

"Your Honor, my client is a public figure with ties to the community—" I started, but Teresa cut me off.

"Your Honor, Mrs. Kirby brutally stabbed her husband. She is a woman of great means and has contacts in many countries that do not have extradition treaties with ours. The People consider her to be a serious flight risk," Teresa stated.

"My client is not a flight risk and plans to vehemently fight these accusations against her. She is one of the most recognizable people on the planet. There is nowhere she can hide. And her financial state is highly exaggerated," I countered.

"Your Honor, her fingerprints were found on the murder weapon."

"Along with two other sets of unknown fingerprints. Your Honor, if the People's case was as strong as they portray, then they'd be charging my client with first degree murder and not second."

I took a step closer to the bench, locking eyes with Judge Jackson and staring as if she were the only woman in the room that mattered. She looked back, almost as if she was in a trance, and I stared harder, biting my bottom lip ever so slightly as my right eyebrow raised a fraction. It was a gesture that I had no doubt would work to my advantage.

"I'd like to hear a recommendation for bail." Judge Jackson finally forced herself to look away and fanned herself slightly.

*It worked*, I thought as I fought the urge to smile.

"The People request bail in the amount of ten million dollars," Teresa responded confidently.

"Ten million dollars?" I glared at Teresa. "Your Honor, that is outrageous!"

Judge Jackson's eyes went from Teresa to me. "I'm setting bail at two million dollars with home restriction and ankle monitoring. Mrs. Kirby, you will surrender your passport."

"Thank you, Your Honor." I nodded as I pretended not to notice the scowl on Teresa's face. Instead, my attention went to Savannah, who looked confused by everything that was happening, and I gave her a reassuring nod.

"I'll hear opening arguments two weeks from today. Court is adjourned," Judge Jackson announced before hitting the gavel.

"Now what?" Savannah began to panic as the deputy reached for her. "I thought . . ."

"It's okay, Savannah." Carla's voice was soothing. "They're just taking you back until your bail is posted, that's all. I'll be back to talk to you in a minute."

Savannah was taken through a side door. I was packing up my briefcase when Teresa walked over. From the somber look she wore, I could tell that she wasn't pleased with the bail hearing. That still didn't stop me from reminding her about the rain check.

"We still on for Saturday?" I asked with a hopeful tone.

"I haven't made up my mind yet," she said in a low voice that only I could hear. "I don't make it a habit of screwing my opponents, except in the courtroom."

As she walked away, I couldn't help but stare at her plump derriere. I wasn't satisfied with her answer and went to follow her.

I'd almost caught up to Teresa when Billy K appeared out of nowhere, blocking my progress.

"I thought you said you were going to get her out!" Billy said angrily. "Where the hell are we supposed to get two million dollars?"

"We know we aren't getting it from you, that's for sure. But calm your nerves," I said and pointed to the courtroom doors that Teresa had walked out of just as my father entered. "Her bail money just walked through the door. Dad!"

My dad and two other gentlemen made their way down the aisle, followed by Mike, the new guy he'd recently hired, and I walked toward them.

"Gentlemen, this fine lawyer here is my son, Lamont Hudson," Dad boasted. "Lamont, this is Howie and Snow. Howie was Savannah's old manager."

"Yeah, before she decided she'd rather work with trash instead," Howie said, nodding his head toward where Billy was left standing.

"Let's play nice, Howie," Dad told him. "We're here to make sure Savannah gets out safe and sound. Mike, will you take these gentlemen to where they can take care of the bail? I'll be down shortly."

"No problem, Mr. Hudson," Mike said, then motioned for the men to follow him. "Right this way, gentlemen."

When they were gone, Dad gave me a pat on the shoulder. "You did good in here today, son. I couldn't have done a better job myself."

"Thanks, Dad. I'm glad we got bail set. That's a start. But we're not out of the fire yet." I sighed.

"No, we're not. Where's Carla and your sister?"

"Carla went to check on Savannah. Dez is somewhere around here."

"I'm going to speak to Savannah before she's processed out. She's going to have to make a statement. Find your sister and see if she has something appropriate for Savannah to wear."


Two hours later, Savannah was processed out, wearing a dress and shoes that Desiree had brought for her. We exited the building as a group, and my father paused at the press podium on the courthouse steps to address the crowd. He waited for the commotion of what seemed like hundreds of people with microphones and cameras to settle down before he started to speak into his mic.

"I just want to reiterate that my client is innocent until proven guilty, and I ask that you not rush to judgement. I'm sure some of you remember the name Anthony James. He was indicted by the press but later found innocent in court." After his brief statement, he stepped aside so that Savannah could have the mic.

Savannah had been fully prepped on what she should and should not say, but she still looked nervous. She spoke so quietly at first that reporters were leaning forward to make sure their mics picked up her voice.

"First, I would like to thank Howie and Snow from Innovative for posting my bond." She paused for a moment and took a few deep breaths, and the crowd leaned in eagerly to see if she would say more. Her voice was stronger when she continued. "Guys, I can't wait to get back in the studio and work with you again once we have cleared my name of this heinous crime. Secondly, I want everyone to know that I loved my husband, and I am not guilty of doing anything but loving him. I look forward to proving my innocence and helping to bring the real killer to justice before the law and before God." She stepped back into Howie and Snow's awaiting arms. Howie kissed her forehead as he helped her from the podium.

When I went to shake Dad's hand, I noticed Billy staring at Savannah with Howie and Snow. I would've thought he'd be happy about her release. Instead, he looked angry and disappointed. Something wasn't right. I already didn't trust Billy for shit, and now I had even more reason to question his motives.

# 12

## *Lamont*

*Nothing is promised to me and you, so why would we let this thing go? Baby, I promise that I'll stay true. Don't let nobody say it ain't so.*

Jagged Edge was playing softly in the background of my home as I waited to hear from my favorite ADA. It was almost midnight, and Teresa still hadn't called. I guess I'd wasted my time planning a meal for her. Last time we spoke, she said she was contemplating our Saturday night plans, but it was becoming apparent that she'd made up her mind without giving me a heads up.

I was disappointed and more than a little pissed off. Our showdown in the courtroom didn't need to affect whatever we had going on in our personal lives. I was surprised she was taking it so personally. Teresa wasn't the type of woman to trip off a loss. At least I hadn't thought she was.

Putting the last of the food in the refrigerator, I sat on my couch and opened the bottle of vintage Bordeaux we were supposed to be sharing. It felt good to be able to relax. With everything going on with Savannah's case, the last few days had been nonstop late nights and early mornings at the firm. Of course, it would have been nicer to relax between Teresa's soft thighs. No matter how expensive the wine was, it was no substitute for tasting her sweet center.

As I downed half the bottle, my thoughts wandered to our last time together. Teresa was like a damn Olympic athlete. When it came to screwing, I'd never met another woman with more endurance than she had. Images of her legs in the air and my face buried between them flooded my mind. She was always very vocal during sex, and now her moaning and screaming echoed in my head. Before I knew it, I was hard as a rock.

*Damn,* I thought. *I better call it a night before I end up in front of my laptop with some lotion and a box of tissues.*

I got up from the couch a little unsteadily, more buzzed than I'd realized. As I slid my feet into my Gucci slippers, the doorbell rang.

"Seriously?" I snapped when I opened the door and saw Teresa standing there.

"What do you mean?" she asked. "You said you were going to cook. I brought the wine. And these." Her hands came from behind her back, and she showed me a row of gold-wrapped condoms.

The condoms were tempting, but she wasn't getting off the hook just yet for standing me up. I opened the door for her to come inside. "It's damn near midnight. Dinner got cold three hours ago."

She shrugged. "I guess I am a little late."

"A little? A phone call, even a text would have been nice." I closed the door and looked her up and down. She looked fucking amazing in a clingy red dress and stiletto heels. I had to fight the urge to reach out and run my hand up her bare legs.

"I know, but it took that long for my hormones to overrule my work ethic and force me to come here," she said, making her way to the sofa. She wobbled a little bit, and I realized I wasn't the only one who'd been drinking.

"So, there it is. The eight-hundred-pound gorilla in the room," I told her. "You couldn't have given me a heads up that you were the lead prosecutor? I had to find out in court?"

Teresa sighed as she put her arms around my neck. I let my arms rest on her hips, but when she leaned in for a kiss, I turned my head.

Teresa pouted when she realized she wasn't getting out of this so easily. "Well, I didn't see you blowing up my phone to tell me your father's firm was representing Savannah Kirby."

"It was all over the TV!" Did she think I was stupid?

"Oh, yeah." She giggled. "It was, wasn't it?"

"You really should recuse yourself," I said with a look that said unlike her, I wasn't playing around.

"I'm not doing that." She shook her head so adamantly that her long hair fell in her face. Suddenly she was serious. "This is the biggest case of my career. You should recuse *yourself*."

"Hell no. And what excuse would I give my old man? Sorry, Dad, I can't be counsel on this case because I'm screwing the ADA and it may be a conflict of interest. Hell, my old man would skin me alive if he even thought we were sleeping together."

"So we have a secret," Teresa said, leaning in for another kiss. This time, she held my head firmly in her hands until I finally gave in. Our lips met for a brief moment, and I felt the spark between us melting any resistance.

She leaned back and said, "Let's make it interesting, shall we? Why don't we make a wager?"

At this point, I was only halfway listening to her words. I was too distracted by untying her dress to uncover her gorgeous curves. She kissed me again, sucking my bottom lip. At this point, I was ready to agree to anything so she would shut up and get to work on my rock-hard member.

"What do you have in mind?" I asked in a low tone.

"When I win—and trust me, I will win—you have to cook for me every weekend for a month. Breakfast in bed, lunch, and dinner, wearing only an apron and chef's hat."

I countered with, "When I win, you have to clean for me every weekend. Naked."

"I'll take that bet," Teresa said as she pulled at the waistband of my sweats. "Now, I came over here for dinner, and since it seems that I won't be getting that, I guess you'll have to give me something else."

Without missing another beat, I slid her dress from her shoulders. It fell to the floor, revealing her body in all its naked gloriousness. She never wore underwear when she came to see me, and that shit was so hot.

She pulled me in for another kiss, and my hands roamed her smooth cocoa skin. As our tongues intertwined, I scooped her up into my arms and carried her over to the couch. Trying to make it to the bedroom would've been a waste of time. I needed to feel her right then and there.

As I sat down, she maneuvered herself so that she straddled me, grinding her wetness against my erection.

"Take these pants off, baby," Teresa instructed me. "I want to ride it."

She didn't have to tell me twice. Within seconds, I had kicked my pants to the side and leaned back so she could slide a condom on my thick, hard manhood.

"Mmm," she moaned, gripping it in her hand. "I've been thinking about this since the last time I had it."

She positioned herself over me and slid down, throwing her head back and hissing as I entered her. The sensation of her wet walls sent chills down my spine. I gripped her hips and started matching her motion, thrust for thrust.

"You forgive me for missing dinner?" she whispered in my ear.

"Yes," I breathed.

"You're not mad at me, are you?"

"No."

"Good." She leaned back, using one hand to brace herself on my shoulder and the other one on my thigh. With the precision of a professional bull rider, she moved up and down on top of me.

I glanced down, enjoying the view. My breath quickened, and my heart raced. From the look on her face, I knew that Teresa was well on her way to an orgasm.

"Lamont . . ." she gasped

"I know, baby."

"Lamont . . ." she called out again, and then her walls tightened around me as her body shook and she screamed through her first climax.

As far as I was concerned, we were just getting started. Still inside her, I stood up with her on my lap and then laid her onto the couch on her back. I threw her legs over my shoulders and went to work, drilling into her slippery love canal. Her second climax was even harder than the first, and this time, I met her at the finish line.

I collapsed next to her on the couch, and she buried her head in my neck, stroking my sweaty chest.

"Whoa. That was . . . whoa," she said when she'd caught her breath.

"Yeah, see what you would have missed if your ass didn't finally show up?" I teased.

She rolled her eyes. "Wow. So much for basking in the afterglow."

"Hey, what can I say? I don't like to be stood up after I've slaved over a hot stove all afternoon."

"Speaking of food, I'm starving. What did you make?" she asked, getting up and heading toward the kitchen.

I followed behind, watching her ass jiggle. I caught up and slapped it playfully. "Oh, you missed out on that when you rolled up here three hours late. However, I will serve you up a delicious bowl of cereal."

She giggled. "Only if you have Cap'n Crunch Berries."

# 13

## *Bradley*

The wake for Kyle Kirby was a first-class affair. Everything was white: the casket, the flowers, the family cars and limos, and the custom-made suit Kyle was sporting as he was laid to rest. The funeral home was packed with close friends, family, and A-list celebrities from near and far gathered to pay their respects.

I could feel the eyes on us as I entered the sanctuary with Desiree and Savannah and led them to the row where Carla, Lamont, and Perk were already seated.

"Hey, honey," I whispered to my wife and kissed her cheek after I took my seat beside her.

"Hey, baby." She looked past me and reached out to touch Savannah's hand. "How are you holding up, Savannah?"

"Well, I'm here," Savannah murmured, her face covered by oversized shades.

Lamont, who was sitting on the other side of Carla, asked, "Would you like to go up to the—"

"Not yet." Savannah cut him off, shaking her head.

"Just take your time," Carla told her.

"Right," I said and gave Lamont a slight frown. "Nobody's rushing you into anything."

I began reading the program booklet one of the ushers had handed me when we walked in. Kyle's extensive but brief life had been filled with mega hits, and he'd won awards from just about everyone—the Grammys, BET, MTV, Soul Train, the NAACP, and even a GMA Dove award for a gospel song he was featured on. His former high school had dedicated a scholarship and a classroom named in his honor. It was an impressive career.

I was so engrossed in the obituary that I didn't realize Perk was saying something to me until I felt him tap my shoulder.

"Huh?" I turned around and saw him sitting behind me, leaning in close.

"Has anyone started to look into Kyle Kirby's personal life yet?" he asked quietly.

"Just the basic internet and police searches. You know, domestic violence, police contact, stuff like that," Carla answered. "We'll get more into a psychological profile when we get closer to trial and start wrestling with picking a jury."

"You come across him having a gambling problem?" Perk pressed.

"No, he's into boxing and collectible angels, but I can do a more intensive search," Carla told him.

Perk nodded. "Do that."

"Why?" I wondered where his question was coming from, especially now, while we were sitting at the man's funeral. "What's up?"

"Probably nothing, but let's check it out anyway," Perk said then slipped out of the pew to get back to work.

Suddenly, Savannah stood up. "Excuse me," she said as she made her way out of her seat.

The church became eerily quiet as every person in attendance watched her slowly walk down the aisle toward the front of the church. When she finally reached the casket, she snatched off her sunglasses and looked down for a moment, then leaned into the coffin, reaching for Kyle's body. She started sobbing like a baby, and the noise rang through the sanctuary.

Truth be told, I was a bit put off and skeptical. What sort of widow purposely draws attention to her grieving?

As I was about to lean over to Carla and comment on it, Savannah's sobs were overpowered by a shrieking voice.

"Get off him! Get off my son!" Cathy Kirby, Kyle's mother, came rushing up the aisle.

"Oh, hell," I mumbled as I rose to my feet in a flash. Lamont was right behind me, his Hudson instincts kicking in without me having to say anything. We needed to intervene before our client had even bigger problems. We made it to Savannah's side before Cathy could reach her, but we couldn't stop her from speaking up.

"Momma Kirby . . ." Savannah's voice trembled.

"Don't you Momma Kirby me, you murderous bitch!" Cathy screeched.

"I didn't!" Savannah pleaded, still teary-eyed. "I swear to God I didn't kill him. You have to believe me. I love Kyle, and I wouldn't ever think of hurting him."

"Liar! You loved his money, that's what you loved. His money and yourself! You murderer!"

"No, I'm not."

Savannah tried to take a step toward her mother-in-law, Cathy slapped her so hard that it echoed in the church. Lamont stepped in, grabbing Cathy's arm before her follow-up strike could make contact with Savannah's face.

The entire congregation jumped up to get a better look at the commotion between the two women. I looked around, wondering where the hell security was. With none in sight, I reached in to restrain Savannah.

"Oh, hell no! Let me go! Let me go!" Savannah fought against my hold.

"That woman murdered my son!" Cathy shouted hysterically, pointing her finger in Savannah's face. "Do you hear me? She murdered my baby!"

Cathy continued to spew hateful words as Carla arrived and helped drag Savannah, kicking and screaming, out of the church. As soon as we stepped outside, Perk appeared and helped us get into the Rolls Royce, which was fortunately still parked nearby.

"Thanks," I said to him as we leaned in to shield Savannah from the lenses of the paparazzi who were crowding outside the windows.

"No problem, boss. What the hell happened in there?"

"Kyle Kirby's mother, that's what. She hauled off and slapped the hell out of Savannah like she was a rag doll."

"Damn," Perk said.

"My thoughts exactly."


"How bad is it?" I was sitting at my desk later that day, hoping to get an idea of what damage the altercation at the wake had done to Savannah's already questionable reputation. I rubbed my temples, trying to prepare myself and remain calm.

Carla stood next to me with her headphones on, holding her iPad. She rapidly scrolled through different social media feeds and news outlets, her attention laser focused on whatever was on her screen.

"Well . . ." She sighed.

"Please tell me it's not that bad," I asked with a hopeful tone.

"Bad is an understatement. It seems as if every cell phone in the room was set to record. The video is already viral." It was Desiree who spoke. She and Lamont were in chairs near my desk as we all tried to wrap our heads around the shit show we had witnessed that afternoon.

"She's right," Carla said, turning her iPad so I could see the screen. "Almost a million hits on World Star Hip Hop alone, and it's only been a few hours. What we need to do is get ahead of this. Talk about disrespect for the dead."

Perk entered the room, interrupting our pity party. "I got some info. The other fingerprints on the knife came back as Kyle and his mother. Obviously, we know Kyle didn't stab himself in the back, but—"

"We don't really think his mother killed him, do we?" Desiree interjected. "I mean, let's be serious."

"The cops don't," Perk said. "They're verifying her alibi as we speak."

I tapped my fingers on the desk, already formulating a strategy. "The cops don't, but the public is still up in the air." I glanced toward Carla. "Maybe we need to float the possibility on some of those sites."

"Daddy." Desiree wore a disappointed expression. "You can't go out there pointing the finger at the victim's mother. Especially if she's innocent."

"We don't know if she's innocent. As far as I'm concerned, she's just as much a suspect as our client. The same client that we're supposed to be defending," I reminded her. "The media is running with the narrative that Savannah killed Kyle. We have to do what we can to distract people from that assumption. That's our job."

"Didn't you see that woman today? She was *broken*. Does anyone in this room believe in the power of karma?" Desiree looked at everyone and got nothing but blank stares back. Defeated by our indifference to her question, she sighed. "Great."

"Dez," Lamont said. "This has nothing to do with karma. We're just planting the seeds of reasonable doubt. It's what we do."

"Well, it's the part of the job that I can't stand," she huffed. "I can't believe you all are willing to ruin that woman's life like this. She just lost her son."

"And our client just lost her husband," I retorted calmly, unmoved by Desiree's pleas. I hesitated for only a moment before I launched into my argument. "Someone killed that man, and we can't be sure who it was until we get all the facts straight. A distraught mother doesn't always mean an innocent one—and deep down, you know that. We're just giving our client a proper shot at proving her own innocence before blindly believing in someone else's. If Kyle's mother is truly free of blame in this situation, we will figure out another strategy."

Desiree shot me a look of pure disdain. It was obvious that my daughter still wasn't happy with the moral quandary that we were proposing. Without saying another word, she exited the room.

"Dez!" Lamont called after her.

"Let her go, Lamont. I'll talk to her when this meeting is over," I told him.

"All right," Lamont said, still looking at the door. He'd always been protective of his baby sister. "She kind of has a point, though, Dad. I mean, how will that make Hudson and Hudson look if we throw that woman under the bus and it turns out she isn't the one who killed Kyle either? This is kinda savage."

"They will say we did our job," I said with a simple shrug. "Shedding light on Cathy Kirby as a potential suspect is just us doing the same thing that the world is doing to Savannah. Fair game. There are only two other sets of fingerprints on the murder weapon, and one does belong to Cathy Kirby."

"I agree with you, honey," Carla said, placing her hand on my shoulder.

"All right, well, let's get on it then," Lamont said, pushing away from the desk.

# 14

## *Desiree*

I'd been secluded in my office for almost an hour, going through the case files on my desk. I needed something to take my mind off the fact that my father was going to put Cathy Kirby in the line of fire and accuse her of murdering her son.

I was surprised when I looked out the window and saw the sun setting. There were still a few phone calls I wanted to make before leaving, so I picked up my desk phone and dialed a number.

"Hello?" A husky voice answered after a few rings.

"Adam?"

"Yes."

"Hi, it's Desiree with Hudson and Hudson. My father, Bradley Hudson, asked me to give you a call to find out if you'd rather we served notice to you or your client in regards to the Barbara Simpson negligence case."

"I didn't realize you were with Hudson and Hudson, Ms. Hudson," Adam stated.

I rolled my eyes at how inadvertently stupid he sounded, but I kept my tone professional when I responded. "Well, I am, and if you could just tell me who we should issue service to, I won't take up any more of your time."

"You know what? There's no reason for us to be wasting a whole bunch of money or time. I think I can get my client to a seventy-five thousand settlement. You think that would work?" he asked.

"If you can get it to one hundred and fifty thousand, we can make that work."

There was a brief pause, and then he said, "I think we can do that. I'll get back to you within the hour."

"Perfect," I said, smiling as I placed the phone back on the receiver. At least something good had happened that day.

"I see you've learned something from me after all."

I looked up at my father, who stood in the doorway.

"Another one of your pro bono cases?" he asked as he entered the room.

"Uh, yes," I answered, wishing he hadn't overheard that. I hated discussing pro bono work with him because I knew he didn't value it, so I always ended up feeling belittled. "St. Mary's Hospital gave the name of the battered women's shelter to our client's husband. I don't understand how anyone could be so stupid."

"We all make mistakes." He shrugged. "But you're right, that was a stupid one."

"Yeah, well, he showed up and beat her up pretty bad. A hundred and fifty thousand is not a lot, but it's enough for her to start over somewhere far from here," I told him.

"Good. I'm glad we could help. Glad the Hudson name could help."

I loved my father, but I resented his comment—and I hated the fact that he was right. My pro bono work was always amplified by my association with Hudson and Hudson. Being the daughter of one of the country's most successful and sought-after defense attorneys often worked in my favor. I knew I was smart—I'd inherited my father's tact and legal abilities—but more often than not, I also used the Hudson name to my advantage. The moment opposing counsel heard the name Bradley Hudson, they were far more inclined to settle rather than go face to face against the high-profile firm with a stellar success rate.

"Here." Dad reached in his pocket and pulled out a small paper that he placed on my desk.

"What's this?" I asked, picking it up and unfolding it.

"That's the number to John Shapiro. He runs the Legal Aid Society. Just give him my name, and he'll hire you on the spot."

I suppressed a gasp. "Wait. Are . . . are you firing me?"

"No, honey, but I've noticed that you don't seem happy here. The only time you truly seem excited about your work is when you're doing these pro bono cases. I'm glad to support you to do those, but we need that level of dedication on *all* the cases at Hudson and Hudson," he explained.

"I never said I was unhappy. I just expressed my empathy for Kyle's mother. Who wouldn't feel sorry for her? That poor woman is being put through the wringer. What if that was me, Daddy?" I countered.

"But it isn't, and we've been hired to defend Savannah Kirby. We took her money and an oath, so if you can't get with that program, then you can't work for this firm. I love you more than life itself, Desiree, but that's the cold reality. Now, hopefully I'll see you here tomorrow, which means you understand where I'm coming from. If not, good luck with John, and I'll see you for Sunday dinner."

Dad walked out of my office as quietly as he'd come. When he was gone, I stared at the piece of paper in my hands for a little while longer before tossing it to the side. My father had always been cutthroat, even in his parenting. But suggesting that I leave our family's firm was unexpectedly aggressive, even for him. I mean, we butted heads from time to time, but what parent and child don't? This move hurt my feelings.

Placing my fingers on my temples, I leaned on my desk and tried to gather my thoughts with anxiety balling up in my stomach. Cathy Kirby wasn't the only one being put through the wringer, that was for sure.

A knock on the door startled me from my reeling thoughts. I didn't know who was knocking, and I didn't care.

"Now isn't a good time," I called out.

"Even if it's your favorite brother?" Lamont asked, poking his head through the doorway.

"Even if it's my brother who isn't so much my favorite." I didn't try to hide the irritation in my voice.

"Well, I guess I'll just take these cream-filled doughnuts with chocolate frosting to my own office and eat them by myself." Lamont turned to head back out the door.

"Wait!" I stopped him before he could leave. "I guess you could come in for just a minute."

"Yeah, that's what I thought." He grinned.

I rolled my eyes as he strolled in, carrying a white box filled with my favorite kind of doughnuts. Obviously, the sugary treats were his way of apologizing for not having my back earlier. I was still mad at him, but I wasn't going to say no. Besides, I was hungry.

Lamont placed the box down and sat on the edge of my desk. I grabbed a napkin from my drawer and reached for a doughnut, but he put his hand over the top so I couldn't open it.

"Hold up, greedy," he said.

I groaned. "All right, what do you wanna know?"

"What's really got you so riled up? I haven't seen you this upset since Clifton Thompson asked your best friend to the prom."

"Hey, she knew I liked him, and she still said yes. I haven't talked to her since." I glared at him. He definitely could've thought of something a little less painful to use as an analogy.

"Holding grudges has always been your strong suit, sis. We all know that. But in this case, you were right in doing so. She was a bitch." Lamont said, raising his eyebrow playfully. When he saw the smirk on my face, his tone softened. "Talk to me, Dez."

"I guess this case is taking a little bit more out of me than I thought, and it's only been a few days," I admitted. "I know Savannah is our client, and I know it's the police's job and not our job to make sure whoever did the crime does the time, but . . ."

"But what if she did it?" Lamont finished my question.

"Yeah." My eyes met his. Hearing him say it brought me a little comfort, because I had felt like I was the only one at the firm who had considered that possibility.

"I had that same thought, too, when Billy first brought us the case. But whether she did it or not doesn't matter. She's our client, and she says she didn't. It's our job to make sure she gets a fair trial—and that she isn't proven guilty by a jury of her peers."

I frowned at him.

"Come on, Dez. That's Law 101, and you know Dad is going to do whatever he has to do to make that happen. Hell, any good lawyer would, and this firm is the best. You're part of this firm, so that's just as much your responsibility as anyone else's, sis."

"I understand." I nodded and picked up the paper from Dad again.

"What's that?" Lamont asked.

"John Shapiro's number. He runs the Legal Aid Society for New York. Daddy said Shapiro will give me a job if I want it."

Lamont began to chuckle. "That's what Dad said?"

"He feels that I'm unhappy here at Hudson and Hudson." I sighed. "His words, not mine."

"Damn."

"Exactly."

"Look, don't let it get to you. This is a high-profile case, and everyone's on edge, including Dad. I'm sure he just wants to make sure we're all on the same page. It will make things go more smoothly."

"Well, he could have just said that," I grumbled and swatted Lamont's hand from the box of doughnuts.

"Ouch!"

"Boy, that didn't even hurt." I picked up a doughnut. "You want one?"

"Nah, I actually brought that whole box for you. I felt like you needed it more than me. I have something to do tonight," he told me.

"Mm-hmm. You think you're slick in those tight-ass suits," I said before taking a big bite.

"What do you mean?"

I savored the sweetness and swallowed another big bite before I answered. "Lamont, who do I look like, Boo Boo the Fool? I always know when somebody has your boxers in a bunch. Who is she?"

"I don't know what you're talking about," he said unconvincingly. "I'll catch you in the morning.

I shook my head as he jetted toward the door. A small smirk made its way to my lips as I watched him leave. I was grateful to have him as a brother. Whether it was the conversation we had, the sugar rush from the doughnut, or a combination of both, I felt better.


When I woke from my deep slumber, I stretched and yawned, then snuggled under my favorite Egyptian cotton sheets. Or at least that's what I thought I was doing until I realized that instead of my two-hundred-dollar luxury sheets, I was feeling some basic, bargain-brand cotton. I sat up and blinked to focus my eyes, confirming that I was in someone else's bed. I spotted my blouse and skirt folded neatly on a nearby chair, then I glanced down at my naked torso. I was about to scold myself for doing something I knew I shouldn't have, but my thoughts were interrupted by the sound of my phone.

"Shit!" I scrambled to my feet, noticing both the time and the caller on my watch. It took a few moments, but I found the phone before it stopped ringing.

"Hello?" I answered.

"Everything okay?" Carla asked. "I've been calling and texting you all morning."

"Ummm," I said sheepishly. "I got drunk last night and got myself into something I probably shouldn't have."

"I've been there a time or two. You okay?"

"Yeah, I'm fine. What's up?" I asked.

"You tell me. What's this I'm hearing that you quit? You really going to work for Legal Aid?"

It took a few moments for me to remember the conversation with my father the night before.

"No, Carla, I did not quit. And I am not going to go work for Legal Aid. I love my job. I'll be in the office in thirty minutes. Cover for me with Daddy, will you, please?"

"No can do. This is between you and your father, but if you get your butt down here soon, today might be your lucky day anyway. Your brother and your father are on their way to talk to Savannah. He won't be back for at least an hour. Now, find your panties and get your ass to work."

I looked down at the phone and then at my naked body, slightly embarrassed. How the hell did she know I wasn't wearing panties?

I turned around to pick up my clothes just as Perk entered the room wearing his boxers.

"Good morning, counselor." He had a satisfied smile on his face, but that disappeared quickly when I cursed at him.

"You're an ass," I said.

"Why am I an ass? You're the one who showed up uninvited, looking for a booty call."

I felt slightly queasy as the details of the night before came back to me. After leaving the office, I hadn't gone home. I just didn't want to. I wanted—*needed*—something to take my mind off the hellish day I'd had. That was how I ended up on the other side of Perk's door after a few shots of tequila.

"You're an ass because you let me do it. I thought we agreed that we wouldn't do this anymore."

"No, you asked me to move out and told me we weren't doing this anymore. I didn't agree to anything. I like doing this."

Perk and I had been through this so many times, and every time I tried to put an end to it, I'd end up backsliding right into his bed again. We had been roommates at one time, and we had a pretty tight bond. He was like a best friend to me, someone I felt totally comfortable with, but my father would lose his mind if he ever found out we were sleeping together. So, as much as I enjoyed our chemistry, I knew it was too dangerous to pursue.

"Not everything we like is something we should do, Perk," I said as I put on my skirt and fastened the belt.

"Why not? Because I'm not a lawyer, I'm not good enough for you?"

I paused, resisting the urge to snap at him. I'd explained to him a million times why we couldn't do this, and he knew damn well it had nothing to do with his lack of a college degree. Still, he didn't deserve my attitude now, since I was the one who was constantly breaking the rules I had set.

"No, Perk. because you're like a son to my father. And what man wants his son screwing his daughter?"

"Ain't much he could say about me screwing you if I was his son-in-law."

"Is that a proposal?"

"Should I get on one knee?" Perk asked in all seriousness.

"Hell no!" I retorted as I slipped on my heels. "Are you crazy? I can't marry you. This was a mistake that won't happen again."

"I've heard that before." Perk moved closer to me, and I could see him hardening beneath his boxers.

"I have to go, Perk." I stepped out of his reach and grabbed the rest of my belongings, then gave him a wave as I left his bedroom and headed toward the front door—even more confused than I'd been when I first walked in.

# 15

## *Teresa*

When an alert chimed on my phone, I didn't need to check the screen to know who was texting me. Lamont and I had been exchanging funny gifs and memes all morning to describe our days. His humorous personality was almost as sexy as his athletic body, and it brought out a side of me that I almost forgot existed. Being a district attorney was a serious job that took a lot out of me, and I rarely got the chance to laugh. Lamont allowed me the chance to do that, and it was one of many reasons I enjoyed him. We weren't what I would consider an item yet, but if he wanted to take our "situationship" to the next level at some point, I would be open to that happening. Right now, however, things were complicated by Savannah Kirby's case. To avoid any appearance of a conflict of interest, it was best that things stayed as they were. We would remain just two people who enjoyed each other's company and had great sex—magnificent, satisfying sex—that no one else in the world could find out about.

I left my phone in my purse and rushed to catch the elevator before the doors closed. After an extended lunch break, I needed to get back to my office and get serious about working. I had too many looming deadlines to play around.

When I settled in front of the pile of papers on my desk, though, I couldn't resist checking my phone one more time.

I need to see you again.

I smiled at the words on the screen. If I didn't know any better, I would think he was a little sprung. Granted, I'd tried to leave a lasting impression on him that morning when we were together, but I hadn't expected this much attention.

I was about to respond to his message when I heard someone knocking. I looked up and saw my colleague, Avery Cook, standing in my doorway. The freckles on his pale skin looked even more prominent than usual. It must have been the reddish-brown suit he was wearing.

"Good afternoon, Teresa," he said. "When you get a chance, can you look at these?"

"Sure. What are they?" I asked, placing my phone on top of my desk.

"We need to dig even deeper into who Savannah Kirby is. She's hiding something, and I want to know what." He entered my office and handed me a manila folder. "We need to come up with a solid motive. Have the lieutenant talk to that manager of hers."

"Got it," I said as I flipped open the folder and focused on the contents, which included Savannah's mug shot and the initial background check we had ordered.

It wasn't until I felt Avery standing over me that I realized he was still in my office. I glanced up to see that he was no longer standing in front of me. He had moved beyond my desk and was hovering uncomfortably close to my side.

"Was there something else?" I asked.

"Have dinner with me tonight," he said bluntly. "We can talk business or . . . about anything else. I can pick you up at eight."

"Oh, Avery, I'm flattered. I really am, but I—" I tried to think of a suitable excuse. "I just have so much work to do. Maybe another time."

It wasn't the first time I'd been invited out by a coworker. I'd learned early on that it came with the territory of being an attractive woman in a male-dominated field. I'd responded with a polite "no, thank you" more times than I could remember. Usually, if the proposition was inappropriate or crossed the line, I had no problem being assertive, but Avery was a genuinely nice guy and was always respectful, so I wanted to let him down easy.

"You said that the last time I asked you to come to dinner with me." He sighed. "Just tell me flat out. Is there someone else? I would understand completely if there was. I mean, you're a gorgeous woman."

"Avery, I appreciate the compliment, but I prefer to keep my personal life separate from my professional one. We're colleagues and friends, and you're a nice guy, but—"

My sentence was cut off by the ringing of my phone. I looked down at Lamont's name and tried to grab my phone before Avery could see, but it was too late.

He narrowed his eyes at me. "Lamont Hudson? Bradley Hudson's son?"

I opened my mouth to answer him, but nothing came out.

"What's that about?" Avery took a step back and folded his arms.

I wanted to tell him it was none of his damn business, but he was also working on our prosecution of Savannah Kirby, so whether I liked it or not, he was entitled to an answer about her lawyers. Besides, if I protested too much, it would only make me look guilty. So, I lied to him.

"What do you mean? He's part of Savannah Kirby's defense team. We've been going back and forth on our witness list for the past few days."

"Shouldn't that conversation happen on your office phone, not your personal cell?" he challenged.

I maintained eye contact as I lied to his face. "I'm all about multi-tasking, Avery. I gave him my cell so he could contact me even when I'm not in the office. This is the biggest case we've got right now, and I don't want anything slipping through the cracks because someone can't reach me." I dropped my gaze back down to the folder on my desk. "I'll go through Savannah's background again. Is there anything else?" I asked in a dismissive tone.

"No, not at all," Avery relented and turned to leave.

*Shit, that was close.* I didn't exhale until he stepped out and closed the door behind him.

Shoving my phone in the top drawer to avoid any more distractions, I got to work reading through the file Avery had left. It was a lot of information to sift through, so I settled into my chair, expecting to be there well into the evening.

An hour later, I had just started reviewing Savannah and Kyle Kirby's financial records when there was another knock on the door. This time it was my boss, District Attorney Daniel Shepherd.

"Ms. Graham, how's everything going?" he asked.

"All good, boss. Avery brought me the information you sent. I'm going through the financials now, and it's pretty interesting.

Our case is going to be pretty strong, and it's not looking too good for Mrs. Kirby," I told him.

"That's good to know. Speaking of interesting, something else has been brought to my attention," Daniel told me.

"Something else to help our case?" I picked up a pen, ready to jot down notes.

"No, this was about you." Daniel sat in the chair in front of my desk and crossed his leg over his knee. I'd worked with him for three years and had learned all of his nuances. Crossing his leg meant that whatever he was about to say was serious.

*Oh, shit.* I put the pen down.

"What about me?"

"You're dating Lamont Hudson."

I couldn't tell if it was a question or a statement, but either way, I wasn't about to confirm it was true. I mean, technically I wouldn't call what we were doing "dating" anyway.

"That's absurd, Daniel. And I can't believe you'd even approach me with something like this."

Daniel smirked. "You're good, Teresa. One of the best. That's one of the reasons I hired you. And just like any skilled lawyer— or politician—you've avoided answering my question directly."

"Because it's invalid," I said.

"You've worked for me long enough to know that I'm just as serious about winning as Bradley Hudson. I have the highest number of case victories in the state and plan to have it stay that way. Right now, I'm being considered to be nominated for the position of State's Attorney General. All eyes are on me, this office, and you. We will win this case." Daniel's eyes were dark and intense. "I don't give a shit if you're dating Lamont Hudson, but I would hope that if you are sleeping with him, you use it to your advantage."

"Daniel, what are you saying?" My voice was barely above a whisper. I was totally caught off guard by this entire conversation.

"I'm saying it's a well-known fact that Bradley Hudson will do any and everything to keep that murderer out of jail. You would be wise to do everything in your power to make sure she's prosecuted and justice is served."

# 16

## *Bradley*

The ride in the Rolls Royce over to Billy K's that morning was a quiet one. Normally my son would be full of conversation, but he was unusually mute for some reason. Something was on his mind. This wasn't the first high profile case we'd worked on, but this was a major one. We'd been pulling some long hours, and everyone was stretched a little thin even though the trial hadn't even begun. I needed him to be focused, not distracted. I cleared my throat to get his attention, but he didn't turn his head from the window. It was almost as if he didn't hear me.

"Son," I said loud enough to get his attention.

"What's up, Dad?" Lamont finally acknowledged my presence.

"You've barely said two words since you got in the car. Everything all right?"

"Yeah, everything's cool," he replied.

"You sure?"

"Yeah, I mean, I just hope Savannah is all right, I guess. After that slap to the face and the online world assassinating her character, it's too much for even the strongest person," he said.

"I couldn't agree with you more. And that's why she hired the best of the best." I gripped Lamont's knee affectionately and directed the conversation back to the task at hand. "Did you read the email that I sent out this morning?"

"About Kyle Kirby's phone?" Lamont let out a breath. "Yeah, I got it. Things aren't looking too good."

"Which is why we need to get some answers. Head in the game, chief. We're here."

The Rolls Royce slowed down in front of Billy K's residence, and we got out. We stood out in front of the lavish house for a few moments when no one answered the doorbell. I was about to call and ask him where the hell he was when he finally opened the door and waved for us to come inside.

I did not like what I saw. We followed Billy down the hallway and arrived into what looked more like a QVC warehouse than a living room. Bags and boxes of unopened merchandise were everywhere, covering the furniture and much of the floor.

I glared at Billy. "Where's Savannah?"

He gestured to the sofa, where I was startled to realize that I hadn't seen her because she was camouflaged by all the damn shopping bags around her. She was thumbing through some sort of catalog, with her phone pressed between her shoulder and her ear.

"Oh, sorry. You know how customer service can be. Keep you on the phone forever," she exclaimed when she finally ended the call and acknowledged our presence.

I cleared my throat. "I hope you were calling them to make some returns," I said as my eyes traveled over the mounds of merchandise in front of us.

She looked at me like I was speaking a foreign language. "Returns?" She laughed. "Anyway, I'm glad you're here. I have something for you." She started rummaging through one of the bags on the couch.

"Where the hell did you get the money to buy all this stuff?" I asked, unable to keep the anger out of my voice.

"Billy gave it to me," Savannah said nonchalantly as she continued her search.

Both Lamont and I turned to Billy, who looked as if everything was normal.

"I think it's in the bedroom," Savannah said, jumping up and leaving the room.

"Where the hell was all this money when Savannah needed to be bailed out?" I asked Billy. "You said you were broke."

"I was. I am." Billy shrugged. "But when you brought that asshole Howie and that scumbag Snow around to bail her out, you gave me an idea. If they were willing to help her, how many other people were willing to do the same? So, I started a GoFundMe page for her. Plenty of people are down to help out an innocent, distraught widow. Especially guys who have always fantasized about Savannah and are maybe a little excited at the prospect of her newly single lifestyle." He chuckled. "I mean, their chances are already slim, but if she's serving life in prison, the possibility goes down to zero. So, they send money to help with her defense."

"And then you let her use the money to go shopping. Asshole," Lamont said. The look of disgust on his face mirrored the one I wore.

I closed my eyes for a brief second. "Please tell me this is a joke," I said to Lamont, who had pulled out his phone.

"Nope." Lamont held up his cell so I could see for myself. "If it is, the joke's on us."

"The Savannah Defense Fund?" I hissed. "How the hell did this get past Carla? This should have been picked up by Google alerts."

"Looks like dumbass over there spelled her name wrong," Lamont said as he scrolled through the GoFundMe page.

I suddenly imagined myself wrapping my hands around Billy's throat. I was furious. How the hell could this guy be so foolish? I should've let Lamont kick his ass in the office when he wanted to.

"You stupid idiot! Do you have any idea how this is going to look?" I growled. "Howie and Snow have already paid her legal fees. This is fraud!"

"What did you think I was gonna do, let that prick Howie outdo me?" Billy's voice was just as belligerent as mine. "I'm Savannah's manager! Not him, me!"

I took a step forward to get in Billy's face, but Lamont grabbed my shoulder.

"We didn't come here for this, Dad," he said as he pulled me back. "We have more important things to deal with, remember?"

A smiling Savannah re-entered the room, oblivious to the tension, and approached me with a shopping bag. I stared at her, noticing how her demeanor had changed tremendously since the last time I saw her. She was no longer the frightened, grief-stricken widow facing a murder trial. She was giddy, excited, and seemingly happy. It was eerie.

"I found it! I hope you like cuff links." She offered the small bag to me.

"I don't want any gifts, Savannah. What I want . . . what I *need* is some answers so that I can keep you out of jail. And this time, I'd appreciate the truth."

"What are you talking about? I always tell you the truth." Savannah's outstretched hand dropped to her side, and she gave me an innocent stare.

Lamont must've sensed my growing frustration because he quickly stepped in to assist.

"Savannah, the police have Kyle's phone."

"Yeah, and?" Savannah rolled her neck with a slight attitude.

"And Cathy gave them the password. Rumor has it the last text message Kyle received was from you, and it's more than enough to prove you had motive to kill your husband," Lamont told her.

"You go to trial in less than two weeks. If this is true, they'll be upping your charges to first degree murder. So, I don't have time to wait for discovery. I need to know what's in those messages, and I need to know now."

In spite of the seriousness of what she was facing, Savannah groaned like a petulant teenager. She glanced over at Billy, expecting him to speak up on her behalf, I guess. He shrugged and gave her a look that told me he knew what we were talking about. Savannah exhaled loudly and took her phone from her pocket, unlocking it before handing it to me.

"His contact is the one that says—"

"Love of my life," I said, opening the message thread to read. By the time I got to the last message, I felt as if somebody had wrapped their hand around my heart. There was no doubt my blood pressure was up, and for good reason.

"Shit! What the hell made you send him this?"

"He . . . he made me so mad that night. I just snapped. But I would never want to hurt my husband."

"I need to know everything if you want me to keep you out of prison," I said.

Savannah swallowed hard and began to fill in the details of her story.

*The who's who of Hollywood were packed in the SoHo night-club to enjoy the festivities. The lights were dimmed, the music was jumping, and the drinks were flowing. Savannah and Billy sat in a VIP section reserved for Gregg Anderson. Everything about the night had gone perfectly for Savannah, including her appearance on the red carpet in a dress that left little to the imagination. She had been hesitant to wear it initially and voiced her concern, but her stylist and her manager had convinced her otherwise.*

*"Sex sells, and we need to sell," Billy had insisted.*

*He'd been right. She was the talk of the night, getting the attention of everyone: media, artists, and even a few big-name music producers. When Gregg Anderson sent one of his handlers to invite her over to his section at the club, she didn't hesitate to accept. Billy made sure he was right on her heels. They sat beside each other, grinning and sipping expensive champagne.*

*"Gregg, I would really love to work with you in the future," she boldly announced. The several glasses of liquid courage she drank gave Savannah the push she needed.*

*"Is that right?" He gave her an amused smile.*

*"It sure enough is! It would be a great honor."*

*"Well, you know what they say about great minds. They're always in sync. I was just thinking the same thing. You'd be perfect as the female lead in my new film,* Dirty South," *Gregg said.*

*Savannah squealed and looked over at Billy, who was all smiles as Gregg explained his vision for the project and what her role would be. She was nearly on the edge of her seat while she listened to the details of the action-packed movie. It would be the perfect opportunity for her to finally break into acting, the same way Kyle had done. Billy was just about to hold his glass up in a toast, but Gregg put his hand in the air to stop him.*

*"I am very excited about the film and would be even more excited to have you as my leading lady, Savannah. But there is one deal breaker," Gregg said.*

*"Lay it on the table. I'm sure we can sort it out," she said eagerly.*

*"I need you to get your husband to play the male lead," Gregg responded in all seriousness. "I'm sure he would love to see you as the leading lady on the big screen, and with him by your side, this film has no choice but to shoot to the top."*

"No problem. He'll do it," Savannah assured him without hesitation.

"Savannah, I wouldn't—"

"I said he'll do it!" Savannah said, cutting off Billy's skepticism.

"I'm sure he would do anything for his beautiful wife," Gregg added.

"Gregg's right, Billy. My husband would do anything for me." Savannah leered at her manager.

"You sure?" Gregg asked. "I need an answer by tonight, 'cause I'm supposed to meet with Taraji tomorrow. This role could win someone an Academy Award."

"Me," Savannah said confidently. "It will win me an Academy Award."

She stood up from the table. "I'll be right back." Savannah excused herself and stepped outside for some privacy. She selected her husband's contact, praying he would answer the phone. She wanted to lock down this deal before the night was over.

She heard his smooth voice after a few rings. "Hello?"

"Baby!" she all but shouted into the phone. "You're never going to believe this. Gregg Anderson just offered me the lead female role in his new film."

"That's fantastic," Kyle said. "You always said hiring Billy was gonna jump start your acting career. I was skeptical of him, you know that, but he came through. I'm so proud."

Kyle's response was just what she had hoped for, so she felt sure he would do what she needed to help her secure the role. "I know, right? And guess what else?"

"What's up, babe?"

"Gregg wants you to play the male lead," Savannah said, her voice full of excitement.

"Tell him I said no." Kyle's flat response was the opposite of what she'd expected.

"No? What do you mean, no?" Savannah was confused and disappointed by her husband's words.

"Exactly what I said: no. I'm not interested."

"But I already told him you'd do it. I'll look like a complete fool if I go back over there and tell him no. Kyle, this is a big opportunity for me!" Savannah didn't try to hide her anger.

*Here she was telling him they'd been offered the opportunity of a lifetime, and he was flat out rejecting it. Not even giving it a second thought. Damnit, this wasn't just about his career! It was her career, and as her husband, he should be helping her. It was Gregg Anderson, for God's sake! How could he risk fucking this up for her?*

*"You shouldn't have told him that I would star in his movie without speaking to me about it first."*

*"Kyle . . ."*

*"Look, make sure that man understands I'm not doing that movie," Kyle said, then ended the call.*


"He hung up on me." Savannah concluded her story. "And that made me so mad. It was like a ball of fury was eating at my insides. I called him back a few times, but he wouldn't pick up. So, I sent him a text."

I looked down at the cell phone in my hands and read the message out loud.

"I can't believe you're embarrassing me like this. When I get home, I'm gonna kill you."

The room was quiet. Savannah avoided making eye contact with any of us. I passed her phone back to her, already racking my brain for a strategy that could salvage her defense after such damaging evidence had emerged. Add this text to the fact that she'd fled the scene without calling the police, and it would be easy for the prosecution to convince a jury of her guilt. The more information we discovered, the worse it looked, and the harder my job became.

"Why didn't you tell us about this before?" Lamont asked.

"Wives tell their husbands that they're going to kill them all the time!" Savannah said. "It wasn't the first time I'd sent him a text like that. Hell, he's said even worse stuff to me."

Her excuse sounded ridiculous to me, but Billy finally jumped in to defend her. "She's right," he said. "I've seen some of the stuff he's sent her. It ain't all nice, either."

"Yeah, well, Kyle isn't the one on trial now. She is," I snapped. "God damn it. Once the press gets a hold of this, it's going to be everywhere."

"Everybody already thinks I did it anyway, so does it really matter?" Savannah flopped down on the sofa, causing a couple boxes to fall to the floor. "You're making a big deal out of nothing. It's just a text."

"Just a text?" Lamont glared at her.

"Savannah, listen to me." I walked over and looked her square in the eye. "This isn't some game! That judge isn't going to care that you're a famous singer. You are being charged for murder and could spend up to forty years in prison. What you're thinking is no big deal is exactly what the prosecution can use to put your ass behind bars. Now, I'm gonna need you to start acting like your life is on the line, because it is. Is there anything else you haven't told me, either one of you?" I turned toward Billy to make sure he understood I expected his input as well.

"Nah. I told you everything I know," he said.

I turned back to Savannah. She glanced at Billy and then back at me.

"No," she said.

"Good. Don't let there be any more surprises, or I promise you, I will drop your case faster than your previous label after your last album flopped," I warned.

The frown on Savannah's face indicated that my words stung, but I wanted them to.

"There won't be, okay?" Billy assured me.

"There better not be." I turned on my heels, accidentally stepping on one of the shopping bags in the middle of the floor. "And send all this crap back. Come on, son. Let's go."

# 17

## *Lamont*

Sneaking around with the opposition was not easy, but we were trying to make the best of it. Teresa and I both had full plates and tight schedules with Savannah's case, so the closer we got to the trial date, the harder it became to find time to see each other. We had less than a week before the start date, and Dad had everyone working around the clock in an effort to perform a miracle and get Savannah off. I'd been in the office since the break of dawn, and from the way it looked, I was going to be there all night. I had to cancel the late-night plans I'd made with Teresa the same way she'd had to cancel three days before.

I sent her a text to let her know, then sat back in my chair and stared at the pile of folders in front of me hopelessly. I had plenty of work to do, but I couldn't concentrate. I couldn't stop thinking about Teresa's curves and all the places I wanted to put my tongue.

The loud knocking on my door jarred me back to reality. I closed the file I was attempting to work on, annoyed that my fantasy had been interrupted.

"Just a moment," I grumbled as I got up.

"Pizza delivery."

*What the hell—?* The voice on the other side of the door sounded weird, like an adolescent boy with a cold.

"I didn't order any pizza. You might want to check down the hall," I said as I yanked open the door.

"No, I'm in the right place." Teresa was standing there, grinning at me. She was wearing a baseball cap pulled low over her eyes and carrying a pizza box.

I broke out in a goofy grin. I was so flattered that she'd made the trip to my office that I couldn't even laugh at how absurd the disguise was. Thank God my family members had all stepped out to dinner a while ago.

"So, are you gonna let me in, or are you going to risk getting caught?" she asked.

I stepped back and let her in the office, quickly poking my head out the door to make sure no one was in the hallway who might have spotted her. I turned around to see that in the seconds it took for me to close and lock the door, she'd stripped down to nothing but her underwear. I had truly never met a woman like her before.

"What are you doing here, Teresa? My dad would have my head on a stick if he saw you." I was aroused by the sight of her, but still nervous about being discovered. The combination was a thrill.

"That's why I wore a disguise," she said with a wink. "I think I would make a fine-ass boy."

"I like you better as a girl," I said, unable to conceal the smile that was spreading on my face. "But seriously, what are you doing here? And how did you find me in this office?"

"Well, I'm here because I thought you might be hungry," she said and motioned to the pizza that she'd set on my desk. "Oh, and I also want some dick. The receptionist lady told me you were down this way."

"And what if that receptionist lady comes looking for you when you don't leave soon?" I pointed out.

"Are we really gonna go back and forth with the what-ifs?" Teresa reached her hand out to me. "Or are you going to come and feel how wet this pussy is? I miss you. It's been too long since I had you inside of me."

"Are you trying to tell me I'm a drug and you're a fiend?" I asked, unbuttoning my pants as I slowly advanced toward her.

"I wouldn't go so far as to say a fiend," she said and unsnapped her purple bra. "But close to it."

By the time I made it to my desk, Teresa had pushed the pizza to the side and was sitting on the desk with her legs spread open, giving me the perfect view. Her panties were pulled to the side, and her wetness glistened under the overhead light like diamonds. Unable to resist any longer, I dropped to my knees and buried my head between her thighs.

"Lamont, yesss!" she whispered. "I love it when you do it like that."

My tongue went to work until I felt her love button swelling. My fingers joined in on the action, and it wasn't long before her body was shuddering with release. I didn't stop until the last tremors had left her body.

"You really turn me on, you know that?" I asked as I stood up and cupped the side of her face with my hand.

"Good," she breathed. "Now it's your turn."

She turned around and offered her backside to me, knowing that I loved to hit it doggie style. I dropped my pants to the floor, ready to tear that ass up, but then I remembered one very important thing.

"Shit. I don't have any condoms."

"Check the pizza box." She winked.

I reached over and opened the box. Sitting in the center of the pepperoni pie was a single, gold-wrapped condom. I picked it up, and it was time to get busy.

As our bodies mashed together, the friction was intense. It was so hot and wet inside her walls that I could barely control myself. If we weren't in my office, she would have had me hollering at the top of my lungs. She started moaning a little too loudly, so I quickly clamped my hand over her mouth. We released at the same time, hard and fast, leaving us both breathless.

"Shit, woman. You sure do know how to take the edge off," I whispered as I slipped from inside her.

"I could say the same for you." She turned around and wrapped her arms around my shoulders. After a deep kiss, she pulled away. "You are everything, Lamont Hudson."

As she gathered her clothes, I headed to the bathroom connected to my office to get rid of the condom. "I'll be right back," I told her.

"Take your time."

In the bathroom, I flushed the condom and wet a few paper towels to clean myself up.

"So, I was thinking —" I said as I came back to the office, but I stopped abruptly, feeling like I'd just been punched in the gut. "Teresa, what are you doing?"

Now fully dressed, she was sitting at my desk, thumbing through some papers. She looked up at me, frozen like a deer in headlights. I walked over and confirmed my worst fears: the folder for Savannah's case was open in front of her.

"What the hell are you doing?" I asked, not trying to hide the accusatory tone of my voice.

"Lamont, it's not what you think." Teresa stood and stepped back.

I snatched the papers and shoved them back into the folder. "Then what the hell is it?"

"I was just straightening the desk up, that's all." She pointed to a few other papers that were on the floor nearby, then quickly picked them up and held them toward me. "See, we knocked them over."

I took them and stared at her, wanting to believe her. Teresa and I had known one another long enough for her to understand that I was no fool. She couldn't be dumb enough to think she could play me. Or could she?

I pointed to the door. "I think you should leave."

"But what about the pizza? I thought we would eat some of it together."

"Take it with you. I'm not hungry. I have work to do, and I'm sure you do, too."

"Lamont, really?" She frowned. "You can't be serious."

"I am."

"You know I would never—"

"Bye, Teresa," I cut her off and pointed her toward the exit.

"All right," she said with her head hung low. I saw that her feelings were hurt, but I didn't care. What the hell did she expect?

She tucked her hair under the baseball cap, picked up the pizza box, and made her way to the door. Then she turned around and looked me in the eye. "I guess the next time I'll be seeing you is at trial then."

"I guess so."

As the door closed behind her, I gathered the papers and folders and flopped in my chair. The scent of our lovemaking was in the air, and I shook my head, knowing that pizza and sex were certainly not the only reasons she had shown up.

# 18

## *Bradley*

"I'm nervous."

Savannah was a bundle of nerves as she sat beside me in the back of the Rolls Royce. Billy, who was seated on the other side of her, placed a reassuring arm around her and gave her a small squeeze. We'd just arrived at the courthouse. Carla, Lamont, and Desiree were in the car behind us.

Freddy opened the door to let us out. I stepped out, but Savannah and Billy didn't follow. She sat frozen, a petrified look on her face and tears flowing freely. Billy looked at me helplessly for a minute before he realized it was his job as her manager and supposed friend to calm her down.

He leaned closer to speak to her, and I was surprised by how gently he spoke to her. This wasn't the Billy K I was used to. "Everything is gonna be all right. We're gonna prove to all these sons of bitches that Savannah Kirby could never do something so horrible. Isn't that right, Bradley?"

I nodded. "We need to go now, Savannah." I reached my hand out to her. "We don't want to be late. That would look bad to the judge."

"But they hate me." Savannah peered out at the large crowd gathered nearby.

"They don't hate you. They don't understand you, and that's why we're here today," I said. "But you won't get the chance to tell your story if you don't leave this car."

Savannah took a deep breath. Her eyes went from the swarm of people in front of the courthouse to Billy, then to me. She slipped her oversized sunglasses on her face, then finally took my hand and got out of the car. Lamont, Carla, and Desiree joined us, and we all took the first steps toward the courthouse together, interrupting the press conference that ADA Teresa Graham was giving on the steps of the building.

"Mr. Hudson! Mr. Hudson! Anything you care to say about the trial?" a young male reporter called out.

"Today, Savannah Kirby begins her fight for justice," I stated as I walked past. "And we as citizens have the opportunity to see if the system really works. Thank you."

We were led by a set of officers to the designated courtroom. I sat at the defense table, along with Savannah and Lamont. Carla and Desiree sat directly behind us. It was standing room only; every single seat was taken. The jury had been selected, pre-trial motions and opening statements made. Today the prosecution would begin presenting their case. It was time for me to do what I was hired to do: make sure my client was found not guilty.

How I was going to do that, I wasn't exactly sure yet. But it was early in the trial, and I still had a little time. It wasn't the first trial I'd entered with no solid plan of defense. I had enough faith in myself and my team to know that when the time came to rest our case, we would have delivered our case effectively enough to at least cast reasonable doubt. Well, I hoped that we would.

I tuned out everyone and everything and focused my thoughts on the job ahead of me. My focus was interrupted when the bailiff called the court to order and Judge Jackson took her place behind the bench. The state called their first witness: Lieutenant Steven Barnes.

"So, Lieutenant," Teresa started, "as the lead investigator on this case, can you share your findings as to who murdered Kyle Kirby?"

"That would be his wife, Savannah Kirby," Lieutenant Barnes answered.

"That's a very straight-to-the-point answer. Can you explain how you came to that conclusion?" Teresa casually paced back and forth.

"There were quite a few reasons, but mainly, Mrs. Kirby sent her husband a threatening text message shortly before returning home that night. Her fingerprints were found on the murder weapon. Add that to the fact that her first inclination was not to call the police, but to run to her lawyer. Seems like a no-brainer to me."

I felt Savannah begin to squirm a little. I touched her hand underneath the table to steady her and leaned in so that only she would be able to hear.

"It's all part of their game," I whispered. "Don't let anyone see that they're getting to you. Emotions inside, poker face outside. Understand?"

I pulled away, and she gave a tiny nod, straightening her shoulders as she sat up. Our attention went back to the assistant district attorney.

"Now, we've heard testimony from the medical examiner that Mr. Kirby was stabbed seven times in the back. As a veteran police detective, what does that say to you?"

"That this was a crime of passion. Most likely done by a spouse or a lover. In this case, Savannah Kirby," Lieutenant Barnes explained.

"And why do you say that, Lieutenant?"

"Because of the viciousness of the crime," Barnes said, shaking his head. "To stab someone that many times is overkill and most likely done out of pure rage. Nothing was taken from the home, so this wasn't a robbery. You have a clear-cut crime of passion."

"Thank you, Lieutenant. No further questions, Your Honor," Teresa said with a confident smile as she returned to her seat.

"Mr. Hudson," Judge Jackson announced, "you may begin."

"Thank you, Your Honor." I stood and smoothed my ties as I approached the witness stand. I looked Lieutenant Barnes square in the eye. "I really only have a few questions for you. You say my client stabbed her husband. Were there any witnesses? Or perhaps a video tape?"

"Not that I'm aware of."

I strolled across the courtroom to the evidence table and picked up the knife, staring at its sharp blade for a few moments before I turned back to face Barnes. "Detective, this is the murder weapon, correct?"

"Correct." Barnes nodded.

"And Mrs. Kirby's fingerprints weren't the only ones found on this knife, were they?"

"No." Barnes shifted slightly in his seat.

"And whose fingerprints were also found on it?" I asked a little louder.

"Kyle Kirby and Cathy Kirby, the victim's mother." From the tone of his voice, I could tell Barnes wasn't too eager to share this information.

I set the knife back down and walked back toward the defense table. Stopping a few steps short of the table, I turned around as if I'd suddenly remembered something important. I looked back at Barnes. "One last question, Lieutenant. How many other individuals did you look into concerning Mr. Kirby's death?"

"One. That I know of."

"And who was that person?"

Barnes stared at me, his eyes full of contempt.

"Your Honor, would you please instruct the witness to answer the question?" I requested.

"Lieutenant, please answer the question," Judge Jackson instructed.

Lieutenant Barnes cleared his throat before he answered. "The victim's mother, Cathy Kirby."

"No further questions, Your Honor." I smirked at Barnes before glancing over at the jury. Their expressions told me I had their attention.

"No further questions, Your Honor." Carla gave me a nod of approval as I returned to my seat. I noticed that Perk and Michael had slipped into the seats beside her.

"Lieutenant Barnes, you may go. We will now take a thirty-minute recess," Judge Jackson announced.

"I need to get some air." Savannah stood and made a beeline for the exit before I could stop her.

"Desiree, go with her, please. We don't need her doing anything rash." Instead of chasing behind Savannah myself, I decided to give her a little space to breathe. Besides, Desiree was the best person to deal with the emotional roller coaster our client was on.

"On it," Desiree said.

"I'll come with you," Perk offered.

"No!" Desiree snapped at him. "I mean, I got this. You stay here with Daddy."

"Man, if Savannah's this uneasy now, how is she gonna handle the rest? We haven't even gotten to the hard part," Lamont said.

Carla looked up from her notes. "How would you feel if your life was on the line?"

"Touché." Lamont shrugged.

"She'll handle it fine because she has to," I said to my son. "Come on. Let's go grab a cup of coffee."

Lamont and I entered the cafeteria, and my stomach growled as soon as the aroma hit me. I'd been too distracted to eat the breakfast Carla had prepared for me, and now I wished that I had. Thirty minutes wasn't enough time for a meal, but at least I could grab something quick to hold me over.

We were standing in line to order when I felt a tap on my shoulder.

"You should be ashamed of yourself," Cathy Kirby said before I could even turn around.

"Mrs. Kirby, this isn't the time or place to have a discussion," Lamont warned, coming to my aid. "I know your daughter-in-law's trial is—"

"Daughter-in-law," Cathy scoffed. "That bitch is no daughter-in-law of mine. All she cared about was my son's wallet with that excessive shopping addiction of hers. She killed my son, and you should be ashamed of yourself for defending her."

"If you'll excuse us, we will see you back in the courtroom, Mrs. Kirby," I responded, showing no sign of emotion.

She glared at both of us before she finally walked away and exited the cafeteria. I had lost my appetite again, so we ordered coffee and drank it in silence. This trial was already taking a lot out of both of us.

When court was back in session, Teresa called her next witness to the stand: Cathy Kirby. I felt the acid from the coffee burning my stomach.

"Good afternoon, Mrs. Kirby," Teresa greeted her.

"Good afternoon," Cathy responded tersely, shooting a nasty side-eye in Savannah's direction.

"Mrs. Kirby, the defense wants us to believe that you had something to do with your son's death." I had floated the possibility of other suspects in my opening argument, and evidently,

Teresa anticipated where I planned on going with that line of defense.

"The defense is a bunch of asses!" Cathy exclaimed and turned to the jury. "They're trying to confuse you and get that murderous tramp off. But you can't run or hide from the truth."

"Uh, Mrs. Kirby?" Teresa regained Cathy's attention. "You were with your son the night of his death, weren't you?"

"Yes. I come over once a week to cook all of his favorites for the week. His wife's idea of a homecooked meal is to call Uber Eats," Cathy sneered.

The jury and courtroom audience chuckled. Savannah tensed up. I placed my hand on her arm and could feel the heat radiating off her angry body. Luckily, she held her composure. Judge Jackson banged her gavel, and the laughter stopped abruptly. No one wanted to be thrown out of court for misbehaving after they'd been lucky enough to get a seat in the crowded room.

Judge Jackson motioned for the ADA to continue.

"Ms. Kirby, your fingerprints are all over the knife that killed him. Why is that?" Teresa asked.

"My fingerprints are all over that house. Hell, I'm the only one who cleans up over there. The dishes are always piled up. If I didn't wash them, they didn't get washed," Cathy said.

"Now, after you made your son's meals for the week, how long did you stick around?"

"Kyle drove me home about eight o'clock, 'cause it takes an hour to get to my building, and I wanted to get home and watch the *Family Business* on BET," Cathy answered.

Teresa pulled out a jump drive from her pocket. She held it up so that the judge could see.

"Your Honor, People's fifteen."

A television was rolled into the courtroom so that she could play the drive. She stood in front of it and explained to the jury what they were seeing.

"These are surveillance tapes of Mrs. Kirby's apartment building the night of her son's death. It is time stamped 8:56 p.m., and you can clearly see her getting out of her son's car, saying hello to a gentleman in front of the building, and walking into the lobby." The ADA narrated the video as it played on the screen.

Cathy looked directly at the jury as she spoke. "Yes, that's exactly what happened."

"Nothing further," Teresa said.

"Mr. Hudson, your witness," Judge Jackson said.

I looked down at the notes I'd taken and waited a few moments before standing. I glanced behind me at Carla, who shook her head.

"No questions for this witness at this time, Your Honor," I announced. "I would like to reserve the right to recall and question at a future time."

"All right." Judge Jackson checked her watch. "This might be a good time to break for the weekend. We will resume at 9:30 on Monday morning."

"Good job today, baby," Carla said as I gathered my things and put them in my briefcase.

"Good job?" Billy K made his way over to the table. "Bradley just got chewed up and spit out by that sexy lawyer bitch."

"Watch your mouth," Lamont said. "My dad knows what he's doing. Unlike you, Mr. GoFundMe."

"Yeah, whatever. Come on, Savannah. I got us a ride home," Billy said, taking Savannah by the hand.

Savannah looked at me, and I told her, "It's fine. I'll call you later. It's been a long day. Go home and get some rest."

"Thank you, Bradley," Savannah said. "And she's right. You did a good job."

"I can't stand that motherfucker," Lamont said when she and Billy were gone.

"Me either," I told him, noticing Perk, who stood staring at the now-blank TV screen. "You all right, Perk?"

He jerked his head in my direction like I'd startled him out of deep thought. "Yeah, I was just thinking about some business I need to attend to."

"Well, you do that, and Lamont, don't you have some business to attend to as well?" I said to my son.

"I'm already gone," Lamont said and left the courtroom.

"Michael, why don't you come and ride with me?" Perk suggested.

"Sure," he said a little too excitedly. "And by the way, my friends call me Mike."

"Got it, Michael," Perk said. "Now come on. All these white folks in here are giving a brother anxiety. I'll call you later, boss."

"I finally have you to myself, eh?" Carla smiled at me. "Or you don't have an hour to spare for your wife?"

"An hour? No, I don't have an hour," I told her. The look of disappointment on her face didn't last long after I grinned and said, "I have two."

# 19

## *Michael*

"So, we got a lead on something? Is it an alibi for Savannah? Man, she could really use an alibi. Things aren't looking good," I said. Perk and I had been driving for almost twenty minutes, but he hadn't spoken to me once, so I had no idea where we were going.

"Do you always talk this much?" Perk asked as he whipped through traffic.

"I just asked one question."

"And you've been sitting over there looking like you were practicing it in your head for the last ten minutes. Has anybody ever told you that you need to relax? Just enjoy the day."

Perk usually worked alone, so when Bradley told him to bring me, I was kind of excited. I didn't want him to know that, though. Although I'd graduated top of my class at Harvard Law, I was the youngest at the firm, with the least amount of experience. Everyone at the office referred to me as "the rookie," and I wanted to change that stigma. I was hoping this could be my opportunity.

"Yeah, all right, man," I said, staring out the window.

"Plus, today's the day you become a hero."

"What?" I turned my attention back to him.

"Bradley wants you to ride with me, so you ride with me."

"Got it," I said and sat back. His response was a reminder that this was our boss's idea, not his.

I tried to relax like Perk had instructed me to do, but as we arrived in a part of the city that Savannah Kirby wouldn't be caught dead in, I knew our destination had nothing to do with the case.

"Where are we going?" I asked again.

"Look, if you must know, I have some business to take care of. A father refusing to give his daughter back to the mother after a visit. Court order says he has to, so that's where I come in," he explained.

The car slowed in front of a run-down apartment complex. A couple of old guys were leaning on the building, passing a bottle back and forth. The broken glass on the sidewalk told me this wasn't their first bottle. The area was filthy. This was certainly no place for a child—I knew because I'd grown up in the same conditions. My siblings and I lived with our mother in a junky studio apartment in a neighborhood just as bad, or maybe even a little worse. I couldn't remember how many times I'd seen my mother shoot up right in front of me. We were lucky, though, because she finally got help and cleaned herself up. By the time I went to high school, we were in a better neighborhood, and she had a steady job at a hotel. Still, the images of those early years were some I'd never forget, and what I saw now made me feel bad for any kids living there.

"You coming in or staying in the car like a pussy?" Perk asked, pulling me out of my trip down bad memories lane.

"Yo, I'm not a pussy," I snapped. "But every wise man knows not to go into a situation blind. What if he has a gun?"

"You don't have a gun?" Perk looked at me like I was crazy.

"How was I supposed to know that I was going to need a gun today?"

"You're a black man. You need a gun every day," he deadpanned. "I'm hoping you won't need one, though. Come on." Perk stepped out of the car.

"Hoping?" I whispered as I followed.

The strong smell of urine hit my nose before we made it to the front of the building. When we went inside, it was even worse.

"Public housing." Perk shook his head. "You'd think they would take care of their shit."

I tried not to be offended, because he had no idea how I'd grown up. But knowing Perk's personality, I figured it was best not to lecture him about it now. I walked silently beside him to a door on the first floor. Perk placed his head close to the door and motioned for me to do the same. The sound of footsteps on the other side, along with a deep voice, let us know that someone was inside.

"No matter what happens, hold onto your balls," Perk murmured. He knocked on the door and placed a finger over the peephole. There was no answer. Perk knocked again, this time louder.

I heard a faint shuffling. Someone was right by the door. My eyes met Perk's, and he gave me a nod, letting me know he heard it too.

"Who is it?" a gruff voice finally asked from inside the apartment.

"My name is Perk Simmons. Are you Mr. Thomas Clyde?" Perk asked.

"What's it to you?"

"Well, I'm looking for Mr. Clyde. I have a check here for him. Are you Mr. Clyde?"

"A check?" the man asked. "Yeah, I'm him."

There was a click of the lock. As soon as the door opened, Perk kicked it open with a loud thud and burst into the apartment. Gun or no gun, I was right on his heels. The man on the other side of the door had fallen into the wall behind him and was struggling to get to his feet.

"What the fuck are you doing?" Thomas shouted as he regained his footing. "Get the fuck out my house before I call the police!"

The inside of the place was no cleaner than the outside. There was junk everywhere. Dirty dishes were piled in the sink, overflowing onto the counter, and the floors looked like they'd never seen a mop.

"I wouldn't call this a house. And I am the police." Perk flashed a badge, and Thomas's eyes widened at the sight of it. "I'm here on behalf of the mother of your child. She would really like it if Melanie came home."

"You son of a bitch! You tricked me." Thomas's nostrils flared as he spoke. "Well, Melanie ain't here. And unless you have a search warrant, you can go now."

"I don't think so." Perk shook his head. "Michael, go check out the back of this dump."

"Uh . . ." I was thrown off by his instruction. He had a badge, but I didn't, and I damn sure wasn't a police officer. Neither one of us was, so I had no clue what I was expected to do.

"Go check out the back," he repeated, this time a little slower, like I was stupid.

I paused for a moment, then nodded. I heard Thomas yelling all types of threats and obscenities as I walked down a small hallway, stepping over a mess of dirty clothes and toys. The bedroom door was slightly open, so I pushed it a little wider and stepped inside. The room was tiny, with a mattress and box spring on the floor, covered in another pile of dirty clothes. When I turned around to leave, I spotted a pair of small brown eyes staring at me.

My heart went out to the kid, who looked to be about five or six years old. She was crouched in the corner, wearing a pair of unicorn leggings, a raggedy T-shirt, and a look of fear. Her hair looked like it hadn't been brushed in days.

"Are you Melanie?" I asked.

"Yes," she whispered.

"Hi, Melanie. I'm Mike." I knelt in front of her. "We're gonna take you back to your mommy. Is that okay?"

"My mommy? She's here?" She looked relieved.

"No, but she's been looking for you." I reached out to her, and she took my hand and let me lead her out of the room.

When we got to the kitchen, Perk and Thomas were right where I'd left them. Thomas was sweating bullets, still cursing and complaining, and Perk was unbothered.

"You ain't giving my baby back to that whore and her new man! For what? So Melanie can grow up just like her? My kid's not going nowhere." Thomas went to grab me, and I felt the little girl squeeze my hand tighter.

Perk grabbed him. "You don't have a choice here, Mr. Clyde. And if you put your hands on my partner, you'll be sorry."

"Oh, yeah? What is this little pussy boy gonna do to me?" Thomas challenged, snatching his arm away and trying to get at me again.

Perk stepped in front of him and puffed out his chest. "You need to calm down before I knock your ass down."

I rushed Melanie out of the apartment building, and by the time we arrived at the car, Perk was right behind us, unlocking the doors. I placed her into the back seat and buckled her in, then slid into the seat beside her.

"Now to reunite a daughter with her mother," Perk said as he got into the car and started the engine.

"I'm sure she'll be happy to have her back. Especially after all that," I said when we drove off. "Poor girl was living in filth because of his jealous, trifling a—" I stopped myself from cursing in front of the little girl.

"Lucky for her, she had Michael Butcher to save the day." Perk grinned at me in the rearview mirror.

"Yeah, yeah, whatever. You helped out a little too." I laughed and looked down at Melanie, who now leaned against me, her eyes closed. Poor thing probably hadn't gotten a good night's sleep since she left her mother's side.

We spent the rest of the drive in silence, and when we arrived at the little girl's home, her mother was already waiting on the porch. As soon as we pulled up, she rushed to the car.

"Melanie!" She had tears rolling down her face. "Oh, my baby!"

Perk opened the back door, and after I unhooked the seatbelt from Melanie's tiny body, he lifted her into his arms and passed her to her mother. She hugged her daughter tight as she carried her into the house.

"Get back in the car. I'll be there in a few," Perk said. He went up onto the porch and waited until the mother came back out. She handed him a small envelope, then wiped away a few tears and threw her arms around his neck. Perk didn't exactly look emotional, but the scene was still oddly touching.

Perk tucked the envelope in his pocket as he walked back to the car.

"What was that she gave you?" I asked.

"Damn, here you go again with the questions. It was her payment," Perk said, backing the car out of the driveway.

"Payment? She's a client of the firm?"

"Yes, payment. She's my client. As much as I'd like to do nice things like that for free, I still have bills to pay. I do a lot of work for hire, most of the time for the Hudsons, but sometimes I pick up something on the side. I like to stay busy," Perk explained.

"I would think that you'd be busy enough with the Kirby case."

"You'd think, huh?" he agreed.

"Do you think Bradley is going to get Savannah off? I mean, the evidence against her is pretty steep," I said, taking advantage of Perk's sudden willingness to talk.

"If she's innocent, Bradley will prove it. But if she's guilty, she'll end up where she needs to be." Perk glanced over at me. "Even when a client gets sent to jail, they can never claim that they got an inadequate defense. Bradley puts in a hundred and ten percent at all times, and he expects his team to do the same."

"Makes sense," I said.

"Speaking of which, I'm headed back to the office to go over the crime scene photos again. Another set of eyes wouldn't hurt."

"Sounds like a plan. Let's go," I said casually. I was trying to play it cool, but inside I was glad that Perk was finally treating me like an equal, a part of the team. Maybe his hard surface was starting to crack just a little.

"And I heard what you said back there," I continued. "You called me your partner."

He laughed and shot me a look that told me I was wrong to think his attitude had softened. "That was just for effect. I work alone. And if I did have a partner, it wouldn't be a lawyer who doesn't even carry a gun."

# 20

## *Lamont*

I entered the Granger Gallery dressed in the same suit I'd worn in court. The scent of rich folks was in the air, and I double-checked my reflection in the window to make sure I'd fit right in. As I made my way through the room, I couldn't help but pause and admire the artwork: life-sized portraits of the Obamas and other well-known African Americans, past and present. The portrait that caught my eye was a life-sized still painting of the late Nipsey Hussle. Much like Kyle Kirby, Nipsey's life was taken too soon. He'd touched a lot of lives with his music, and his lyrics would be something to chant for a lifetime. I stared at the painting for a few moments before continuing toward the auction block.

The auction being held at the gallery featured rare items and collectibles. As I followed the signs that directed me to the event room, I couldn't help but notice a few women checking me out like they wouldn't mind bidding on me. I might have stopped to get some numbers, but I had a mission, and the auction was already underway.

I entered the room and found a seat near the back. About two dozen people were in there, and the mood was lively, mostly because of the auctioneer at the lectern. He looked a little like Samuel L. Jackson—if Sam could speak seven hundred words a minute.

The item up for bid, a comic book, was on the easel next to him as he worked to push the price higher and higher.

"Five hundred! Can I get five-fifty? Five-fifty! Can I get six? Six! Can I get six-fifty? Six-fifty! Six-fifty going once . . . ladies and gentlemen, this is a Dondi Jones original. Six-fifty going twice!" The auctioneer paused for a second and eyed the room. "Sold for six hundred fifty dollars to number 823!"

I watched the winning bidder silently cheer while a woman replaced the item on the easel with another. This one was an encased comic book.

"Ladies and gentlemen, the next item up is a very special treat," the auctioneer said with a wide smile. "Right here, we have the very first appearance and highest CGC graded copy of *Hero for Hire* number one! The first appearance of Luke Cage. This brother was so bad they made a TV show about him. Why don't we start the bidding at a thousand dollars?"

Instantly, a man raised his paddle to bid a thousand. A second one joined in, and the bidding went back and forth between them. It looked like the first guy had reached his limit, because he put his paddle down at twenty-five hundred. The other guy was grinning like a fool, thinking the book was his now. But then another black man in a suit almost as nice as mine raised his paddle.

"Five thousand dollars!" he called out, and the room was stunned silent.

"Five thousand going once . . . is that all?" The auctioneer goaded the room. "This is Luke Cage we are talking about. Five thousand going twice!"

"Six thousand!" Every eye in the room turned to stare at me in the rear of the room, holding my own paddle.

"Six thousand from the man in the back. Do I hear seven thousand?" the auctioneer asked.

The suited man raised his paddle.

"Seven thousand! Do I hear eight thousand?"

"Eight!" I called.

"Eight thousand. Do I hear nine?" The auctioneer turned his attention to my competition, now standing and glaring at me.

"Ten thousand dollars," he said.

I waited a beat, matching his stare. Then, a grin slowly spread across my face, and with a nonchalant shrug, I said, "Fifteen thousand dollars."

Both the auctioneer and my competition were visibly shocked. For a second, the man looked like he wanted to raise his paddle, but he ended up shaking his head and mumbling something to himself as he took his seat.

"Fifteen thousand going once, twice . . . sold to the man in the back, number 899!"

I couldn't take possession of my book until the auction was over, so I sat in the back and watched for a while. The guy I'd beat sat with his arms folded across his chest for the rest of the event. He didn't place one more bid.

Afterward, I wrote a check and picked up my comic, tucking it in my briefcase. I headed toward the exit, taking my time because my mission wasn't finished yet. When I felt a tap on my shoulder, I smiled. I knew exactly who it was before I turned around.

"Excuse me, sir?"

"Yes?" I said, now facing the man who'd been bidding against me. "Can I help you?"

"I was wondering if you'd be interested in trading that comic book you purchased tonight. It's all I need to complete my set." He spoke politely, but he was probably steaming mad that he had to come grovel.

"Well, that depends on what you have to trade, Mr. Jeffrey Bowens."

"Do I know you?" He frowned, obviously uncomfortable that I knew him, but he didn't know me.

"No, but we travel in the same circles. You're an entertainment lawyer, if I'm not mistaken?" I continued.

He nodded cautiously. "How'd you know that?"

"I'm a lawyer too—name's Lamont Hudson. My firm represents Savannah Kirby. We've been trying to set up a meeting to talk to you about Kyle Kirby for the past few weeks."

There was an instant look of recognition on his face, followed by uneasiness. He took a step back. "Look, I have a lot of respect for your father and your firm, but I'm an entertainment lawyer. All of Kyle's buddies are my clients. How would it look if I met with his killer's attorney in my office? I'd lose half my practice."

"I guess I can understand that," I agreed. "But the prosecution has you on their witness list."

He shook his head. "They're not going to call me. I told them everything between my client and me was privileged."

That made me feel a little better. Seeing his name on Teresa's witness list had been alarming, and we wanted to get a heads up on what he had to say before he got on the stand. That was what had brought me to this auction. I'd read that he was an avid comic book collector, and I collected a little myself. So, when I heard about the auction, I knew there was a strong possibility he would be there too. I was glad that I'd taken the chance.

"Well, I'm not going to ask you to waive privilege, but there's nothing against two comic book collectors talking shop and swapping hypothetical stories, is there?" I tapped my briefcase a few times. "We could consider it part of our trade."

Jeffrey eyed my briefcase hungrily. I could tell that he really wanted the comic book inside. And I had no problem departing with it, but it all depended on how far he was willing to go to get it.

"What do you want to know?" he asked after pondering my offer for only a few seconds.

"Did Kyle have any enemies? Anybody that might have wanted to kill him?" I lowered my voice in case anyone was close enough to overhear our conversation.

"Nope. Everybody loved Kyle. And those that didn't love him sure liked him a hell of a lot."

"What about stalkers? Any overzealous fans?"

"No, even his stalkers were pretty tame by industry standards. Mr. Hudson, the only person I know that Kyle had an issue with was his wife."

This was not what I wanted to hear, and I sure hoped he was right about not being called to the stand to repeat that in front of the jury.

"Was it because of her shopping?"

"No, because of her cheating."

He looked like he was surprised I didn't already know that, but I damn sure didn't. During trial preparation, we'd discovered a lot about Savannah, but this was the first time I'd heard anything about her cheating. There had to be some kind of mistake.

I pressed him for clarification. "Cheating?"

"Yeah. Kyle loved Savannah, but he swore up and down that she was cheating on him. He was on the verge of filing for divorce."

As I processed the information, it was hard to hide my shock. Just when I thought things were going to get better, they seemed to get worse. No doubt this would be the most damaging information if it were to get out.

"On the verge? Why didn't he file?" I finally composed myself enough to continue the conversation.

"Prenup. If he could prove that she cheated, he wouldn't have to give her a dime. And if he couldn't prove she cheated, there was technically no need for divorce. He was just waiting on the private investigator's report."

"Interesting," I told him, instinctively realizing my window of opportunity. "Well, seeing that you have something that I want, and I have something valuable that you want, I propose a swap of some sort."

He raised an eyebrow. "Exactly what are you proposing?"

"Why don't you give me the name of that PI and a check for ten grand, and we'll call the trade even?" I said.

Without hesitation, Jeffrey pulled out a pen and a checkbook.

# 21

## *Bradley*

I was lying on my back with one arm behind my head, watching a cloud of cigar smoke rise to the ceiling as I enjoyed the electric shockwaves pulsing through my body. The last waves of my climax finished, and I blew out a satisfied breath. "Shit, woman," I whispered, "I will never, ever get tired of that feeling."

Carla appeared from underneath the covers in the bed we shared. The wicked grin on her face told me that she already knew she was damn good—better than any woman I'd ever been with.

She rested her head on my shoulder and softly stroked my chest. "Your heart's racing."

"You're surprised? After a performance like that, I don't even think I should still be alive." I took another drag from the cigar.

Two hours had turned into an evening of lovemaking for us, allowing me to release all the tension I'd built up in the courtroom. I appreciated my wife knowing exactly what I needed.

I placed a soft kiss on her forehead. "Have I already told you how much I love you?" I asked.

"All the time, but more importantly, you show it. You are my favorite man in the whole world, Bradley Hudson. Have I told you that?" She looked up at me and smiled.

"You married me, didn't you?"

"Best decision I've ever made in my life." Carla rose from the bed. "I'm gonna go hop in the shower. Join me?"

"Of course." I didn't have to be asked twice.

Before we made it to the bathroom, the doorbell rang.

We both stood naked in the middle of our bedroom. Carla checked the slender, diamond-studded Rolex on her wrist, then looked up at me as if to ask who would be at the door this late. I put the cigar out, grabbed my underwear and pants, and slipped them on.

"I'll go see who that is. Go ahead and shower."

She turned around, and as she walked past, I smacked her bottom. She giggled as she sashayed away, and I watched her until she made it into the bathroom and closed the door behind her.

I headed downstairs and opened the door to see my son standing there. "Kinda late, ain't it? I thought I would've head from you hours ago," I said when I let him in.

"It ain't that late, Dad. It's not even nine o'clock. The auction ran a little late." He looked me up and down. "Uh, am I interrupting something? This can wait 'til in the morning."

I glanced down at my bare chest. Not only had Carla put it on me so good that I thought it was damn near midnight, but I also forgot to grab my shirt. "No, I was about to jump in the shower when you rang the damn bell, that's all. I need a drink."

"I bet you do," Lamont teased as he followed me into the den.

I went to the bar in the corner and poured us both a glass of brandy. "So, I take it things went well." I handed him a glass.

"Well, it depends on your definition of *well*." Lamont sat down on my Italian leather sofa and finished his drink in one gulp, then set the empty glass on the coffee table. Had my wife been in the room, she would've yelled at him for not using a coaster.

"What does that mean?" I asked.

"I made contact with Kyle's lawyer, but he didn't exactly have great news for me."

"What did he tell you?"

"So, apparently Kyle was looking to divorce Savannah."

"Because of her shopping addiction?" I reached under the table and took out a coaster, placing it under his glass.

"That's what I asked too, but no. He thought she was cheating. Even hired a PI to prove it."

"Cheating? With who?" I asked, taking a hefty swig of my drink.

"Bowens didn't know, and Kyle died before he got the PI's report."

I blew out a frustrated breath. So much for the good vibe Carla and I had just generated. I was stressed the hell out again. "Shit. This could be really bad for Savannah."

"Actually, he's not going to testify. The guy's a businessman, and he just wants to keep his clients happy. He doesn't want anything to do with this mess, so he used the old attorney-client privilege excuse, and he doesn't think they're gonna call him."

"That's good news."

Lamont sighed. "Yeah, but the rest of it isn't."

"What do you mean? What else did he say?"

"It wasn't him. It was the private investigator that Kyle hired."

"You found him?"

"It cost me five grand, but I got his name from Bowens. I went to see the PI, and he gave me this." He pulled out a manila envelope and handed it to me.

There were about ten photos in the envelope, and there was no denying that the woman in the photos was Savannah. There were several shots taken at different times and in different locations. They all had one thing in common, though. The man with Savannah in every picture was the same.

"Savannah was having an affair with Billy King?" I asked, despite having the answer right in front of me.

"'I don't think *was* is the correct word. I'm sure they haven't stopped screwing each other." Lamont stood up. "You need a refill?"

I shook my head. "I don't think a drink will do anything for me right now. They've been lying to us this whole time!"

"Believe me, you're going to want to drink when you see the email that was CC'ed to all of us a while ago." Lamont took out his phone and logged into his account. He passed it to me.

I stared at the message from an unfamiliar address. Its subject line was *Pay or I'll Post*. I opened the message and instantly wished I hadn't. The video was enough to send my blood pressure through the roof. It was like watching a bad horror movie, but as horrible as it was, I couldn't look away. There on the screen were Savannah and Billy K naked in bed, doing things to each other I would never be able to unsee.

I handed the phone back to Lamont. "Why the hell did I agree to take her on as a client?" I asked, rubbing my temples.

"Whoever sent that is demanding fifty thousand in cash by five o'clock tomorrow," Lamont said. "They're blackmailing her. If that video gets out—"

"It's over for Savannah. They're going to argue that she wanted Kyle out of the way so she could live life with her lover," I thought out loud.

"With her dead husband's money."

"Damn it!" I exclaimed, feeling every muscle in my body tense up.

Lamont stated the obvious. "Dad, we can't let that video get out. We have to pay the money."

"No, *we* don't have to do anything. The GoFundMe account that Billy and Savannah set up has almost two hundred thousand dollars in it. They can cover their own expense. This is on them. They're the ones who got themselves into this position, not us," I snapped.

"Should we head over there now?"

"No," I shook my head. The only place I was going was back upstairs with Carla. "It's late. You head over there first thing tomorrow."

"Me? Alone? You're not coming?" he asked.

"I can't even think about looking at that girl right now. I think it's best if you handle this one for me. Take Perk with you in case you need to be restrained," I told him.

"All right." Lamont gathered his belongings and headed toward the door.

"Son."

He stopped and turned to me. "Yeah?"

"Tomorrow, when you see Billy K, try not to knock his ass out for all of the trouble he's caused. I'll do that myself when the time is right."

He smiled. "I'll try not to. But I can't make any promises."

# 22

# *Lamont*

*Before I let you go, before I let you go, can I get a kiss good night, baby?*

The music was playing so loud that Perk and I could feel the vibrations under our feet as we stood on the steps in front of Billy's door, waiting for someone to answer. I rang it a second time, and still got no answer.

"Shit, no one's gonna hear the bell over that music anyway," Perk said, taking a step back like he might be thinking of kicking the door down. He was pissed when I told him about the pictures and the video.

I didn't need him damaging Billy's property, though. "Hold up," I said. "Let's just try one more time."

"The hell with waiting," he said, reaching for the doorknob.

To our surprise, there was no need to break down anything, because the door was not even locked. Billy's irresponsible ass had left it open. Anyone could have walked in and taken what they wanted—and they had plenty to choose from, considering the place was still overflowing with the goods from Savannah's online shopping frenzies. We passed through the mess of boxes and bags on our way to the back of the house. The aroma of barbecued meat let us know that we would likely find Billy in the back at the grill.

Sure enough, Billy was flipping steaks at the grill, singing along with the blaring music. Savannah was in the hot tub, sipping a tall glass of wine. She spotted us and hit the pause button on her phone. Billy turned around to look at her when the music stopped.

"Babe, why'd you—"

"Look who's here!" she said cheerfully. "Y'all grab a glass. This is some of that good French wine. It cost five hundred dollars a bottle. I can't even pronounce the name." She giggled, clearly buzzed to the point that she didn't even notice the unhappy expressions on our faces.

But Billy did. He turned abruptly and held up his tongs as if he could use them to defend himself if he needed to.

"Well, can either of you pronounce *scandal*?" I asked, not even attempting to hide my disgust. "Because that's what we're about to have."

"Scandal?" Billy came from around the grill and stepped right in my face. "What the hell are you talking about?"

His invasion of my personal space sent me over the edge. I punched him so hard in the jaw that it sent him and his tongs flying into the pool. I wished he hadn't gone down so easily because I wanted to hit him again. Perk stood by and watched as I went to the edge of the pool and glowered down at Billy.

"That's for lying to me, you piece of shit," I hissed at Billy, who luckily had enough sense to make his way to the other side of the pool away from me before climbing out.

"Oh my God!" Savannah screamed and scrambled to get up.

Billy, who was soaked from head to toe, rushed to help her out of the hot tub. They grabbed towels off the table, and Savannah affectionately touched Billy's face where I'd socked him.

She turned to me. "Have you lost your mind?"

"No, I haven't lost my mind," I answered. "The question is, have you lost yours? From the jump, all we asked was for you to be honest with us. But you lied! Both of you! My father is so disgusted that he couldn't even force himself to be here right now. What the hell were you two thinking?"

"Disgusted about what? What are you talking about?" Savannah tilted her head down and looked up at me through her long lashes.

"Cut the innocent act, Savannah. It's bullshit, and it's not gonna work. Not this time," I snapped at her.

"What act? Innocent about what? I don't know what you're talking about," Savannah whined.

"We're talking about *this*. It was sent to us at the office last night." Perk took out his phone and played the video.

Billy and Savannah watched in horror. Savannah's hand flew to her mouth, and Billy went about four shades paler. It was obvious that neither one had any idea the recording existed.

"Lamont, I–I—" Billy stuttered when he was finally able to speak.

"Save it. I don't even wanna hear whatever bullshit that's about to come out of your mouth."

"Oh, God. Is it viral?" Savannah asked.

"Not yet," Perk answered. "But the person who sent this clip wants fifty thousand dollars by five o'clock today, or he's going to be selling it to the highest bidder."

"Then pay the man and get the damn tape!" Savannah shouted in a panic.

"I'd be glad to," I told her. "I just need access to the GoFundMe account that you guys set up."

We all looked at Billy.

"Ain't no money in the account," he confessed.

"What do you mean, there ain't no money in the account?" I asked, hoping I hadn't heard him correctly. "There should be close to two hundred grand in that account!"

"Don't look at me." Billy nodded toward Savannah. "She spent it. All of it."

"You spent two hundred thousand dollars in a month? One month? How?" I couldn't believe what he was saying. There was no way.

"Well, first of all, there couldn't have been that much money in that account. I can't go through that much that fast. It was probably more like twenty grand, not two hundred. You're wrong. And regardless, it was my money to spend," she said.

Savannah's nonchalance was pissing me off.

"You've gotta be kidding me." I threw my fists in the air, then let them fall in exasperation. "What is wrong with you? I've never met someone this confident in their stupidity."

"I'm still Savannah Kirby!" she responded. "Just because I'm going through something doesn't mean I have to look like it. Plus, my nerves have been so bad lately, and shopping is the only thing that calms them."

"So you spend two hundred thousand dollars on clothes and other shit that you don't need? You know what?" I pointed at her and Billy. "You two deserve each other, because you are truly something else."

I felt like I was being pranked. Surely this had to be some sort of cruel joke and there were hidden cameras somewhere, because what I was dealing with couldn't be reality. I was at a loss for what to do, and from the look on Perk's face, he was too.

After a few breaths, I pulled out my phone, dialed a number, then held it out to Savannah.

"What?" Savannah stared at my phone as if it had cooties. "Who is it?"

"Take it. It's my dad. You explain to him why you don't have the money to stop this from happening," I told her.

Savannah's eyes widened as she took the phone from my hand. She opened her mouth like she was about to speak, but then snapped it shut and ran into the house with my phone.

"So, what now?" Billy asked.

"What happens now is that at five o'clock today, all hell is gonna break loose. For Savannah and for you. You should've told us this shit from the beginning. You must be dedicated to screwing us over, huh?"

"That's not what I wanted to . . . I thought we . . ."

"No one gives a shit about what you wanted or what you thought. All we care about is the truth so we're not blindsided by shit like this. Do you know how this is gonna look once it gets out? And trust me, it's gonna get out." I shook my head in disgust.

"We're all screwed," Billy said.

"You're screwed, she's screwed. We? Nah," I told him.

"Damn, Billy. Fucking your client," Perk commented. "That ain't good business."

"Don't act like you've never pissed where you lay," Billy said, then suddenly smiled like he had a happy thought. "Hey, at least if it gets leaked, we won't have to sneak around anymore. Maybe this is a good thing."

"You idiot!" I lurched at Billy, but Perk intervened just in time. "Do you have any idea what you've just done? By sleeping with Savannah, you've given them a motive for Kyle's death."

Savannah strolled out of the house, all smiles, looking nothing like a woman who'd just had her ass handed to her by her defense attorney. Giving me my phone, she proudly announced, "Your father said he would take care of it and add it to my bill."

Billy clapped. "See! Nothing to worry about. Your old man has us covered."

The celebration lasted less than five seconds. My cell phone immediately began vibrating, and so did Perk's. We exchanged glances, knowing that something was up. The headline that appeared with the notification from TMZ almost made my heart stop.

"No, he doesn't." I couldn't look away from the screen.

"What do you mean?" Savannah frowned. "He just told me."

"The sex tape has already been leaked. It's everywhere." I sighed.

"It's official," Perk said. "Ladies and gentlemen, we now have a scandal on our hands."

# 23

## *Savannah*

"Oh God, what are we gonna do?" I groaned.

It was late Sunday night, and Billy and I were lying in his bed. The last twenty-four hours had been hell. Not only had the world accused me of being a murderer, but now I was being called a cheater and a whore. It was all just too much. The one thing I was grateful for was Billy. He stayed by my side. Granted, that fact was ironic, considering it was my being with him that had caused the latest drama. Kyle was gone, but I still had Billy.

"We are gonna lay here and enjoy this joint," Billy said, taking a long drag of the weed between his fingers. "Trust me, this will blow over in a couple of days."

I sat up and frowned at him. "I am on trial for murder, and you're saying it'll all blow over? Really? I am a married woman caught on video sleeping with my manager."

"Were," Billy corrected me.

"What?"

"You *were* a married woman. Kyle is dead, remember?"

In that moment, I understood exactly why Lamont Hudson had punched Billy in the face, because that was exactly what I wanted to do. Instead, I snatched the joint from his fingers and placed it to my lips, inhaling deeply and welcoming the lifting sensation it gave me. I relaxed and flopped back down on the bed.

"Where the hell did that video come from, anyway?" Billy asked the question I'd been pondering since seeing the leaked sex tape.

"Your guess is as good as mine." I tried to think of who'd want to do something so hateful. For a moment, I'd even wondered if

Billy had been the one to leak it to the press, but that didn't seem likely. He may have been money hungry and somewhat of an opportunist, but this was low, even for him. Besides, Billy loved me.

"Savannah, tell me something." Billy interrupted my thoughts.

"What?"

"Off the record. You know you can trust me, right?" He rolled over to face me.

"Of course I know that I can trust you." I propped my head on my elbow. "I wouldn't be here if I didn't trust you, Billy. You're my rock." Okay, maybe that last part was an exaggeration. Kyle had been my rock. But Billy was all I had now, so I needed to keep him happy.

"Yeah, I am. But . . . you know you can tell me, right?" He looked at me with raised eyebrows.

"Tell you what?"

"Did you do it?"

"You think I leaked the video? Are you crazy? Why the hell would I do something like that? Of course I didn't do it," I snapped.

"I'm not talking about the fucking video, Savannah." He leaned in close and looked me dead in the eyes. "Did you kill Kyle?"

I stared, searching his face for some indication that he was joking, but the only thing I saw was a serious expression as he waited for my answer. My heart raced, and I swallowed the lump that was in my throat.

"I can't believe you just asked me that." I moved so fast that I became entangled in the silk sheets I'd purchased a few days earlier.

"Savannah, wait." Billy grabbed my arm, but I quickly snatched away from him.

"Fuck you, Billy King!" I shouted, putting my finger so close to his face that I almost touched his nose. "You hear me? Fuck you!"

"I'm just saying, you were pretty angry at him that night. And you also drank half the bar at the party. Don't you think it's possible that you just don't remember doing it? Maybe you were blacked out. If you did it, I understand, Savannah. Just tell me," Billy pleaded.

"I did not kill my husband!" I rushed out of Billy's bedroom and locked myself in the bedroom down the hall.

"I didn't kill him. I didn't." I wrapped my arms around myself and rocked back and forth, repeating those words over and over in the darkness. I couldn't believe Billy actually thought I was guilty. He was the one person I was sure was in my corner. Now, here he was not only accusing me of doing the unthinkable but trying to justify a motive. Yes, I was angry at Kyle and got drunk at the party, but I remembered everything that happened that night. At least, I thought I did.

# 24

## *Billy*

The tension in Bradley's Rolls Royce was thick as we rode to the courthouse. Savannah still hadn't said two words to me since leaving my bed the night before. Not that she didn't have a good reason to be pissed, but I still didn't regret asking what I'd asked. All morning I'd tried to apologize, but she ignored me, and when I tried to touch her hand to help her out of the car, she snatched away. It wasn't the first time Savannah had been angry with me, and it wouldn't be the last. I just needed to give her some space until she calmed down—or she wanted to buy something.

Instead of walking with her and the rest of the Hudson team and fighting off reporters, I opted to sneak to the side of the building. Even though I felt guilty for leaving her, I wasn't in the mood for reporters bombarding me with questions about the tape and photographers shoving their cameras in my face. Unlike Savannah, I didn't have one of the best lawyers by my side. Bradley would make sure she was okay. I had to fend for myself.

I was able to slip into one of the side entrances. I was smoothing the black Tom Ford suit Savannah had purchased for me when I felt a strong arm on my shoulder, forcing me to turn around. I expected to see Lamont Hudson, but instead, I locked eyes with Lieutenant Barnes, the officer who'd testified the last time we were in court.

"How you doing, Billy?"

"Who's asking?" I jerked my shoulder away.

"The whole world apparently," Lieutenant Barnes said. "I saw that little sex tape you did."

"So? What's it to you?" I shrugged. "Jealous?"

"I think not." His eyes became small, and I knew I'd struck a nerve. "Why don't you and I take a little walk and talk about it?"

I folded my arms and planted my feet wide to show that badge or no badge, he wasn't intimidating me. "How about you wait just like the paparazzi, eh? And I'm gonna tell you the same thing I would tell them: go straight to hell." I turned to walk away, but two large officers blocked me.

"I wasn't asking." Lieutenant Barnes's voice came from behind him. "Right this way."

I looked at the oversized law enforcement goons and realized there was no escaping this. "After you," I said sarcastically.

# 25

## *Bradley*

We took our seats in the courtroom. Savannah seemed even more anxious than usual, which was understandable, considering that in a matter of forty-eight hours, her life had gone from bad to worse. She twisted in the seat beside me, clearly looking for someone. I reached for her hand, but she moved it from the table before I could touch her.

"Where's Billy?" she whispered. "He's supposed to be here."

"Who knows, and who cares? I haven't seen him since he got out of the car," Lamont answered her. "I don't even think he came into the building. He probably skipped out."

"No." She shook her head. "Billy wouldn't do that to me."

"In case you're forgetting, your manager is the same guy who skips out on his lawyer's fees and sleeps with his married client," Lamont replied. "All things considered, you may want to think about cutting ties with him. I wouldn't be surprised if he's the one who leaked—"

"Enough," I said to my son. "This isn't the time or place."

"All rise!" The bailiff's voice called us to attention.

"Ms. Graham, please call your first witness to the stand," Judge Jackson said to the ADA when the trial got underway.

Teresa stood up with a newspaper in her hands. "Gladly," she said with a smirk. "Your Honor, the People would like to call Billy King to the stand."

Both Savannah and I wore the same look of shock as the side door opened and Billy walked into the courtroom. He kept his head down as he passed us on his way to the witness stand, and even after he was seated, he avoided looking in our direction. We'd been in the car for damn near an hour, but the slimy bastard hadn't mentioned anything about being called as a witness.

"What the hell is he doing?" Savannah's voice trembled as she stared at Billy.

"I don't know, but it can't be good," Lamont answered.

"Well, do something about it! Object or something," she hissed.

"We can't object. Not yet. We don't have any grounds for any objections," I explained as the bailiff instructed Billy to place his hand on the Bible to be sworn in.

"So, we can't do anything?" She blinked back the tears that had formed in her eyes.

"We can listen to whatever it is he's about to say and pray he says something we can use to our advantage," I explained, hoping I was right.

Once Billy had been sworn in, Teresa stepped closer to the stand and folded the newspaper in her hands before placing it under her arm. "Good morning, Mr. King. Doing good today?" She smiled at him.

"I've had better days." Billy's discomfort was obvious to everyone.

"No worries. We won't take that much of your time. Can you tell us why you were in the news this morning?" she asked.

"Because of my relationship with Savannah," he grumbled under his breath.

She put her hand to her ear. "What's that? I'm sorry. I didn't quite catch that."

"Because of my relationship with Savannah Kirby," Billy said, loud enough for everyone to hear.

"Now, when you say *relationship*, do you mean your capacity as her manager, or something else?"

"We're lovers."

"And how long has this affair been going on, Mr. King?"

He shrugged. "I don't know. It started not too long after she hired me."

"Your Honor, I'd like to introduce exhibit number twenty-one," Teresa said, then went back to her table and picked up a photograph printed on extra-large paper. She carried it dramatically to the judge, then walked it slowly past the jury box so each juror could see it clearly. Then she brought it to the defense table and held it up long enough to make sure everyone seated behind us could also get a good look at it. It was a blown-up still shot of a scene from the sex tape. Savannah was on top of Billy with her face twisted in full-blown pleasure. Sure enough, she got the reaction she'd hoped for, and I cringed when I heard the groans and gasps that came over my shoulder.

Teresa walked back over to Billy. "Just so we're clear, Mr. King, what is this a photograph of?"

"It's a photo of me and Savannah making love," Billy told her.

"And are the two of you in love?" Teresa asked him.

"Objection, Your Honor," I called out. "Relevance?"

"I'll move on," Teresa responded. "Mr. King, we've had testimony that you picked Mrs. Kirby up from the crime scene the morning of Kyle Kirby's death. I'd be remiss if I didn't ask what your part was in the murder of your lover's husband."

"I didn't have a part in his death," Billy said.

"Would you be so kind as to replay what happened the night of his murder?"

"I picked her up from their house, took her to the premiere and the party that night. Then I dropped her ass off at home at about one o'clock." He spoke directly to the jury.

"I see. So, what was her demeanor when you dropped Mrs. Kirby off?" Teresa moved slightly in the direction he was looking toward.

"She was uh, a little angry and inebriated."

"Angry? About what, exactly?" Teresa pried.

"She'd been arguing with Kyle about this role Gregg offered her. He'd told her that she could only be in the movie if Kyle agreed to be in it too."

"And I take it that he declined the offer for the role?"

"He did, and that lit a fire inside of Savannah. She'd been blowing his phone up the whole ride, talking shit about how she was gonna kill him when she got home. She even sent it in a text."

Before I could stop her, Savannah was on her feet, pointing a finger directly at Billy.

"Billy!" she shouted. "You know I didn't mean that shit literally!"

It took both Lamont and me to get her back into her seat. Her hands were balled into fists, and Lamont whispered something in her ear. She looked distraught, but she didn't take her eyes off Billy.

"Control your client, Mr. Hudson," Judge Jackson warned.

"I'm sorry," Billy said sheepishly, as if there was nothing he could do about it. "But I ain't going to jail for you or nobody else."

Teresa cleared her throat. "Mr. King, if she was threatening to kill him, why did you drop her off at her house? Weren't you concerned?"

"Savannah's bark is much worse than her bite. I thought she was just talking shit. I didn't think she would actually do it!" Billy exclaimed.

"No further questions, Your Honor." Teresa gave a satisfied nod.

"Your witness, Mr. Hudson," Judge Jackson said.

I went to stand, but Lamont stopped me. "I got this, Dad."

I leaned back in my seat. I didn't know what Lamont had planned—neither of us had been prepared to question Billy—but I was confident in his abilities. He wasn't me, but he was damn near close.

Lamont straightened his tie as he went to stand in front of the witness stand. "Billy, how many times did I ask you if you and Mrs. Kirby were having an affair when you met with our firm?"

"I don't know." Billy couldn't make eye contact with Lamont.

"Understandable, since we met numerous times. But, ballpark figure, how many would you say?"

"Maybe around five or six," Billy finally said.

"And each time you were asked, what was your answer?"

"I said no."

"Interesting." Lamont poked his bottom lip out slightly and nodded his head. "So, you lied five or six times?"

Billy blinked a few times and shuffled in his chair, but he didn't answer.

"Mr. King, did you lie each time you were asked if you and Savannah were involved?" Lamont asked aggressively. When Billy remained quiet, Lamont looked over to Judge Jackson. "Your Honor, a little help, please?"

"Answer, sir," the judge said.

"Yeah, okay. I lied. But I was only trying to protect Savannah," Billy snapped.

"But now you're lying to protect yourself," Lamont pointed out.

"No, now I'm telling the truth!" Billy raised his eyes to glare at Lamont.

"Billy, why don't we call it what it is? You lied then, and you're lying now." Lamont shook his head and turned to Judge Jackson. "Your Honor, I have no further questions for this liar."

Teresa jumped to her feet, but before she could object, the judge was already issuing a stern warning.

"Don't push me, Mr. Hudson."

"Sorry, Your Honor. I meant no harm." Lamont returned to his seat.

I gave him a nod of approval then turned around to Carla, who gave me the signal to let me know that the jurors had been receptive to Lamont's cross-examination. It was a small victory, but we were in the middle of one hell of a war.

# 26

## *Billy*

I wasn't a religious man, but I damn sure was praying for a miracle as I exited the courtroom after testifying. I knew there would be severe repercussions for being a witness against Savannah, and I had no doubt that Lamont was probably going to assault me again as soon as the opportunity presented itself. It was going to take an act of God for me to slip past the press, the Hudsons, and Savannah. Making a clean getaway was going to be damn near impossible, but I was going to try.

*SLAP!*

A palm connecting with the right side of my face stopped me in my tracks. Savannah stood in front of me, her eyes full of rage as tears rolled down her cheeks. Seeing her made me feel even worse than I already did, and I imagined this was exactly how Judas must have felt.

"How could you? You testified against me!" Her words sounded forced. "How could you do that to me? To us?"

"They made me, Savannah," I gulped, glancing around to make sure none of the Hudsons were around. "They said if I didn't testify, I would be considered an accessory after the fact. I love you, but I can't go to jail."

"But I can?" Savannah scoffed. "And don't say you fucking love me, you traitorous coward."

"Savannah, listen—"

"You know what?" Savannah cut me off. "Fuck you, Billy King. You go straight to hell!"

She turned to walk away, but I grabbed her by the waist and pulled her to me, whispering in her ear. "Please don't walk away from me. I'm sorry. You gotta believe me. I don't want to lose you."

"You never had me, Billy." Savannah sniffled. "The Hudsons are right. You have no loyalty to anybody but yourself." She peeled my arms from around her waist and stormed off.

She stopped after she'd gotten a few feet away, and I hoped she'd had a change of heart.

"Oh," she tossed over her shoulder, "you're fired. I'll be by later to get all of my things."

There was no coming back from what I'd done. It was over, and I'd lost her as a client, a lover, and a friend. It would be hard to find someone as talented and well-known as Savannah, especially with that sex tape out there staining my reputation. Then again, there was that old saying that all press is good press. Maybe the attention would bring me some new clients. I adjusted the collar of my suit, put on my shades, and held my head up proudly as I headed toward the front door to exit.

# 27

## *Lamont*

I was still mad at Teresa after the stunt she had pulled in my office. Outside of court, we hadn't seen or talked to each other. But regardless, she stayed on my mind, which was why, when I had the chance to go head to head with her by cross-examining Billy, I took it. The way she looked at me after my questioning let me know that she'd missed me just as much, and for a split second, I imagined bending her over the defense table, lifting her skirt and—

"Lamont!"

My father's voice interrupted my brief fantasy and pulled me back into the reality of the conference room. I leaned back in my chair, chewing on the end of my pen while my dad paced in front of the window. I'd been so caught up in my thoughts about Teresa that I hadn't even realized Carla had entered the room until I saw her sitting at the far end of the table.

"My bad, Dad. I was just—uh—thinking about court earlier." I sat up.

"Well, I need your head in the game, son."

"Understood," I said. "Any word from Savannah? You think she's really done with Billy for good?"

"Yeah, we confirmed that she picked up all of her belongings from his house," Carla said. "And I'm glad. He didn't mean her any good anyway, and he damn sure wasn't helping her case. Hell, he did more harm than anything."

"Billy has always been out for self. I don't even understand how she got hooked up with that clown anyway. He can't manage nothing." I shook my head. "So, where is she staying?"

Dad sighed. "We couldn't risk her staying in a hotel. The media would definitely find out. And going back to her house wasn't an option, of course. She's staying with Dez for now."

"You think that's a good idea?" I asked.

"Desiree can handle her," Dad assured me. "Right now, we need a game plan, a strategy."

"What are you thinking?" I asked.

"If we don't come up with anything soon, I'm thinking . . ." His voice trailed off.

"Thinking what?" Carla asked before I did.

"After this Billy fiasco, we may have to put Savannah on the stand."

"Dad—"

"I know." He began pacing again.

"If that's the case, they may as well put her in an orange suit right now. She can't do it. Trust me. You know Carla and Dez have been trying to prep her for weeks. She's her own worst enemy," I reminded him.

"You got any better ideas?" he asked.

"Savannah's got a lot of celebrity friends, right? Let them talk her up. Maybe a juror or two will get star struck and hold out on convicting her," I suggested. "It can't hurt."

"Son, I can drag character witness after character witness in front of that jury, but sooner or later, the jury is going to want to hear from Savannah. Maybe her looks and her talent will blind even just one juror to the details that have already been presented."

"As much as I hate to say it, he's right, Lamont," Carla chimed in.

We were all right. Savannah was going to make a horrible witness. Still, the jury needed to hear what she had to say about everything: her marriage to Kyle, her relationship with Billy, and what happened the night of the murder. What other options did we have at this point?

"Maybe it's time to sit down with the DA and cut a deal," I said.

Plea bargains were always the last resort for Bradley Hudson. My father was all about winning, and to him, cutting deals didn't equate to a win. But, at this point, all the evidence pointed to our client being the guilty party, and winning no longer seemed possible.

Dad wasn't ready to accept defeat. "There's got to be another way." He turned to look back out the window.

"You mean like giving them the real killer?"

We turned to Perk, who walked in the room and tossed copies of a photo on the table.

"Who the hell is this?" Dad asked, picking up one of the pictures.

I grabbed my own copy and stared at the familiar man in the photo.

"That right there is Todd Townson," Perk said.

"He's the guy you were staring at during the wake," I said, suddenly remembering where I'd seen him.

"Yeah, that's him," Perk confirmed. "He's also the man in surveillance footage from the security cameras around the Kirby residence. And Todd may very well be the man who killed Kyle Kirby."

# 28

## *Desiree*

Being part of the defense team for Savannah Kirby kept me busy. Most of my assignments were the typical duties that came with all cases: background checks, financial records, legal briefs, and evidence submissions. It was no secret that Dad gave the harder stuff to Lamont, and the more trivial undertakings were my responsibility. Usually, I didn't complain too much, but being tasked as Savannah Kirby's babysitter was a bit much.

*"Savannah will be staying with you for the duration of the trial. She's getting her things from Billy's place and should arrive shortly. She has a key."*

My father's voice played in my head as I parked my car. He didn't even ask if Savannah could stay with me. Instead, I was advised via voicemail that I would be hosting a woman who could possibly be a murderer in my home, for God knows how long—and she had a key to my place. By the time I got the message, Savannah had already arrived. All I wanted to do was go home, finish the leftover chicken salad in my fridge, and go to bed. Now, I had a house guest to entertain.

"Savannah?" I called out, closing and locking the door behind me. "I'm home. Sorry it took me so long. Traffic on the highway was backed up." I hung up my keys and tossed my purse on the dining room table before kicking the heels off my throbbing feet. When I turned on the light in my living room, I almost didn't recognize the place. In addition to multiple suitcases and bags on every piece of furniture, there were boxes piled high all over the floor. I knew Savannah had a shopping addiction, but to see it firsthand was damn near overwhelming.

I headed toward the guest room. The door was closed, but I could see from under the door that the lights in the room were on. I was about to knock, but the ringing of my phone stopped me. I hurried to catch it before it stopped.

"Hey, Daddy," I answered.

"Hey, honey. Did you make it home yet?"

"Yeah, I'm here." I didn't try to mask the attitude in my voice, hoping he would pick up on it.

If he had, he didn't acknowledge it. "How is Savannah settling in? Did you make sure she's comfortable?" he asked as if I were a hotel concierge.

"From the boxes piled in my living room, I'd say she's made herself at home."

"Good. Can I speak to her? I've been trying to call her, but she didn't answer."

I sighed. In addition to being the babysitter and the concierge, I had to be Savannah's personal assistant. "All right. Give me a second."

"Okay. Thanks, honey."

I knocked on the guest room door. "Savannah? My dad wants to talk to you. Can you open the door, please?"

There was no answer. I turned the doorknob and stepped into the room. The lights were on, but Savannah wasn't there. I checked the small attached bathroom, and it was empty as well. Just as I was about to turn the light out and break the news to my father, I spotted a piece of paper on the edge of the bed. I snatched it up and read it.

> To the Hudsons,
> I'm so sorry for all of the trouble I've caused you. But I can't do it. After today, I just don't see how any of you will be able to keep me out of prison. Nobody is listening to me, and nobody believes me. The only way to protect myself and anyone else is to run as far away as possible. I'm sorry again.
> Savannah

She was gone.

*Shit!* I thought in a panic. *This heffa done skipped bail.*

I looked at my phone and contemplated just hanging up. My father was going to be furious, and there was no doubt in my mind that he would find some way to blame me. That was exactly why I couldn't tell him. Savannah couldn't have been gone for more than an hour, which meant I still had time to find her.

"Uh, Daddy? Savannah is in the shower right now. Can I have her call you when she gets out?"

"Yeah, sure," he said. "I'll be up for a while."

"Perfect. Okay, love you. Bye!" I ended the call before he could say anything else. What the hell was I going to do? It took me a few minutes to think of a plan, and I really didn't want to do it, but I finally made a call to the one person I knew could help me locate Savannah in record time.

"Well, this is a surprise," Perk answered. "I thought you said we were only to have contact during office hours."

I rolled my eyes. "This is business-related. I need your help."

"Oh." He sounded disappointed. "What's going on?"

"Savannah's missing."

"Missing? What do you mean? She's at your place, isn't she?"

"If she was at my place, do you think I would be calling you and saying she's missing?" I tried not to sound irritated, but I was anxious, and his questions weren't making me feel any better. "Look, can you make a call and run a locator on her phone and see if you can track it, please?"

"Not a problem."

"Thanks," I said, feeling a little relieved. "Oh, and Perk?"

"Yeah?"

"Let's keep this between you and me, at least for now."

"Isn't that always how it's always been? Gimme fifteen minutes. I'll call you back with the information," he said, then hung up.

I told myself that this wasn't the time to worry about whether his comment was sincere or sarcastic. The only thing I needed to be thinking about was finding Savannah before anyone else did, especially the press. Lord knows we didn't need any more negative spotlight. I poured myself a glass of wine and anxiously waited for Perk to call.

"Found her," was the first thing he said after calling me back less than five minutes later.

"Oh my God! Where?" I didn't know how he'd found her so fast, but I wasn't surprised. Perk was damn good at his job, and he would always get the information he needed however he had to. I was just relieved he'd worked his magic again this time.

"Someplace called Jeremy's. It looks like it's not that far from your place. I'll drop her pin to your phone. You want me to meet you there?"

"No, I got it. But thanks, Perk. You're a lifesaver. I owe you," I said, slipping back into my shoes and grabbing my wallet out of my purse.

"Anytime," he said. "Let me know when you get to her."

Jeremy's turned out to be a hole in the wall bar ten minutes from my house. I'd never heard of it before, and had it not been for Savannah, I would never have stepped foot inside. The moment I opened the door, the smell of cheap perfume and liquor hit me. There were only a handful of people in the small tavern, and they were all spaced out. Some were sitting at tables on the side, while a few were at the bar or playing darts. I scanned the dimly lit area, searching for Savannah, but I didn't see her.

"Looking for someone?" an ancient-looking, scruffy guy behind the bar yelled.

Seeing that his question was directed at me, I nodded as I walked over. "Yes. Yes, I am."

"I figured. It's not often we get ladies as beautiful as you in here," he said with a whistle. "I bet I know exactly who you're looking for, and let me tell ya—she is something. Gorgeous model chick with long hair and a bad attitude?"

"That's exactly who I'm looking for," I told him, amazed that he hadn't recognized her. Was he living in another century or something? "Is she still here?"

"Yep, and she hasn't paid her tab. She's up to four shots of Patrón and two of Grey Goose."

"Where is she?" I looked around again.

"She's been in the bathroom for the past twenty minutes. I was just about to send someone in there to check on her to make sure she ain't puked all over the place. She's drunk as a skunk."

"Thank you. Which way is the bathroom?"

"Down that hallway and straight back." He pointed his finger to the other side of the bar. "Don't be tryna run out on the bill, either!"

I pulled a crisp hundred-dollar bill out of my wallet and set it on the bar to cover Savannah's tab. When I got to the ladies' room, I tried to open the door, but it was locked. There was noise coming from inside that sounded like crying.

"I didn't do it. I didn't do it," she was saying over and over.

"Savannah?" I knocked softly on the door. "Savannah, open the door. It's me, Desiree."

"Go away!" Savannah yelled tearfully. "Didn't you get my note?"

"Yeah, I got it," I answered.

"Well, if you're here, you obviously didn't read it."

"I did read it, all of it. But I don't think you meant anything you said."

"And how do you know that? You don't know me! You probably didn't even want me staying at your place."

"Savannah, you're upset and have every right to be. Your life is in shambles, and you need some support." I sighed. "That's why my dad . . . our firm decided my place was the best place for you to be right now. Open the door, Savannah, please."

There were a few moments of silence, then the click of the door as it opened. Savannah stood in the doorway, her face wet with tears and mascara running down her cheeks. She looked nothing like the glamorous star that she was. Standing in front of me was a woman who was hurting, confused, and scared.

"Oh, Savannah," I said, feeling sorry for the poor woman. "Come here."

As soon as I opened my arms, she fell into them, sobbing hard into my shoulder. I rubbed her back, doing my best to comfort her as she released her pain. It was then that I realized this woman had no family, no friends, and now that Billy was gone, no one else. All she had was us, the Hudsons. I also understood why Dad had her come to my place. She really didn't have anywhere else to go.

"It's going to be okay," I said, pulling away and looking into her eyes. Placing my hands on each side of her face, I wiped away her tears with my thumbs. "You're going to be okay."

"I don't know what I'm going to do, Desiree. Nobody believes me. I didn't kill him."

"I understand that." I shook my head. "But you can't run away. That's not how it works. It doesn't matter if a billion people said you did it. If you didn't do it, you stand on that. Understand me?"

"Do you believe me?"

"Yes," I said. "And so does my father."

"He does? How do you know?"

"Because despite the fact that you've pissed him off several times, he hasn't dropped you as a client. That tells me a lot. You're not alone in this, Savannah. But you're gonna have to start taking things seriously and cooperating with us." My voice was stern as if I were scolding a child who didn't turn in her homework.

"Okay." Savannah nodded obediently.

"All right, get your face straightened up." I reached for some tissue and handed it to her. "My car is out front. Let's get the hell out of here before they think we're snorting coke back here."

By the time we made it back to my place, Savannah was asleep. She woke up long enough for me to help her inside, but once we made it to the guest room, she passed out on the bed, fully dressed and on top of the covers. I grabbed a blanket from the closet and placed it over her. Before I turned the lights off, I stared at her. I may not have believed Savannah before, but now, something in my spirit told me that Savannah Kirby was innocent.

"Everything okay?" Perk asked. "I was starting to get worried."

I had called him after I took a hot shower and finally got settled in my bed. "Yeah, everything's fine. We're home, and she's asleep."

"Good."

"Thanks again. You came through for me, and I appreciate it."

"That's what I do. Get some rest. I'll see you both in court," he said.

After we hung up, I tried to go to sleep, but for some reason, I couldn't get Perk off my mind. He really had saved me that night, as he'd done several times before. If Savannah hadn't been there, I might have invited him over so I could thank him properly. I allowed my mind to wander for a few minutes, imagining all the ways I could do that. But eventually, I remembered the promise I'd made to myself many times, that I would stop having sex with him. I deserved more than that, and so did he. Perk was a great guy. Maybe if things were different, we could be together, but as long as we both worked for my father, there wasn't a chance in hell.

# 29

## *Bradley*

As soon as court was called to session the following morning, Lamont and I approached Judge Jackson to discuss a new motion. Teresa stood beside us, not trying to hide her displeasure at what we were discussing.

"Your Honor, I don't think this is a good idea," she said, shaking her head.

"Your Honor, the People introduced this surveillance video as evidence," I spoke directly to Judge Jackson. "All we'd like to do is call a rebuttal witness."

"Your Honor, we have no idea who this man is and how he is relevant to these proceedings," Teresa said.

"You did open this up, Ms. Graham, so I'm going to allow it," Judge Jackson said.

Teresa turned away from the judge's bench and rolled her eyes at us before going back to her seat.

"Thank you, Your Honor," I said.

I gave Carla a satisfied grin as I sat down beside Savannah, who was noticeably calmer that day. She sat with her back straight and her hands clasped together on top of the table.

Desiree appeared with a bottle of water that she passed to her. "You good?" she whispered to Savannah, who nodded. "Okay, remember I'm right behind you, okay?" She took her seat as the judge spoke.

"Mr. Hudson," Judge Jackson said loudly. "Who is your next witness?"

I stood up and addressed the judge. "We are calling Todd Townson to the stand, Your Honor."

The doors opened, and Todd Townson, wearing a church suit, was escorted to the witness stand. He looked around the courtroom with a shocked look as he took the stand. As soon as he was sworn in, I lifted the remote that controlled the television screen we'd had brought into the courtroom earlier. I pressed play, and the surveillance video began playing on the screen.

"Mr. Townson, is that you there on the television screen?" I asked when I paused the video.

"Yeah," Todd said, looking uncomfortable. "Yeah, that's me."

"And is that you getting in the car?"

"Mm-hmm, that's me," he said.

"And could you please tell us who, exactly, was driving that car?"

"Kyle Kirby."

"So, that's you driving away with Kyle Kirby the night he was murdered?"

Todd's eyes grew wide, and then his forehead crinkled as reality dawned on him. He wasn't there on the stand as a witness; he was there as a suspect. From the gasps in the crowd, it was apparent that they'd reached the same conclusion.

"Oh, hell no!" Todd shouted. "Y'all ain't pinning this shit on me! I didn't kill Kyle."

"Language, Mr. Townson," I warned. "Might I add that you still haven't answered the question."

"Your Honor." Todd turned to Judge Jackson. "I think I need to speak to an attorney."

"I think that might be a good idea." Judge Jackson picked up her gavel. "This court is in recess for two hours."

I returned to the defense table and smiled at Savannah, who sipped her water.

"Who is that?" she asked.

"That is who I'm hoping can provide reasonable doubt," I told her.

"That dude looked like a deer caught in headlights," Lamont commented to Perk, who sat behind us. "Good job."

"Don't 'good job' him yet," I said. "We still need to connect Todd to the crime."

# 30

## *Lamont*

I decided to take a walk and get some air while court was in recess. I exited through one of the back doors of the building to avoid the press that was camped outside. If this were a regular murder trial, it would have faded from the news by now, but Savannah's stardom meant people were glued to the news, hungry for details. The crowd of reporters and cameramen was just as large as it had been on the first day of trial.

"Out here all by your lonesome?"

I didn't even have to turn around to know that Teresa was behind me. I stopped and leaned against the stone building.

"What do you want?" I asked.

"I'm trying to figure out what you and your father are trying to pull with this Townson guy," she answered.

"Oh, you decided to ask me directly instead of using pizza and pussy as an opportunity to sneak through my files?"

"Lamont, I was not snooping in your damn files." Teresa stepped directly in front of me, forcing me to look at her. "I swear."

Even if she was being honest, I wasn't ready to make amends just yet.

"We're not pulling anything with Townson. He's a witness, the same as Billy King," I told her, trying not to notice how sexy she looked in the black dress that revealed just enough cleavage to hold my attention.

"Your client is guilty, and I'm open to a plea agreement right now. Tomorrow, I may not be so generous. If you'd like to meet later and discuss—"

I interrupted her. "My client is innocent. My father and I are going to prove that. So we don't need to meet later for anything."

Teresa opened her mouth and then quickly shut it. The two of us squared off in what became a staring war. She blinked first.

I smirked and shook my head. "Counselor, we should get inside."

"I just hope you're prepared to lose," she said, then turned and walked off.

I battled temptation, but my eyes found their way to her rear end as she switched her hips. When she was gone, I let out a large breath.

"Women, huh?"

I turned my head around and stared at Billy. The casual outfit he wore let me know that he damn sure wasn't there for court.

"What the hell are you doing here?" I growled. "Haven't you done enough interviews?"

Less than twenty-four hours after Savannah fired him, Billy had already done at least ten interviews with various news outlets. He was using his fifteen minutes of fame from the leaked sex tape to promote his so-called talent management. It was utterly disrespectful, but typical Billy.

"Hey, I'm just trying to make the best out of a bad situation." Billy shrugged. "Since Savannah's no longer a client, I need to make sure I'm still gonna be able to eat. You feel me?"

"You know, you should really be ashamed of yourself. The only decent thing you've ever done for Savannah was to bring her to our firm. But you didn't even do that to help her. That was you trying to protect your meal ticket. She really trusted you, and this is how you repay her. Trying to get clout off her trial and kicking her when she's already down. If I didn't know any better, I'd think you leaked that fucking video."

"I wouldn't expect you to believe me," he started, "but I ain't leak shit. Although, if I did do something like that, I'd say I did her a favor. Her music is up three hundred thousand streaming hits, and her videos have millions of views. It sounds crazy, but whoever did leak it did her a favor. She's on the come up because of it. Kinda like a Kardashian. I'm not here to do an interview.

I'm here to talk to Savannah and convince her to hire me back. We can turn this into a goldmine."

"Just when I think you can't get more fucked up than you already are," I spat. "You are truly a piece of work. She's on trial for murder, facing life in prison, and you came here not to apologize, not to support her, but on some bullshit. Get the fuck out of my face, Billy, before those news cameras get you on video catching these hands."


When the court resumed, Todd Townson was back on the stand.

Dad began his line of questioning. "Mr. Townson, before we recessed, I asked if that was you driving away with Kyle Kirby the night he was murdered."

"On the advice of my attorney, I am invoking my Fifth Amendment right not to incriminate myself." Todd's voice was robotic, like the line had been rehearsed and he wanted to make sure he got it right.

A collective murmur went throughout the court.

"Order in the court!" Judge Jackson banged her gavel.

The audience quieted down, and Dad continued. "Did you kill Kyle Kirby? Did you murder my client's husband?"

"On the advice of my attorney, I am invoking my Fifth Amendment right not to incriminate myself," Todd stated again, this time with a little more confidence.

"Your Honor, I have no further questions for this witness." Dad strode back to the defense table with his shoulders squared and his head held high. He'd just landed a point toward establishing reasonable doubt. Invoking the Fifth Amendment didn't prove Todd had murdered Kyle, but it sure didn't make him look innocent, and that could only be good for Savannah.

From the corner of my eye, I saw Teresa lean over and whisper something to her colleague. From her demeanor, I could see that her confidence level had waned. We'd blindsided her the same way she'd done us, and it showed. That was probably the reason she was willing to discuss a plea agreement all of a sudden.

"Your witness, Ms. Graham," Judge Jackson said to her.

"Your Honor, because this witness was brought to our attention just today, we'd like to ask for a brief recess."

Judge Jackson's eyes went from Bradley to Teresa, and then to Todd Townson.

"Very well," she said. "I think that's fair. The court will resume tomorrow at nine thirty a.m."

# 31

## *Bradley*

Todd Townson took his seat on the witness stand the following morning. Surprisingly, the ADA's demeanor was much more confident than it had been the day before. Teresa strolled to the front of the courtroom to begin her questioning like she owned it. I wondered why she'd even called him to the stand. Wasn't it obvious he'd be pleading the Fifth? Either she was buying time, or there was something we didn't know, and that made me nervous.

I glanced over at Lamont, who seemed to be thinking the same thing. Teresa had already proven herself to be a worthy opponent during the trial, and I knew better than to underestimate her.

"Good morning, Mr. Townson. How are you today?" She was pleasant. Too darn pleasant.

"I've seen better days." Todd shrugged.

"I bet. This is a very stressful time."

"It sure as hell is." Todd was already sweating, and she hadn't even asked a question.

"Well, let me see if I can take a little of that stress off you. I only have a few questions." She smiled again, and he nodded his head. "What time did you leave Mr. Kirby the night he was murdered?"

"On the advice of my attorney, I am invoking my Fifth Amendment right not to incriminate myself." Like clockwork, he repeated the same answer he'd given the day before.

"No further questions for this witness, Your Honor," Teresa said.

"What the fuck is going on?" Lamont mumbled.

"I don't know, but they are definitely up to something," I replied, now even more curious as to why she'd called Todd back to the stand. It made no sense. She'd basically handed us the case.

"Mr. Hudson, do you have any further questions for this witness at this time?" Judge Jackson asked me.

With Todd Townson pleading the Fifth, reasonable doubt was basically a forgone conclusion. We'd already decided that Lamont was right; putting Savannah on the stand would be the equivalent of shooting ourselves in the foot. Although she'd been on her best behavior the past few days, there was still a huge chance that she'd crack during cross examination and do more damage than good. With Todd's appearance, we didn't need to take that risk.

"No, Your Honor. The Defense rests," I stated.

"Okay then, we will begin—"

"Excuse me, Your Honor." Teresa stood and interrupted the judge. "The People would like to present a rebuttal witness."

Well, it looked like the shoe had finally dropped. I glanced at Lamont, who wore a bewildered expression. I glanced down at the witness list. Nobody on it could hurt us, so what the hell was she up to?

"Okay, Ms. Graham. Please, call your witness."

"The People call Officer Paul Jones."

*Paul Jones? Who the fuck is he?*

A tall white police officer with blond hair and blue eyes made his way down the aisle of the courtroom. If he wasn't wearing that uniform, you might think he was a college student. He took a seat on the witness stand and tried to sit up confidently. It was pretty obvious he hadn't testified in many cases.

I leaned over to Lamont and whispered, "He wasn't one of the officers at the crime scene, was he?"

Lamont shook his head. "No, he couldn't have been. Perk vetted all of them during pre-trial discovery. I don't know who this guy is."

"Officer Jones, at approximately nine fifty p.m. on May twelfth, did you happen to have contact with Todd Townson?"

"Yes, I did." Officer Jones looked down at a note pad. "My partner and I pulled Mr. Townson over for a broken taillight on his vehicle."

"I see." Teresa began to pace near the jury. "And was he ticketed?"

"No, ma'am. Mr. Townson's license came up suspended, so we arrested him for operating a motor vehicle on a suspended license."

"Interesting, and how long was he in custody?" Teresa asked.

Officer Jones looked down at his note pad again. "He was arraigned the next morning at eleven thirty-nine a.m. and released on his own recognizance by the judge."

Teresa was practically strutting in front of the jury now. I felt myself sinking into my seat and had to sit up straight so they wouldn't notice how defeated I felt.

"So, he couldn't have been in Rockaway killing Mr. Kirby between ten p.m. and two a.m.?"

Officer Jones paused and looked at the jury and then back to Teresa. "No, ma'am, that would be virtually impossible. Unless, of course, he had a clone or a twin."

"Which he does not," Teresa replied smugly. "Your Honor, I'd like to enter into the record Mr. Townson's arrest record from the night of Mr. Kirby's death."

"So noted, Ms. Graham," the judge replied.

"Uh-huh, that proves it. That bitch killed my son!" Cathy Kirby shouted from her seat behind the prosecution, and the entire courtroom erupted.

*And just like that, we're fucked!*

"Order, order in this courtroom!" Judge Jackson slammed down her gavel.

Teresa stood there with a faint smirk on her face while she waited for the crowd to get themselves under control. I looked over at the jury and didn't like what I saw on their faces either. Reasonable doubt was no longer a foregone conclusion.

"Your witness, Mr. Hudson."

Teresa strode back over to the defense table. The self-righteous look she gave me was familiar. It was the same one I'd given opposing counsel hundreds of times when I had no doubt that I'd won case my case.

"No questions for this witness, Your Honor," I said.

"Well, in that case, we will have summations in the morning," Judge Jackson said.

As people rose and started exiting the courtroom, I placed my hand on Savannah's shoulder to assure her we weren't finished yet. We had until tomorrow to try to fix this. But obviously she didn't want to hear any platitudes from me.

"What the hell was that?" she snapped, snatching away from my touch and storming off.

"I got her, Daddy," Desiree said.

"Don't let her talk to any press." I reminded her, and she took off after our client.

"Can you please tell me what the hell just happened?" Lamont hissed in frustration.

"We were just knocked out by Mike Tyson in his prime," I said with a sigh. Carla was now at my side. "At this point, nothing short of a miracle is gonna save our client."

"It's not over." Carla rubbed my arm. "We just have to pull a rabbit out of our hat."

"I don't know. I think I'm fresh out of rabbits." And now I had the worst stomachache. I'd let my client down, my firm down, and worst of all, I'd let myself down. I wasn't used to feeling this way.

Carla tried to offer me some comfort. "You still have closing arguments, and if it's one thing I've learned about Bradley Hudson, he *always* has the last word. And jurors *always* listen."

Whether she was saying what she thought I needed to hear or she truly meant it, I didn't care. I was grateful for her vote of confidence, and even more for the fact that I'd married such an amazing woman. She was right. It wasn't over until it was over, and it was now time to go home and write the closing arguments of a lifetime.

# 32

## *Michael*

It was well after midnight, and I was still at my desk, going over some discovery for a case Lamont had coming up. Unlike some of the other associates, I purposely stayed late and found things to do to make myself useful. A former professor I really respected always said that if a young lawyer was going to be successful, it would be because he made himself invaluable to the people he worked for. So, I made it a habit to be the last person to leave, other than the Hudsons, of course—and possibly Perk, who, I was learning, was practically part of their family. Tonight, I'd even outlasted most of the Hudson family.

On my way out, I knocked on Bradley's door to let him know I was leaving.

"Who's there?" he called out.

"It's just me, sir."

"Come on in, Michael."

I stepped into the office, which was lit only by a small lamp on his desk. Carla was asleep under a blanket on the small couch in the corner. Bradley was surrounded by yellow legal pads. He still wrote his closing arguments out by hand—an old school lawyer.

"I was about to head home unless you needed me for something else. I can stay."

"I thought everyone had gone home hours ago," he said.

"No, sir. I was just going over a couple of things. You sure you don't need me to do anything?"

"No, I was just finalizing some things for tomorrow's summation," he said. "I heard Perk had you going over the crime scene photos again earlier. You find anything new worth talking about? A fresh set of eyes is always a good thing."

"Not really. Nothing worth talking about."

"Everything's worth talking about when you're sitting on a loser," he replied. "It might not have any bearing on the final outcome, but maybe it will give me some insight on how to approach the jury. Talk to me."

"Well, I doubt you'd want to talk about the fact that Savannah Kirby and her manager were just grimy," I said, then quickly added, "No offense, sir. I mean, I know she's our client, and this might be a little inappropriate, but she's still grimy as hell."

"Why do you say that?" He gestured for me to sit by his desk. "What's so grimy about her?"

"Mr. Hudson, they had sex in the same bed she shared with her husband. In my book, that's just nasty and disrespectful."

"You're right. That would be pretty disrespectful. But where's this coming from? You don't know that for a fact," he commented.

Usually when he mentored me, his instincts were spot on and I needed to be corrected. But this time, I was confident that I was right.

"Yes, sir, I do. I've watched that sex tape enough to recognize that headboard anywhere."

He gave me a strange look, and I realized how that must have sounded.

"I watched it multiple times for work, of course. Not for pleasure. I'm not into that kind of thing. I mean, I am, but—"

"I know what you mean, Michael."

"Sorry," I said, slightly embarrassed. "I'm talking too much again, arent' I?"

"Rule number one of lawyering," he said. "Never say more than you absolutely have to."

"Guess I still have a lot to learn," I said. "But at least I have the best mentor around."

He brushed off the compliment and got back to the tape. "But what you're telling me is that our client's sex tape was made in the Kirby home?"

"Yes, sir. The same bed is in the crime scene photos and the sex tape. You have to zoom in on the video close enough to see it. I can go back to my desk and get you the file if you'd like?"

"Yes," he replied. "I want to see this."

As I left his office, I heard him say, "Well, I'll be damned."

A few minutes later, I handed Bradley two different photos, both taken in Savannah's bedroom. The first one was taken by Perk when he'd gone to the crime scene. It was a shot of the bloody bed where Kyle Kirby's body was found. The second picture was a still shot taken from the leaked video. It was zoomed past Savannah's face, and you could clearly see the headboard. There was no doubt I was right; it was the same bed.

Bradley studied the pictures for a good five minutes, then rushed over to the sofa and gently shook Carla. "Babe."

"Hmm?" Carla moaned sleepily.

"Get up. You gotta come look at this."

She sat up and stretched, then followed him back to his desk. He placed the photos side by side, and before he could even point out what I had shown him, she saw it herself.

"But if this was in their bedroom, who took the video?" she asked.

"Michael, call Perk and tell him to get his ass down here. Same thing with Lamont. And if either of them doesn't answer, take an Uber and wake them up."

"Sure thing, Mr. Hudson."

"Oh, and Michael?"

I stopped at the door and turned around.

"You may have just earned yourself a raise. And more importantly, my respect."

I couldn't stop smiling as I made my way down the hall.

# 33

## *Bradley*

I stepped out of the Rolls behind my son and once again stood in front of the home Savannah had shared with Kyle. Judge Jackson, along with the stenographer and Lieutenant Barnes, had just emerged from an unmarked police car, while Teresa Graham and Cathy Kirby got out of a very official-looking vehicle parked near them.

"I'm giving you some leeway here, Mr. Hudson, but the rope is very short. I hope you're not wasting the court's time," Judge Jackson warned.

"Not at all, Your Honor," I told her. "I assure you this little field trip will either exonerate or convict my client. I appreciate the court's willingness to grant our request."

"Your Honor," Teresa interrupted. "I would like to reiterate my objection to this circus Mr. Hudson is trying to place upon this court. The jury has been given ample photos from this crime scene. Not to mention the fact that we had to wake Mrs. Cathy Kirby up to unlock the door."

"Duly noted, Ms. Graham, but having jurors travel to the crime scene is not unprecedented," I reminded her. "If I recall, you not so long ago handled the Carlson rape case, where you made a similar request, and it was granted."

"I was reluctant to agree to this, but case law is on Mr. Hudson's side. He does have the right to present live crime scene evidence as part of his defense," the judge said, and then cut her eyes at me. "But not much. Now, let's get started."

I nodded, and the judge checked her watch before turning toward two vans parked across the driveway. She motioned for them to unload, and the jurors exited the vehicles, most looking curious and confused. Lamont, Carla, and Perk joined the crowd, along with Desiree, who was assigned to babysit Savannah.

"If you all would follow me up the stairs," I announced to the crowd as we entered the house.

Savannah looked like she was going to be sick. She hadn't been back home since the morning she found Kyle's body and fled the scene. It was obvious that this was going to be traumatic for her, but it was necessary if we had any hope of proving her innocence.

I led the group into the master bedroom, which was large enough that everyone was able to fit comfortably and still have space left.

"Mr. Hudson, you can proceed," Judge Jackson said once everyone was settled.

"Ladies and gentlemen, this is the bedroom where Kyle Kirby was murdered. My co-counsel is going to hand you pictures of the crime scene, displaying exactly where Kyle Kirby's body lay."

On cue, Lamont began handing out pictures for the jury to review.

"Objection, Your Honor. The jury has already seen these photos and plenty more in the courtroom," Teresa interjected.

"I assure you this is going somewhere, Judge," I responded.

"You're skating on thin ice here, Mr. Hudson," Judge Jackson warned. "Let's get to the point."

"Of course, Your Honor. Now he's going to hand you a copy of People's Exhibit 113, a still photo of Mrs. Kirby and her manager, Mr. King."

Lamont passed copies of the second photo. I watched as Judge Jackson and the jury began examining the photos. It was obvious from their expressions that they didn't understand why they were being asked to compare the two.

"I want you to look at these photos closely. What do they have in common? Lieutenant Barnes, do you mind answering that for me?"

"The headboard?" Barnes's answer sounded more like a question.

"Exactly, the headboard," I said, pointing to the bed in the room. Being in the physical space where it all happened would heighten the emotion and make it more real for them. "Now, I know the focus has been on the fact that Savannah Kirby and Billy King had an affair, and we aren't disputing that fact, but that's not why we're here.

"The prosecution submitted the salacious video, from which you're holding a still shot now. But not only has the source of the video never been disclosed, but the location of the act has not been examined—up until now. It was only recently that we discovered the video was recorded in the very bedroom where Kyle Kirby was murdered. The question is, how? Who took the pictures?"

I paused and watched as my question registered in the faces of the jurors. Their eyes went from the photos, then back to the bed, which was still stained with Kyle Kirby's blood. Then they all looked at me expectantly, waiting for more information for their unanswered questions.

I had them right where I wanted, hanging on my every word. Just like it did in every trial when I held the fate of the defendant in my hands, that power gave me a rush. Especially since I knew the bombshell I was about to drop would change everything. I turned my gaze toward the row of angel statues on a shelf facing the bed, knowing their eyes would follow me.

"Lieutenant Barnes, did you examine these statues during your crime scene investigation?" I asked.

"No. There was no blood spatter, so the evidence collection was confined to the area directly surrounding the bed."

"I see. Well, could you examine them now, please? Specifically, the large one in the center," I directed.

Teresa shifted uncomfortably nearby. It was never a good feeling when you had no idea where your opponent was going next. What she didn't know was that I wasn't sure either where this would ultimately take us.

Lieutenant Barnes eased over to the wall and picked up the statue, turning it over to look at it from all angles. "Well, I'll be," he stated incredulously. "It's a nanny cam—or an angel cam, in

this case." He removed a USB drive from the bottom of the statue, which he could now see was hollow.

Teresa had turned about five shades darker. She looked like
she was simmering with rage. Barnes was supposed to be helping the prosecution. If he had done his job better, the camera
would have been discovered long ago, and she wouldn't be
standing there, looking like a fool now. I had no doubt she was
wondering how the hell I had pulled this surprise out of my hat.

Once we discovered that the video had come from the bedroom, Michael had talked to Kyle's private investigator again
in the early morning hours to see if he knew anything about it.
After a lot of cajoling and the promise of some future assignments from the firm, the PI finally gave up some information.
I understood why he hadn't mentioned the video the first time,
because he was the one who had installed the camera in the
bedroom—without Kyle's knowledge. When he managed to get
so many candid photos of Billy and Savannah together around
town, he decided he didn't need any footage from the angel cam.
This guy was shady, but even he knew that there was no reason
to invade Kirby's privacy any more than he already had. He had
meant to retrieve the camera at some point, but then Kyle died,
and he couldn't get back in the house that had become a crime
scene. His only hope was that the cops hadn't discovered it—and
if it weren't for Michael's keen eye, it would have stayed a secret.

"I think we all would like to see what's on that jump drive,
Lieutenant," Judge Jackson said.

Now, I was taking probably the biggest risk of my career. The
one thing we couldn't get the PI to do was to agree to come in
and testify, and with closing arguments scheduled for that day, I
didn't think the judge would agree to postpone things to issue a
subpoena. So, I had to do something dramatic. I requested that
the jury be allowed to visit the crime scene, in spite of the fact
that we really didn't know what the angel cam footage would
show. Sometimes, though, even a lawyer has to take a leap of
faith when he's left with no good choices. In my gut, I believed
that Savannah had not committed this crime, and I hoped that
the video was about to prove me right.

Lamont reached into his messenger bag and presented his laptop. "We can watch it right now if you'd like, Your Honor."

Once the laptop was powered on and positioned where everyone could see, I placed the drive into the USB port. Truth be told, I was intensely nervous. We were taking a huge chance.

I felt the tension throughout my body as I opened the file, which contained video surveillance of the bedroom over a number of weeks. I fast forwarded until the time/date stamp reached the estimated time of Kyle's death, then watched in shock along with everyone else in the room.

# 34

## *Kyle Kirby's death*

Kyle Kirby made his way into the master bedroom, dropped his pants to the floor, and unbuttoned his shirt. He didn't even have the energy to hop in the shower. He just climbed into bed with his boxers and T-shirt on. He laid on his back for a few moments, scrolling through his phone and checking sports highlights. The lights were off, but the moon lit up the bedroom. He was in the middle of reading a sports article when his phone started to vibrate every five minutes with calls from Savannah. She was fuming after he told her he wouldn't take the part in Gregg's movie.

When he didn't answer her calls, she sent him a string of angry texts. He loved his wife, but she could be so damn difficult sometimes. Between Savannah and his mom, he had his hands full with demanding divas. He would address Savannah's bad attitude with her in the morning, but for now, he just silenced his phone and set it on the nightstand next to his side of the bed.

Turning on his stomach, he put his arms under his fluffy, cool pillow and nestled his head on top of it. Sleep crept up on him before even he realized it, and everything around him faded away. He was having peaceful dreams until he felt a sharp pain in his back. He tried to adjust himself but found that he couldn't. His eyes jerked open, and he realized that there was somebody on top of him. Before he could make a move, there was another sharp pain in his back. And then another. And another. And another. Until his back went completely numb and his breathing became rigid.

He didn't understand what was happening as he faded into darkness. The last thing he saw before his final breath was his phone vibrating and Savannah's name on the screen.

# 35

## *Lamont*

Everybody in the room looked horror-stricken as we watched the hooded figure climb on top of Kyle Kirby and plunge the knife into his back. My father gave me a knowing glance. As horrific as the images were, they would confirm once and for all that our client was innocent. There was no way she was calling Kyle and killing him at the same time. Now, the only real question was, who was the killer?

It wasn't long before the video gave us the answer. The killer's hood had slipped back during the murder, and as she backed away from the bed, the angel cam got a clear look at the murderer's face. There was a collective gasp from the jurors, and even Teresa let out a little yelp as we all recognized the face of Kyle's mother. She stumbled away from the bed and dropped the knife, then she was out of camera range. I paused the video, still reeling from the shock.

"Somebody find me Cathy Kirby!" the lieutenant yelled. She had been in the room with us when the flash drive was taken out of the angel, but I guess we were so engrossed in my dad's presentation that no one noticed that she had vanished.

"Ms. Graham, I expect that your office will be dismissing the charges against Savannah Kirby. And issue a warrant for the arrest of Cathy Kirby!" the judge ordered.

Behind me, I heard Carla and Desiree shout for joy, while Savannah threw her arms around Dad's neck. Her smile was wide, and she had tears in the corners of her eyes.

"Thank you," she said into his chest as she hugged him. "Thank you, Bradley."

"Just doing my job," he said. "I always knew you were innocent."

I glanced over at Teresa, who gave me a congratulatory nod. We'd be seeing each other soon, and I couldn't wait to collect on that bet we'd made.

Dad pulled away from Savannah and approached me with his hand outstretched. "Good job, son. I'm damn proud to have you by my side."

# Epilogue

The manhunt was on—or in this case, the mother hunt. A warrant was quickly issued for Cathy Kirby's arrest, but nobody seemed to know where she was. Well, there was one person who had an idea. Since the beginning of the trial, Perk had taken it upon himself to keep tabs on everyone involved.

Once the judge dismissed them all, Perk, Lamont, and Bradley left Savannah with Desiree and Carla, while they took a little ride to the cemetery where Kyle Kirby was buried. Just as Perk had guessed, Cathy Kirby was there. Kyle's Range Rover was parked in the entrance—that was how she'd managed to get away from the house.

Freddy parked the Rolls Royce, and the men got out of the car, leaving him with instructions to alert the police of their location.

"If she runs, I'll get her," Lamont told them.

"You trying to tell me I'm too old to catch an old lady?" Bradley asked him, pretending to be offended.

"I mean, she did kill her son. And put on one hell of a show, might I add. There's no telling what she's capable of," Lamont reminded him.

But when Cathy saw the men approaching her, she didn't try to run. In fact, she didn't budge at all. She was kneeling next to Kyle's headstone, sobbing and mumbling things they couldn't make out. They circled around her.

"How did you know I would be here?" she asked tearfully.

"My investigator had all of the major players under surveillance during the trial," Bradley told her. "You came here every day. Plus, I knew you'd want to say goodbye to your son." He knelt down near her. "What happened, Cathy? What *really* happened?"

"I got into some trouble," she said, sniffling.

"What kind of trouble?"

"Gambling trouble. All he had to do was give me the money," Cathy said with a tired shrug. "I told him Todd was going to kill me if I didn't pay up."

"Are you saying that Todd Townson was your bookie?" Bradley asked with surprise. He hadn't seen that coming.

Cathy nodded her head and wiped her face with the back of her hand.

"How did you get caught up in that?" Bradley asked.

"Kyle took me there once to play the slots," she said. "Then I started to play blackjack, and next thing I know, I'm playing craps for a thousand a roll. They gave me credit because I was Kyle's mama, and I was good for it. But it just got worse from there."

She paused to wipe her face again. The men exchanged glances but remained silent as they waited for her to continue.

"Kyle paid my debt before, but it wasn't this much. I just couldn't stop. That night, Todd came to my house to collect, and I got scared. I told him to go to Kyle's house and ask him for the money. It was my only hope. But Kyle did something I couldn't believe. They drove back to my house, and he told me in front of Todd that he was done paying off my debts." Her expression transformed, and anger resurfaced from deep within her. "He paid off two million dollars for Savannah's credit card bills, but he refused to give me a hundred grand. He was the one who taught me to gamble in the first place, and now he was cutting me loose. They were going to kill me, for God's sake, and he didn't care!"

She was yelling at this point, clearly furious. It wasn't hard to imagine how someone with this much rage might snap and become violent. "So, since he showed me that my life wasn't worth shit to him, I took his!"

She broke into another fit of tears, and Bradley had to help her to her feet. Perk raised his hand at the two unmarked police vehicles that had just pulled up. Lieutenant Barnes got out of one of them and walked across the cemetery.

"Cathy Kirby, you're under arrest for the murder of Kyle Kirby. You have the right to remain silent." He read off the rest of her rights as he placed her in handcuffs.

Bradley watched with his son as she was escorted away. All the rage had drained out of her, and now she just looked like a defeated old woman who'd lost her only child.

"That right there is a literal example of that old saying, 'I brought you into this world, and I'll take you out.' Remind me to never say that to my kids," Lamont commented, and Bradley raised his eyebrow at him.

"Kids?" he asked.

"I'm just saying," Lamont said. "But yes, eventually, when the time is right, I would like to be a dad. I mean, I learned from the best, right?"

"I've just never heard you talk like that. Would it have anything to do with the ADA?"

"What?"

"I saw the way you looked at her back at the Kirby residence."

"I don't think this is the kind of conversation I'd like to have in a cemetery with my father," Lamont said, gesturing to all the headstones around them.

"Fair enough," Bradley said. "Come on. Let's meet the ladies back at the office so we can take Savannah to dinner. You can invite Teresa—if you think she won't be too busy licking her wounds."

"I can do that," Lamont said eagerly and pulled out his phone. When he saw the knowing look his father gave him, he cleared his throat. "I mean, if she isn't busy."

Bradley and Perk looked at each other and smirked as they headed back to the Rolls Royce. The other cases at Hudson and Hudson would have to wait. The only thing left to do that day was to celebrate one of the biggest wins for the firm. It was a challenging case for sure, and there were many moments he thought he would lose, but in the end, Bradley ended up where he belonged—on top of the world.

*"Tell me what I gotta do to please you, baby. Anything you say, I'll do. 'Cause I only wanna make you happy. From the bottom of my heart, it's true!"*

Lamont stood in the shower, singing along with Joe's vocals as the hot water ran down his body. It was a Saturday, and two weeks had passed since the charges against Savannah Kirby were dismissed. Things had quieted down at Hudson and Hudson, but that was all right with Lamont. After working a case like that, he welcomed a few weeks filled with easy work and being able to leave the office when there was still sun in the sky. And when the weekends finally came, he did no work at all.

Unfortunately, his newfound free time wasn't spent the way he would have liked—in the bed with Teresa Graham. In fact, she didn't talk to Lamont for a whole week after the trial ended, and when she did, she told him to screw himself.

Lamont turned the water off and grabbed a towel, wrapped it around his waist, and stepped out of the shower. He wiped the steam from the mirror and looked at his reflection as he picked up his toothbrush. The aroma of the bacon frying in the kitchen made him smile as he thought about Teresa, standing near the stove in nothing but a pair of heels.

He'd been surprised when she finally came around and showed up at his place the night before.

"You won fair and square," she'd said, and he knew how hard it must have been for her to say those words. "And I'm sorry I acted like that."

He reached out and pulled her into his apartment. "I'm just glad the right person is behind bars."

"Yeah, me too," she said. "Of course, I'm not happy I lost the bet, but I'm a woman of my word, so I'll cook *and* clean for you naked. If you forgive me."

He, of course, forgave her, and their makeup sex was mind-blowing. Flashbacks of the night before had Lamont longing for another round. He turned off the light and headed to the kitchen, wondering if his naked chef in there could multitask.

"Baby," he called out as he let his towel drop to the ground.


Kyle being gone was still taking some getting used to for Savannah, but she was just taking it day by day. Some days she could find small moments of happiness, and others she was a complete wreck. She guessed that was how it would be for some time. Kyle really was the love of her life.

She'd taken Desiree's advice and gotten a new bed, but she still found herself reaching for her husband. She had to constantly remind herself that he was never coming back. The only thing she could do was hang on to the memories she had and cherish all their photos. The angel cam had been sent to the dump along with the bed. It would be a long time before she could feel truly comfortable in the home again, and she might never get over the feeling that someone was secretly watching her. She shuddered every time she thought about how the private investigator had violated her privacy for his monetary gain.

It turned out that the PI had been lying to the Hudsons when he claimed he'd never checked the angel cam. In truth, he'd collected the video of Savannah and Billy a few weeks before Kyle's death and downloaded a copy. Instead of sharing it with Kyle, he decided to keep it to himself, assuming he could sell it to a tabloid when the time was right. The sleazy PI even placed the USB drive back in the bedroom to see what other valuable footage he might collect. After Kyle's death, he thought Savannah might be willing to pay big money to keep the tape under wraps. However, when he found out her shopping addiction had left her broke, he abandoned his blackmail plan and went with a quick payday from one of his online sources. Even he was surprised at how quickly the video went viral. He'd been charged with blackmail and was awaiting trial now. Savannah hoped he would rot in hell, right next to Kyle's mother.

Savannah's financial situation had certainly improved. She was listed as the beneficiary of Kyle's life insurance policy, but she was unable to access the money until after the charges against her were dismissed. When the funds were at last released to her, she promised herself that she wouldn't just blow through it. Still, one small shopping spree wouldn't hurt.

That Saturday morning, she found herself walking out of her favorite boutique, carrying shopping bags on each arm. She strutted in her four-inch Chanel pumps and shook her head gently so her long hair would catch the wind and stay out of her face. Many people snapped her photo as she walked past, and she graced each of them with her beautiful smile. It felt good to be loved by the media again, but she would never forget how quickly they could turn on her. She pledged to live a quiet and private life from now on.

Her hired security guard walked behind her, carrying a stack of shoe boxes to a waiting limousine. She got in and waited for him to load the rest of her things beside her as she fanned herself.

"Hurry up," she said. "I'm ready to get home and lay down."

"Yes, ma'am." When he was done, the guard got into the front passenger seat and told the driver, "Let's take this lady home."

Savannah leaned back in her seat and closed her eyes. Kyle's face appeared before her. She felt her lips form into a smile.

"I love you, Kyle Kirby," she whispered. "I love you forever. Goodbye."


It had been too long since Bradley and Carla had gone on a romantic date, so that Saturday morning, he took her for brunch and bottomless mimosas. As usual, she was stunning in a long-sleeved red blazer dress and a low, sleek ponytail. Bradley wasn't the only man in the room who couldn't keep his eyes off her.

Bradley didn't look so bad himself, wearing a tailored suit with diamond cufflinks on his silk sleeves—a little something-something he'd bought himself as a gift after winning the Kirby case. He had to admit, for a while there he didn't see anything but darkness at the end of the tunnel, but in the end, the right person was charged with the crime and would be punished accordingly.

As for Savannah, he hoped that she would be able to move on with her life, and maybe even get some help for her addiction. In spite of how difficult she could be, he had a soft spot in his heart for Savannah. As close as she and Desiree had become toward the end of the trial, he wouldn't be surprised if he saw more of her. In the meantime, there were other cases to get to, and other people who needed his help.

"Bradley Hudson, you are the man," Carla said as they sat at the rooftop restaurant, watching the sunlight gleaming off the downtown skyscrapers.

"Say it again, baby," he said, and she giggled.

"Bradley Hudson? You are the *man*." She leaned forward and kissed him passionately. When she pulled away from him, she lowered her eyes and opened her legs slightly. Bradley's eyes jumped with delight when he saw that she wasn't wearing any panties.

"Don't let those mimosas make you write a check you can't cash, now," Bradley said.

"And who says I can't cash it?" Carla asked seductively. "If we leave now, I'll cash it in the Rolls Royce."

"Check, please!" Bradley raised his hand to flag down a waiter.

He and Carla were walking hand in hand out of the restaurant within five minutes. Freddy stood by the Rolls Royce and opened the back door when he saw the couple approaching.

"I hope you two had a lovely meal," Freddy said to them.

"It's about to get even better," Bradley told him as they climbed in the back seat.

As soon as Freddy shut the door, it was on. Carla raised the privacy screen that shielded them from Freddy's view, and then she hiked up her dress and climbed on top of Bradley. He fondled her smooth, round bottom as their lips found each other again.

*Brrrrrrr! Brrrrrrr!*

The loud sound of his phone vibrating against the seatbelt distracted him for a second.

Carla pulled back and looked into his eyes. "Don't you dare answer that."

"I wasn't even thinking about it," he said, grabbing her hand and placing it on his growing bulge.

She reached for his belt buckle, unhooked it, and then reached for his zipper. Before his manhood was freed from his boxers, the phone vibrated again. Bradley looked down at the screen this time and saw the caller's name.

Carla let out a deep sigh. She knew how demanding some of his clients could be. The phone would just keep ringing until Bradley finally answered, so she might as well let him do it now. Better to be interrupted at the beginning, rather than when she was in the middle of the orgasm she expected to be having very soon.

"Go ahead," she said.

"Thank you. I promise I'll be quick," he said, giving her a kiss before he answered the call.

"Bradley Hudson speaking." He paused for a moment, listening to the caller, who was yelling so loudly that Carla could hear him. She watched as her husband's expression changed. He had his game face on.

"Okay, what I'm about to say is very important," Bradley said into the phone. "You're about to be arrested. Do not resist, and do not say anything to anyone other than my team. Do you understand what I am saying?"

*Also by Carl Weber*

# Influence

*Please enjoy this sample of **Influence**, the first book in The Hudson Family series.*

*Available at booksellers near you*

# *Langston*

## 1

"Yo, we need gas." The traffic was just starting to ease up as I pushed my Audi Q5 over the Verrazano-Narrows Bridge onto the Staten Island Expressway. It had taken a while to round everybody up, but we were finally on our way back to Howard University after spending Easter weekend back home in New York with our families. My mother had surprised me with the new car as an early graduation present. Elaborate gifts were her way of trying to make it up to us for walking out six years ago. "Hey, y'all, seriously, the gas light just came on. Somebody needs to cough up some cash."

You want to make a bunch of college students shut the fuck up? Put free food in front of them or ask them to chip in on gas. Either way, you're going to hear crickets. I held out my palm while trying to keep my eyes on the road, and let out a couple fake coughs, clearing my throat.

"What'd you say?" my frat brother Krush asked from the seat behind me.

"Oh, so now y'all deaf?" I flipped my sun visor down to block the rising sun from blinding me. "Y'all heard me. Don't every-body go reaching in your pockets all at once." Not one of them made a move to retrieve any money. "Y'all keep playing and the next stop is going to be the Port Authority and the Megabus. You got my word on that."

"Man, why you always got to be so damn dramatic and shit?" asked Tony, who was sitting in the passenger's seat. "You acting more and more like your old man every day."

The car erupted in laughter. Everyone got a kick out of his joke except for me. Tony knew I didn't like anyone joking or talking bad about my father. My pops was my hero. Shit, he was probably their hero too.

"You got a problem with that?" I asked.

There was a quiet pause before Tony said, "No, but you the one with the fancy ride and the rich old man. I'm barely getting by on financial aid and student loans. Give a brother a break, frat." He threw up our fraternity sign, and I heard Krush and Kwesi laugh again from the back seat.

"Tony, leave him alone, bro," Krush said, coming to my defense—or at least I thought he was. "His pops probably didn't have a chance to get to the safe after paying eighty grand in cash for this ride, so he only gave him five hundred to get through the week."

Once again, laughter filled the car, so much so that it was pissing me off.

"First of all, my dad isn't paying for this car," I said, shutting the fellas up. "My mom bought it for me," I mumbled under my breath, only making Krush's point.

"Aw, man!" Tony roared in my direction. "You should have just kept your mouth shut, you little spoiled bitch. Ain't nobody giving your rich ass any gas money."

The peanut gallery cosigned from the back.

I glared at Krush and Kwesi through the rearview mirror. "That's a'ight." I nodded knowingly as I put my eyes back on the road. "Next time y'all want a ride to McDonald's late at night, I hope you got your walking shoes, 'cause I ain't getting up. You got my word on that." This time, I threw up our frat sign.

"Damn, it's like that?" Tony asked.

"Yeah, it's like that." I mumbled under my breath, "See if y'all be laughing then."

I felt something lightly rest on my shoulder. I looked to see Kwesi's hand with a fifty-dollar bill in it.

"For you, my brother," Kwesi said in his African accent.

"Thanks." I took the bill out of Kwesi's hand. "At least one of you was raised right," I added sarcastically.

"Dude, we're all struggling college students," Krush chimed in from the back. "What do you expect?"

"Yeah, besides," Tony said, turning to look at Kwesi, "if my granddaddy's face was on the money in my country, I'd be generous too and whip out fifty bucks." He nodded toward Kwesi. "Ol' *Coming to America* mafucka."

This time even I joined in the laughter.

"That was a good one," I said to Tony. "But even if your granddaddy was Bill Gates, you wouldn't chip in a dime, because you're a . . ."

We all turned to Tony and in unison said, "Cheap-ass bastard!"

Tony gave us the finger, just like he always did. He could dish it out, but he couldn't take it worth shit.

"Eff all y'all," Tony said.

"Eff all y'all," Krush mocked in a feminine voice, letting Tony know he was being a baby.

It didn't matter how many times we clowned Tony about being cheap; he always caught an attitude. I would have thought he'd be used to it by now, since for the last four years at school, that's all we ever did was call him out for being so stingy. Tony, Krush, Kwesi, and I always had each other's backs, but whenever it was time to come up off some money, that's where Tony drew the line. I couldn't remember that last time he chipped in on a pizza or paid for a round of beers, but you best believe he was always full and had his thirst quenched before the night was over.

Yeah, he was cheap all right, despite having two part-time jobs, but then again, I tried to remember where he'd come from. Tony was raised by a single mother in Brooklyn's Marcy Projects. He had two brothers who were Bloods gang members, but he busted his ass and made it to Howard, where he was about to graduate with honors in accounting. Cheap or not, I had to admire him. He'd broken the cycle.

Realizing I was going to have to make do with Kwesi's contribution, I turned my focus back to the road. I hadn't even driven for a tenth of a mile before there was a clicking sound, a hiss, and then the car filled with something other than our laughter and music.

I sniffed the air. "Shit! Tell me that's not what the fuck I think it is."

"Depends on what you think it is."

I glanced in my rearview mirror at Krush just in time to see him take a long hit from the blunt he was caressing between his fingers.

"What the hell?" I shouted. "I know you're not smoking that shit in my car!"

"Yo, stop being such a pussy. Ain't nobody gonna harm your precious leather." Krush took another hit of the blunt.

"I'm not worried about the leather. I'm worried about jail," I said.

"Whatever." Krush snapped his head in my direction and gave me a serious look in the rearview mirror. Krush was what you might call a wannabe thug. He got good grades in school, but he dressed and acted like a gangbanger, despite coming from a middle-class Queens home. "It's weed, bro, not heroin. Ain't nobody gonna throw us in jail over a blunt."

"Yeah, don't get your panties in a bunch, Lang," Tony added, reaching his hand back for Krush to hand him the blunt. Once again, the peanut gallery in the back seat thought the wannabe comedian to my right was hysterical.

"Y'all laughing and shit, but I'm serious. We're four black guys riding around in an expensive vehicle, smoking weed. You don't think anything is wrong with that picture?" I couldn't have been the only smart one in a group of four college students. Impossible. "We're a racist cop's dream."

"Man, fuck the po-lice! Ain't nobody scared of them racist bastards!" Krush shouted.

"He does have a point, Lang," Tony said in Krush's defense. "Don't nobody care about weed anymore. Just drive the damn car."

I thought about their argument that marijuana wasn't a big deal. It wasn't like it was heroin or anything. It was a blunt. We all have a blunt now and then. Maybe I was being a little dramatic, as Tony would say. But hell, I was the son of a lawyer and judge and the sibling of two lawyers; being dramatic ran in my blood. On the flip side of things, I'd just been reflecting on how long and hard we'd worked on getting our degrees. Was this even worth the risk?

"I don't know. If you ask me, I think this is stupid," I said, shaking my head. "We are in New York, not Colorado."

"And if you ask me," Tony said, "you need to take a hit of this here." He extended the blunt to me. "After three days with your pops, you need to decompress. That's one intense brother."

"I know that's right." Krush took the liberty of removing the blunt from between Tony's fingers. Through the rearview mirror, I watched him inhale and then extend the blunt to me.

"I don't need that shit. I got something better than drugs." I lifted my phone to my ear. "Siri, call Symone."

"When in doubt, call the pussy." Tony laughed as the car's Bluetooth took over and the phone rang. "You one whipped brother, Lang."

A sudden whooping sound jolted my attention to the rearview mirror, and my heart dropped at the sight of flashing lights behind my car.

"Oh, shit!" I said, my stomach tying up in knots.

# *Michael*

## 2

I hadn't been there long, but already my dream job at Goldberg, Klein, and Hooper was exceeding my wildest fantasies. This morning, I'd been asked to join some of the firm's top lawyers in the conference room. Sure, I'd dreamed of sitting with the big boys someday, but never expected that it would happen after only a few months on the job. Yet, there I was, along with six other junior associates, around the eight-foot-long conference room table with three partners and three senior associates of one of New York City's most prestigious law firms. We were all facing the door as we waited for the opposing counsel to come in, like a pride of hyenas about to ambush a wounded water buffalo. The aura of power in the room was palpable, and it had my heart pounding with anticipation. My God, it was like having sex for the first time; the only way to describe it was total euphoria.

There were only certain cases that required this type of attention from the firm, and anything to do with The Rockman Group was one of them. They were by far the firm's largest client, and despite the fact that this wasn't a very big or flashy case, our salt-and-pepper senior partner, Walter Klein, had insisted he personally take charge. Walter was the LeBron James of the profession. He was the main reason I'd pursued a job at the firm. I mean, what basketball player wouldn't want to play with LeBron?

"This should be pretty cut and dry," Walter said confidently to Mark Spencer, a senior associate who was bucking for partner. "My guess is we can settle it for half a million."

I watched Mark's uneasy body language. He paused before speaking, probably to make sure he chose his words carefully.

"Well, with all due respect, boss, that might be a little low. The other side does have a pretty good case. And Rockman has authorized us to settle for one point five million, and get it over wi—"

Mark's reiteration of the client's wishes, of which I'm sure our senior partner was aware, was unceremoniously cut off by Walter's icy stare. The entire room became quiet and perhaps even a little cold. It was that type of power that made me want to work for Walter. I wanted the opportunity to be guided and mentored by someone as educated, experienced, admired, respected, and maybe a little bit feared by everyone who came into contact with him.

Despite my stellar grades and the fact that I had passed the Bar on my first attempt, it had been a shot in the dark when I applied to G, K, & H. The firm only hired six new associates each year, and that group had never included more than one African American, if they hired any at all. But somehow, I became one of six hired out of three hundred interviewed, and I was grateful for that fact every single day I came to work and got to watch Walter Klein in action.

"Offer them half a million and they'll be skipping out of here like they won the damn lottery," Walter insisted, pointing at the file in front of him. "I know the firm that's representing the plaintiff. I know them well, and not from having gone against them in the courtroom." He let out a derisive laugh. "They're a bunch of ambulance chasers. Trust me, they'll take this offer."

"How can you be so sure?" asked Dara Grant, a senior associate and the only female in the room.

One of the other senior associates next to her let out a snort. "Haven't you seen those ridiculous commercials they air on cable television?"

"The one with the attorneys mean-mugging the cameras, strutting around and talking about how big and bad they are?" Mark asked.

"Yes." Walter nodded. "The only thing more ridiculous than those stupid commercials is that goofball Steve Robinson who runs the firm. I've had him sitting across from me three times, and all three times his dumb ass has left at least a half a million on the table. Why should this time be any different?"

"You're right. It's best we stay optimistic," Mark conceded, thumbing through the file in front of him. In perfect timing, the conference room phone rang. Mark was quick to hit the intercom button.

"Is that our ten o'clock?" he asked.

"Yes, sir," the receptionist replied.

"Have them take a seat. Someone will be out for them in just a bit," Walter chimed in.

"Will do, sir," the receptionist said then ended the call.

Peter Weisman, one of the junior associates like myself, rose from his seat.

"Where are you going?" Walter barked.

"I was going to get our appointment, sir?" he replied nervously.

"Sit down, Mr. Weisman," Walter ordered.

With a confused look on his face, Peter sat down, curiously eyeballing his colleagues.

"First, you let them stew for a bit." Walter explained his reasoning for not immediately bringing in the opposing party. "Let them wait for you, sit down, get bored with last month's *Sports Illustrated* we have lying out there. Then when you're ready, and only when you're ready, you stick the fork in 'em." We all sat back, delighting in Walter's tactical insight.

Everyone else at the table sat with tablets and pen in hand, ready to take notes when we finally let the opposing counsel in. But not me. I wanted to observe how Walter moved and how he handled this entire meeting from start to finish. He wasn't a senior partner for nothing, and I was blessed with a front row seat to watch and understand why. He was who I aspired to be.

# *Tony*

# 3

"Roll the windows down! Roll down your fucking window, Tony!" Langston yelled at me frantically.

I opened the window, glancing over my shoulder at the NYPD police cruiser with its lights flashing behind us. Can't say I wasn't nervous, but Langston's ranting and raving was just too over the top.

"Oh God. Oh God. I told you. We're going to jail," Langston continued.

"Lang, man, calm down, bro," Krush said quietly from the back seat.

"How you gonna tell me to calm down, Reem? This is all your fault. You're the one who brought that shit in my car."

"Let's not attack each other. We are supposed to be brothers," Kwesi added, but it had no effect on Lang's continued hysterics.

"Put that thing out, Tony! Put that fucking thing out!" he yelled at me.

"Just chill, bro, seriously. All this yelling and shit ain't helping," I replied, putting out the blunt in the ashtray. I slammed the ashtray closed, trying not to sound as nervous as I really was. "We have to keep levelheaded and act like everything is everything. Now, pull the car over before we have a real problem."

"Yes, those are wise words," Kwesi added. I wondered if he was also trying to hide his nerves, because dude sounded as cool as a cucumber.

I glanced back over at Langston, who was finally pulling the car over.

"Now, everyone try to act normal. You got that?" I looked to Krush and Kwesi, who nodded their understanding. The look on

Lang's face and the beads of sweat on his forehead, on the other hand, were anything but normal. In fact, it screamed of guilt.

"Take a deep breath, frat. We gonna get through this," I said softly.

I looked in the passenger's side mirror at a white NYPD highway cop who was flying solo. We weren't in Brooklyn anymore, that was for sure, because the cops didn't fly solo in my neck of the woods—at least not the ones who wanted to stay alive.

"This is useless," Langston said, now waving his hands around to fan the smell out of his driver's side window. "And the evidence is right there in the ashtray."

"Not anymore it isn't." I opened the ashtray and took the blunt out.

"What are you doing, man?" Langston asked me in panic. "You got the evidence all out in the open now. Oh God, we're definitely going to jail.

"What evidence?" I said before putting the blunt in my mouth and swallowing that shit down. "Now, would you calm down? If your old man could see you now, he'd probably disown you."

Langston stiffened in his seat at the mention of his pops. Meanwhile, I glanced in the side mirror, where I could see the officer headed toward us wearing reflective sunglasses, an eight-point stormtrooper police hat, knee-high boots, and a heavy-ass leather jacket. I turned my face forward as he walked up slowly to the driver's side of the car.

"License, registration, and insurance," was all he said.

"Uh, morning, officer. Beautiful day, isn't it? Supposed to be almost seventy today," Lang stuttered as he reached into the glove compartment for his paperwork.

I didn't know what the fuck he was thinking. This guy wasn't the cashier at Starbucks. He was a damn cop, a white cop at that, and he didn't look like the type who'd be interested in Lang's small talk. I wanted to scream at the top of my lungs, but I couldn't because it felt like the cop was staring directly at me. Damn, we really needed Lang's ass to just chill.

"Where you boys headed today?" the officer asked Langston in a casual yet condescending tone.

"School." Kwesi, Krush, and I all spoke in unison. It went without saying that none of us really wanted Langston to do the talking. He might give the guy our life stories.

"We're, uh, all students, sir," Kwesi said. He was doing the right thing, but I was not sure if his accent was helping. "We were visiting with our parents. We are on our way back to the university."

"Is that so?" the officer asked, his tone now laced with suspicion.

"Yes, sir," I answered.

"What school you fellas attend?" the officer asked.

"We attend Howard University," Kwesi continued.

"That's down there in D.C., isn't?"

"Excuse me, officer, uh . . . I didn't get your name," Langston asked as he handed him the documents.

The cop narrowed his eyes at Langston. "Officer Blake. You want my badge number too?"

"No, thank you, Officer Blake. I can see that just fine from here," Lang replied. I stared at him with my mouth open, and I was sure the guys in the back were doing the same thing. "What I would like to know is why you pulled me over," Lang continued.

What the fuck was he doing? He had taken that comment about his old man a little too seriously for me, and now he was using this condescending, lawyer-like tone that was sure to piss this cop off and put us all in deeper shit.

"Yeah," Krush said boldly. "Was we speeding or something?"

I wanted to reach back there and slap him. With a smirk on his face, the officer bent down and began looking in the back seat at Kwesi and Krush.

*Shit, we're in trouble.* I squirmed uncomfortably in my seat. Why couldn't these idiots have just kept their mouths shut?

"No, you weren't. As a matter of fact, you were going a little slow to be highway driving. I thought something might have been wrong. But from the smell of things,"—he sniffed the air, moving back to the driver's window—"I think you were just a little distracted."

Langston let out a nervous laugh. "What do you mean by that, Officer?"

Officer Blake slowly rose back up into an erect, standing position. "Come on, now. You mean to tell me you don't smell that?" He let out a taunting chuckle.

This wasn't looking good. We were so busted, but all hope wasn't lost. Regardless of what the officer smelled, I'd made sure there was no evidence. I would probably be shitting green plants for a week.

"Smoke was damn near seeping through the windows," Officer Blake said. "And the way you all were fanning when I was calling in your plates . . ." His face straightened up. "I think you boys were smoking pot in here."

"No," we all said in unison. I shot a side glance at Langston and shook my head.

"We were fanning because I passed gas, officer," I said, waving my hand in my face. "It was really bad. If you smell anything, that's probably what it is."

"Do you boys think I'm some kind of idiot?" Officer Blake asked, sounding quite offended.

"Noooo," we all said, once again in unison. The fact that the scent of weed was filtering through the car, out of the windows, and probably smack into his face didn't help. In short, we were fucked.

"Look, Officer, despite what you may think you smelled, there's no evidence we were smoking or had any marijuana," Langston stated with confidence. I swear I wanted to punch him in his arrogant-ass face. "So, if you're going to give me a ticket, give it to me, because we have a long ride to D.C.," he finished.

"You know what? You're a real smart-ass, aren't you?"

"He didn't mean anything by it, Officer," I said, making a last-ditch effort to smooth things out. Langston blew up that effort in an instant.

"Don't speak for me, Tony," he snapped. "I have my own mouth to speak with. And no, Officer Blake, I'm not a smart-ass, but I do know my rights."

All I could do was lower my head, because Lang was talking with the swagger of his father. His tone was all ego, and I knew there was no turning back for him now that he was channeling his father's personality.

One by one, the cop gave us the once over. His glare was almost menacing. "Okay, everyone out of the car."

"Thanks a lot, Lang," I grumbled as I reached for the door handle.

# *Bradley*

## 4

"Please have a seat. Someone will be with you momentarily."

Her tone was pleasant enough, but I could see right through the receptionist's fake smile the second she hesitated on the phone. I glanced down at my watch. We were right on time. Certainly, they were all prepared for us and waiting. They had probably met a good fifteen minutes earlier, joking about how easy this win was going to be. The smiley receptionist was just doing her boss's dirty work, but that was okay. That was her job and what she got paid for. Well, her bosses were in for a big surprise when they saw my black face, because while she was paid to be a gatekeeper, we got paid to win cases, big cases. I say "we" as in me and my son, Lamont, my first born and protégé.

I smiled knowingly then looked toward the chairs in the reception area. Turning to walk away, I realized when I reached the chairs that Lamont hadn't budged. He and the receptionist were busy giving each other googly eyes. Had I not known this case was going to be a slam dunk, I probably would have allowed Lamont to use his skills of persuasion to play the young lady to our advantage, but we could tuck that quarter away in his pocket and save it for a rainy day, because this case was over the minute I had agreed to take it. Besides, I couldn't be a hypocrite when it came to Lamont and his overly active libido. That was something I always stayed on him about. The legacy of the Hudson family was that of viciously dangerous, smart lions, not dogs in heat, and I wasn't going to allow him to damage something I had worked decades to create.

"May I, uh, offer you a drink?" the receptionist asked, staring directly at Lamont as she sat up a little straighter so that her ample breasts were front and center on display. "Water? Coffee? Anything?"

"We're good. Thanks." I jumped before Lamont got a chance to rattle off what his choice of "anything" might have been. At least the sound of my voice reminded the two of them that someone else was in the room, as they both shot their attention to me. "Come on, Lamont."

He broke his gaze from the receptionist and settled in to the seat next to me.

I had to give opposing counsel credit for good taste. Their reception area was more comfortable than my office. They showed poor judgement in leaving a hungry shark waiting, but good taste in decor. Clearly, Lamont was impressed as well. He plopped down in a chair, slightly bouncing to test the comfort and durability of his chair.

"Now, see, Pop, this is how we need to model our office to go after the big dollars. Downtown, a view, valet parking . . ."

"We already have big clients, and we are not leaving Harlem. We own the building."

"That doesn't mean we can't have a second office down here."

Watching my son in all of his excitement over the chair, it reminded me of the year he got his first two-wheel bike under the Christmas tree. He had tested out that seat pretty much the same way he was doing now. A slight smile teased my face.

"You've been thinking about this a lot lately, haven't you?"

"I believe we owe it to ourselves to get a slice of the corporate cake, Pop. It's a logical growth area for us, and we've never tapped into it."

I looked around at the flat-screen television with a picture so clear I felt as if Chris Cuomo was sitting in a chair right across from me. The fish tank was large enough for a damn mermaid to live in. I must say that I wouldn't have been mad to have my nameplate attached to one of those heavy cherry wood doors, but that wasn't really my dream. Maybe it was Lamont's, but not mine. I'd always been an uptown guy. For me, the pillar of success was having my adversaries in the courtroom become immediately perturbed at the sight of my name on a court document because they knew I was going to be hard to beat. I took pride in the number of cases that I had won over the years, and although I didn't have the flashy office and wasn't the most well-liked attorney in the state of New York, I had earned the respect of my colleagues and those on the bench. That was my dream, and I'd pretty much lived it for the past twenty-five years.

"I believe we owe it to our client to stay focused on why we're here." I looked straight ahead at the wall.

"But you have to admit that—"

The annoyed look I shot Lamont let him know to dead the conversation and prevented him from finishing his thought. However, it didn't stop him from looking around the office in continued amazement and envy.

"Looks like they're playing right into our hands," Lamont said quietly.

"Yep, it's part of the game, that's all," I said, noticing him anxiously checking his watch. It amused me that now that he was no longer entertained by the receptionist or the exquisite office decor, he was concerned about how long we'd been waiting. "They want us to think they have more important business than what we're here for. They figure we'll sit out here and be impressed by carpets, paintings, and pretty women. Bullshit like that."

"Yeah, but, of course, we know better." He chuckled, and I laughed right along with him. He was still learning, but sooner or later, he'd no longer allow himself to be distracted by the pretty things that opponents would put in his path to try to throw him off his game.

Lamont's phone rang. The volume sounded as if it was on its max.

"Kill that," I said, shooting him an annoyed look.

"All right," he said while checking his caller ID screen. "But it's Dez." He looked at me to see if I would change my position just because his sister was on the line. It didn't, especially since she was supposed to be at this meeting with us.

Just then, I saw a gentleman heading toward us. "I don't have time to listen to her excuses right now. I'll deal with her later. This looks like us."

"Hello," the gentleman approached and greeted. I stood as he extended his hand.

"I'm Peter, one of the associates." We shook hands. "My apologies for the wait. We had some important business to finish up."

*Important business, my ass.* Lamont and I shot one another a look, a smirk dancing at the corner of my mouth.

"I completely understand, Peter," I said.

"Good. Then why don't you follow me?" He extended his hand toward the large, wood door.

# *Langston*

## 5

When you're driving down the highway and you see a black or Latino guy sitting on the side of the road while the cops search his car, have you ever wondered what that guy must feel like? Well, now had I firsthand knowledge of it because my frat brothers Kwesi, Krush, Tony, and I were all sitting on the grass in cuffs, watching the cops search my car. It had to be the most humiliating feeling I'd ever experienced.

There were two cops on the scene now, but Officer Blake, the one who pulled us over in the first place, was the one searching the car, while the other cop stood in front of us. I glanced over at the fellas, but none of them would look my way. I couldn't believe they were blaming this on me when it was Krush who had pulled out the blunt and started smoking it.

After about ten minutes, Officer Blake walked over from the car, looking annoyed. He took a deep breath and relaxed his tense shoulders as if trying to regain his professional composure. "Now, I'm going to ask you boys one time whose pot this is." He held up a quarter-ounce bag of weed, slowly walking by each of us. "And if I don't a get satisfactory answer, I'm hauling all your asses in, and we can sort it out in front of the judge."

*Fuck!* Things had just gone from bad to worse.

Tony, Kwesi, and I shared concerned looks with one another. Of course, we knew who the weed belonged to, but Krush would never fess up. I had already been accepted into law school. No way did I need this on my record.

*Dammit, what would Dad do in a situation like this?*

I really couldn't be sure what my father would do, but he was never one to back down, so I took my best guess that he would put up a fight. Clearing my throat, I tried to display some of my father's strength as I spoke up.

"Officer Blake," I started, "I didn't give you permission to search my car. You do know you're violating my rights against illegal search and seizure, don't you? You didn't have a search warrant, and I didn't give you permission." I sat up and forced myself to stare at him in an imitation of confidence—though I was scared to death at the moment.

"Lang, will you shut the fuck up?" Tony snapped.

Blake laughed walking over to the other cop. "Maybe these kids need to be taught a lesson. Just because you go to college doesn't mean you know everything."

The other cop nodded, looking directly at me. I had obviously misjudged the situation and was starting to wish I'd just kept my mouth shut.

"For the record, young man, the moment I smelled marijuana, I had probable cause to search your vehicle. So, I didn't need your permission or a search warrant," Blake responded.

There was nothing I could say in response.

"Damn, Lang, to be going to law school next year, you sure are stupid sometimes," Tony added. I didn't respond to him either, because he was right.

"So, what do you want to do?" the other cop asked Blake. "You wanna haul their smart asses in?"

Before Officer Blake could respond, Krush raised his hand, surprising us all. "Officer, that's my weed." From the look on Krush's face, he'd surprised his own damn self. As a matter of fact, he looked like he wanted to change his mind and use that raised hand to point his finger at one of us. Thankfully, it was too late. Officer Blake had already acknowledged his admission of guilt. Krush swallowed hard, no doubt realizing he was now at the point of no return. "These guys had nothing to do with it. In fact, Langston tried to stop me." Krush turned to me with an apologetic look on his face. "I'm really sorry, bro. This is all my fault. I take full responsibility."

I gave Krush a forgiving head nod. I really felt sorry for him, but as heartwarming as this Hallmark moment was, we were certainly not out of the woods yet. I turned my attention to Officer Blake to get a feel for how he was receiving this display of brotherhood. Sure, I was glad Krush had stepped up, but I was now scared to death for him.

Officer Blake stood there for a moment, looking from Krush to me. "Get up." He pointed at me and then Krush, gesturing with his hand for us to stand. I don't know about Krush, but I was so scared that my legs felt like jelly as I struggled to my feet. It was difficult to balance with handcuffs on, and I got no help from either officer.

Officer Blake stood in front of Krush. "I respect your honesty, young man, and your loyalty to your friends," he said to Krush. "Anything else in the car? If I call for a dog, is he going to find anything?"

"No, sir," Krush replied.

"You sure? I'm not going to find anything else in that car, am I?" This time he was speaking to us all.

"Yes, sir, the car's clean. Just our suitcases and some groceries from our moms," Krush answered.

"Okay, I'm going to give you a citation for the marijuana, and your wannabe lawyer friend here a ticket for reckless driving." He placed his hand on Krush's shoulder, firm enough to make Krush squirm uncomfortably. "Leave the pot alone, kid. I'm letting you off because you're in college and I don't want this on your record. Next time, you might not be so lucky."

I swear to God, he sounded like he was delivering a public service announcement, like he'd been rehearsing that line in the mirror for years and finally had the chance to put his skills to work. Krush let out such a huge gust of wind I'm surprised it didn't send Officer Blake stumbling backward.

"Thank you, Officer," Krush said.

"And you," Blake said, directing his comments to me, "next time you run into an officer, keep that jailhouse lawyer shit to yourself." He looked at me with a huge smile of conquest on his face. I did not return the expression. Maybe he wasn't the racist I thought in the beginning, but this experience had not made me a fan of the police.

"Thank you, Officer," I said, forcing myself to deliver the words in a respectful tone. "But there won't be a next time. You can trust me on that."

"Sorry about the cuffs, fellas," Officer Blake said as he and his partner uncuffed us. I felt like a freed captive from a slave ship when Officer Blake removed the cuffs from my hands. "But you all had me outnumbered without backup."

We opened our mouths but looked at one another before anyone dared to speak.

"We understand, sir," I finally replied in a humble tone. Everyone else nodded meekly in agreement.

He pointed at the ground. "Now, grab a seat while I write up these tickets and we'll let you be on your way."

The four of us eyed one another and, in unison, exhaled a sigh of relief. We wiped some of the dust off our clothes and the sweat from our foreheads, then sat back on the grass. I'd never been happy to receive a ticket before, but considering the alternative was being arrested, I was grateful and anxious to get that piece of paper in my hand. I just wanted to get the hell out of there.

Before that could happen, a police K-9 SUV pulled up, and a large, overweight black cop stepped out. He looked stern, like he didn't tolerate any bullshit, as he stared at us sitting on the ground.

I remember thinking, *Shit, I'm glad he wasn't here five minutes ago.*

"Blake, Collins, you a'ight?"

"Yes, sir, Sergeant Lanier," Officer Blake replied.

"What you got here?" Sergeant Lanier asked. He turned his attention toward us.

"Just a bunch of kids smoking pot, Sarg." Officer Blake shooed his hand, brushing the situation off. "Boys being boys. You know." He shrugged. "I'm citing one for the dope and the driver for reckless driving."

"Just a little pot, huh?" Sergeant Lanier's eyes lit up, and he might as well have been drooling. As minor as the situation may have seemed to Officer Blake, from the looks of Sergeant Lanier, the molehill was about to become a mountain.

"Yes, sir," Officer Blake replied nervously. Whoever this Sergeant was, he obviously put some kind of fear in Blake's heart.

Sergeant Lanier let out a *harrumph* as he looked to his comrade. "You run all their names through the system for warrants?"

Sergeant Lanier remained silent for a moment. Mental wheels were turning in his head; it was evident from the expression in his eyes. Sensing a shift in the atmosphere, my frat brothers and I exchanged concerned looks. I could feel the sweat beads pooling on my forehead again.

"No, I uh . . ." Officer Blake started. "I didn't think it was necessary. They're just college kids, Sarg." Once again, he downplayed the scenario.

"Hmmm." Sergeant Lanier stood in front of Krush, staring at him hard.

"Is, uh, there a problem, Sergeant?" Blake asked.

"I don't know. You tell me. This one here looks more like a gang member than a student."

This Lanier person, having only spoken a few words, came across as a . . . an Uncle Tom. And if the use of the N-word wasn't so offensive, I'd be inclined to suggest he was one of those house ones. Neither one could mean us any good right about now.

My friends and I eyeballed one another again. Although none of us spoke a single word, our eyes said the same thing: *What's with this asshole?*

Sergeant Lanier walked over toward Officers Blake and Collins with his hands in his pockets, eyeing us suspiciously. I glanced at my boys. We may as well have been riding the largest rollercoaster in the world as green as everyone's faces looked. I felt like I was about to throw up. There was something about this cop that didn't sit right.

"I say we let my dog search the car," Sergeant Lanier said to Officer Blake. "You know I've got a sixth sense about these kinds of things."

"That you do." Officer Blake let out a nervous chuckle.

Sergeant Lanier was throwing his rank around, and it was obviously intimidating Officer Blake. That was apparent from the hard swallow that rolled across his Adam's apple, not to mention the way his face was splotched with bright red. Officer Collins was so quiet that if he weren't standing in front of me, I would have thought he wasn't even there. This entire scene had me baffled. The tables were turned in the most peculiar way. Officer Blake looked so subservient I swear he was about to start calling Sergeant Lanier *massa*. I'd started out assuming that

Blake was a racist white cop, but it turned out it was a black cop who really had bad intentions for us.

"Why don't we run the dog around the car a few times and see what she finds?" Lanier suggested. He was halfway to his car before Blake could even reply.

"Sure thing, Sarg," Blake replied. He turned to us and shrugged his shoulders, looking almost apologetic.

Lanier opened the rear door of his SUV and let out what looked like a black Labrador Retriever. It was on a leash, and it jumped around excitedly as Sergeant Lanier led it over to my car.

He looked down at the dog and commanded, "Find it, Princess."

# *Michael*

## 6

Peter left to retrieve the opposing counsel and came back in no time. As the conference room door opened, the smile on Walter's face was sadistically cheery. He turned toward my end of the conference table with a subtle "We got this" nod. This was one of those moments I had been looking forward to all my life, and I could hardly contain my excitement. I leaned back in my chair, wishing I had a bag of popcorn, because this was going to be quite a show—or so I thought. Within a matter of minutes, things took a dramatically unexpected turn, and the show I'd been hoping for turned into a three-ring circus, and we were the ones who looked like clowns.

The first of the morning's surprises was that the two men who followed Peter into the conference room were black men in expensive, tailored suits. One looked to be in his fifties, and the other maybe around thirty, and both of them obviously spent a lot of time and effort to look as good as they did. Walter had described them as ambulance chasers led by a goofball, and I had imagined a couple dudes in baggy suits with bad haircuts. I sure wasn't expecting these brothers, whose suits clearly cost more than I would make in a month as a junior associate.

I turned to look at Walter, and his reaction told me these weren't the guys he had been expecting either. His face dropped, and all the color left his cheeks. He jumped up from his seat as if someone had lit a fire under his ass. I was confused by his reaction, and from the look on my colleagues' faces, so were they. No one seemed to know what to do or say as these two lawyers strolled confidently into the room.

"Hudson? What the hell are you doing here?" Walter asked, with an edge to his voice.

"You don't sound too excited to see me, old friend." The older man gave my boss a casual smile. "It's been a long time."

"Ah, yes, yes, it has. The Klippinger case, if I remember correctly," Walter replied, sounding nervous. It shook me a little, because I'd never seen him this way before, and just five minutes earlier he'd been so damn cocky about how this meeting would go and how he was going to make them his little bitches.

"Still as sharp as ever, aren't you, Walter?" Hudson replied, adjusting the lapel on his suit.

"So, to what do we owe the pleasure?" Walter asked, very obviously trying to regain his composure.

"I'm here for our ten o'clock. We're representing the Cooper family." The way he spoke sounded almost poetic. This guy had a swagger about him like no other lawyer I'd ever seen before.

Walter shot Mark a perplexed look. "I thought you said the Cooper family was represented by—"

"They are—I mean, they were. . . . There must be some mistake." The paper in Mark's hand shook as he looked helplessly at Walter. "It says right here that their attorney is Philip Hall of Dorf, Robinson, and Associates." Mark turned to Dara, another senior associate, attempting to shift the heat to her. "What's going on?"

"I don't know. I spoke with Philip last night," Dara replied as Mark went back to digging through his paperwork.

"There has to be some mistake," Mark said, peering over his glasses.

The black lawyer looked slightly amused by all of this. I wasn't the one in the hot seat, but even I was feeling embarrassed right about now. This guy, whoever he was, had the upper hand for sure, no matter how long we'd kept him in the waiting room.

"There's no mistake. The Coopers were initially represented by Dorf, but we were brought on this morning," Hudson said to Mark in the manner a father might speak to a half-wit son. Then he turned his attention to Walter, who was looking very uncomfortable. "My son, Lamont, and I will be taking over as lead counsel from here—unless, of course, you have an offer."

Mark looked at Walter, who cast his eyes downward and remained silent. The look of defeat on his face was pitiful.

"Well, Walter, do we have an offer?" Hudson asked.

Walter didn't answer.

Mark suddenly found his courage and seized the moment, speaking up. "We're authorized to offer five hundred thousand."

A sudden laugh came from Hudson's son. Hudson, however, wasn't laughing. He looked insulted as he stood glaring at Walter. My boss remained silent, as if he were still trying to comprehend what was happening.

"Of course, we haven't totally familiarized ourselves with this case, but . . ." Hudson looked at his son and extended his hand. The younger man pulled out a file from his briefcase and handed it to him. "We already see strong class action possibilities," Hudson said, opening the file and flipping through it. "But, considering we're old friends"—he closed the folder dramatically—"I'm thinking five million will make everyone happy." He handed the file back to his son.

Mark burst out laughing, then stopped when he realized none of us had joined in.

"You find it funny that we aren't asking for more?" Hudson said to Mark. "I'm sure we easily could, but five million sounds like a fair and reasonable number. Don't you think so, Walter?"

He focused like a laser beam on Walter, who struggled to make eye contact.

I still didn't quite understand how things had gone so wrong so quickly, but I could tell from Walter's behavior that this was bad—real bad. Finally, in a tone that was as stoic as the look on his face, Walter said, "I'll have the paperwork drawn up and a check over to your office first thing in the morning."

"Great." Hudson nodded. "Good to see you again, Walter. Say hello to that lovely wife of yours."

The son had a smirk on his face as he tucked the file back into his briefcase.

"Will do, Hudson." Walter exhaled loudly.

Peter went to stand.

"Oh, no, we appreciate your hospitality, but we can find our way out. I'm sure you have plenty to discuss," Hudson said, then looked at his son. "Ready?"

"Absolutely." He turned to the others in the room. "Have a wonderful day. It was a pleasure."

Hudson led the way out of the conference room, looking back over his shoulder before they exited to say, "By the way, Walter, nice reception area. It's very impressive."

As soon as the door closed behind them, chaos ensued.

"Five million? What was that?" Mark demanded.

"That was Bradley Hudson," Walter said in a defeated voice.

"Wait a minute. *The* Bradley Hudson? The one who took down Russ Oil and TK Shoes, and got TJ Winter off for murdering his wife?" Mark asked.

"One and the same." Walter sighed.

"We studied his Marcus Hall defense in law school," Dara added, clearing her throat to proclaim, "If the witness blacked out, that's reasonable doubt." She was mimicking a male voice.

Peter must've noticed the look of confusion on my face, because he explained, "That was one of his famous lines from that trial."

"I know," I said. "I just can't believe I didn't recognize him." Hell, every black lawyer knew who Bradley Hudson was. He was half the reason I went to law school. I'd studied all of his big cases. I guess in the confusion of this unexpected scene, I hadn't put two and two together.

"He's a legend," Dara added.

"Dammit, Dara, we know who the hell he is, okay?" Walter said.

But she was right; he was a legend, possibly more like an African god. Anyone who had the ability to instill that kind of fear in Walter was at least that.

"Get the hell outta here, all of you!" Walter shouted to the room.

No one else moved at first, but I quickly gathered my things, rushed out of the room, and headed down the hallway. In the distance, I could see Bradley Hudson and his son waiting for the elevator. I doubled my pace and was able to catch them just as they stepped on. The doors were beginning to close, so I held my hand out to stop them. I glanced around, making sure no one saw me before I hopped inside.

"What floor?" Lamont asked me.

"Uh, all the way down," I said.

He looked at the button for the first floor, which was already lit. I knew I had to talk fast, because the chances of us making it all the way to the bottom floor without stopping for more passengers was damn near impossible in our busy building.

"Mr. Hudson, that was very impressive lawyering," I told him.

"Thanks, young man. I appreciate your approval." Hudson smiled at me. "How long have you been here at the firm?" In this small space without the other lawyers around, he seemed much more personable.

"Only a couple of months. I finished Harvard Law this past Spring," I replied proudly.

"Harvard Law, huh? I'm a Howard University man myself. So is my son, but Harvard is a decent school. I'm sure you'll do well. This is one of the top firms in the city."

I could feel the elevator slowing down, and I realized we were about to stop. I had to move quickly. "Thank you, sir, but I have a question."

"Ask away."

I took a deep breath and blurted out, "By any chance, are you hiring?"

He had an amused look on his face. "Don't you already have a job?"

"Yes, sir, I do." I nodded. "But as one black man to another, there is nothing these people can teach me that you can't and more. I'm sure you understand where I'm going with this."

The doors began to open, and the small crowd of people waiting stepped inside with us. Hudson didn't respond. We spent the remaining ride down in silence. When we reached the lobby, everyone stepped off except the three of us.

Hudson turned to his son and said, "Lamont, give him a card. Make sure it's one with my personal cell."

I was so excited I felt my ear jump into overdrive.

Lamont reached inside of his suit jacket and passed me a business card as they stepped off the elevator.

"Give me a call when you're ready, and we'll talk," Hudson said.

"I'll call you this afternoon," I said without hesitation.

"Understand one thing, young man. We aren't all fancy like they are down here. We work for a living." He smiled at me as the elevator doors began to close.

"I can see that, sir, and I'm ready," I replied, watching him walk toward the exit.

# *Langston*

## 7

Sergeant Lanier and his dog had already searched the front seats of the car, and he was in no way as considerate as Officer Blake, having thrown everything out of my glove compartment and tossing around every item in my center console. I was sweating bullets the entire time. Yeah, I was a little nervous, but I was more pissed. This was bullshit if I ever smelled it. I didn't give a damn if he had a dog or not. If Officer Blake hadn't found anything other Krush's weed, what the hell made this asshole think he would? He was just being a dick—a big, black Uncle Tom dick—and he was just wasting our time looking for something that he wasn't going to find.

"You're not going to find anything, 'cause there's nothing in there!" I shouted. I got the evil eye from Officer Blake and my boys, but at that point, I didn't care. I couldn't wait until Dad ripped these punk-ass cops a new asshole.

"God damn gangbangers," Sergeant Lanier said under his breath as he stood outside the car with his empty hands on his waist. He hadn't found a damn thing, but he wasn't giving up yet. He led the dog to the back seat. "Come on, Princess. Let's find it."

A minute or two later, he was once again assuming the position outside the car with his hands on his hips, shaking his head. It was obvious he was disappointed that he'd come up empty. I thought he would finally give up and agree to let us go, but then he stopped shaking his head and looked toward the trunk of my car. He walked over and pulled on it.

"Open the trunk," he ordered.

For a second, I thought about protesting, because it was within my rights to refuse to let him search the car. But then I realized it wasn't worth it. If I antagonized him, he might just drag us all down to the precinct to spite us. I might as well just let him get the search over with. Then, all we would have to do was clean up the mess he made, and we could be on our way. I aimed the key fob toward my car and clicked the trunk emblem. It immediately popped open. Sergeant Lanier looked as eager as his black Labrador to start searching.

"You're not going to find anything in there either," I said, knocking the smile right off his face.

When the trunk opened, a few bags fell right out onto Lanier's feet. We'd had that trunk stuffed to capacity. Hey, we might have been independent black men, but who doesn't take laundry home to Mama when visiting from college?

"Lang, will you shut up?" Tony snapped.

"Listen to your friend, kid. You're not making this better," Blake whispered as we watched Lanier kick the bags out of his way.

He pulled a Louis Vuitton and a Ralph Lauren bag and dropped them carelessly to the ground. The dog started pacing around the bags.

"What the fuck, man? That's my bag! That shit is worth more than you make in a week." Krush yelled. He was about to stand up, but Blake placed his hand on his holster.

"I'd calm down if I were you, young man."

"But that's my shit," Krush snapped angrily.

"Let the Sergeant complete his search so you boys can get outta here."

"Chill, Reem," I said, looking up at Blake. I could feel the anger in all of us intensifying, but we fell back and let Lanier continue without interruption.

When the trunk was empty, he'd pick up one bag, unzip it, and throw it to the ground so the dog could sniff it. Then they would move on to the next. He looked up at us, laughing as clothes and groceries spilled on the ground.

When he threw one bag, Tony went to make a move, but I held my arm out, halting him. "Don't do it, man. My pops is going to handle this. You best believe that." I said it loud enough for everyone to hear. "This is Staten Island. We don't need another Eric Garner."

"What was that, college boy?" Sergeant Lanier cupped his hand around his ear, daring me to repeat it.

I bit my tongue and tightened my lips, refusing to speak the words again. He was going to get his real soon.

"Thought so." He let out a snicker and then continued digging through the trunk.

I tucked in my bottom lip and bit down to keep myself from crying. I was so heated that tears of anger were starting to form in my eyes. The last thing I wanted was to stand there crying on the side of the road like a little bitch. My boys would never let me live that down. This would all be over in a little bit. I just had to keep my composure and hold on for a while longer.

"Satisfied now?" I asked when he'd gone through all our bags and the trunk was empty. "You gonna put our bags back in the car?"

Sergeant Lanier looked defeated, but not done. "Come on, Princess. Up, girl."

I couldn't believe it, but that fool had his dog jump up in my trunk and start sniffing around. I glanced over at Tony, who was shaking his head, but I shifted my attention back to the car when I heard the dog scratching and barking in my trunk. Lanier turned to us with a satisfied grin as he escorted the dog out of the car and back to his truck. He then walked back to my car and submerged himself in the trunk. After a few tense seconds, he popped back out and strutted over toward Officer Blake, carrying a cloth bag. He said nothing, just simply opened it up wide for Officer Blake to peek into.

The expression on Officer's Blake face did more than concern me. It downright scared me. Something was wrong. That was evident from the way the two cops were ogling the bag.

The fellas and I shot each other questionable looks. Our eyes silently demanded that whoever knew what the two cops had found so interesting should speak up. But no one said a word as Sergeant Lanier placed the bag on the hood of his car. The next thing I knew, he was taking out a rectangular package wrapped in grey duct tape. What the fuck was that? I watched as he used his keys to cut it open. He dipped his index finger into it and tasted the contents of the bag right before a sinister smile took over his face.

"I told you I have a sixth sense about this kind of thing," Lanier bragged to Blake.

"You certainly do, Sarg," Officer Blake replied. The look on his face was a mixture of anger and disappointment. He'd tried to give us a break, and now he had just been humiliated in front of his superior officer.

"Now, would anyone like to 'fess up to this?" Sergeant Lanier asked, holding up the brick of drugs. Nobody said a word. "That's what I thought."

# *Desiree*

# 8

*"Girl, put your records on, play me your favorite song. . . ."*
I woke up to loud, off-key singing coming from the bathroom.
I rolled over onto my side and blinked my eyes in an effort to
focus. Bright sunlight streamed through the blinds and created a
prism design on the wall, causing me to realize it was much later
than I thought. I glanced over at the clock radio.

*Shit. I overslept.*

I stood up, taking a moment for my body to get adjusted to
shaky legs. Where the fuck were my clothes? I spotted my skirt
and blouse laying neatly on the back of a chair in the corner of
the room, but I didn't see the lace bra and thong I had worn
under them. A flashback of hands slipping the lace from my
shoulders, then lips exploring my breasts, filled my head and
gave me a hint of where I might find the lingerie. I tossed the
duvet and sheets back and ran my hands through them. Bingo!
I'd found the bra, but where were my panties?

*Think, Des, think.* I couldn't believe I had allowed this to
happen. I was going to be late again—the third time this week. I
grabbed my cell phone off the desk and called my brother. There
was no answer. I called again. This time, it rang once and went
straight to voicemail.

"Hey, it's me. I know I screwed up, but I need you to cover for
me. I'm on my way. I'll just meet you all at Klein's office in half
an hour." I ended the call.

"Good morning, sunshine." The bathroom door opened.

"Don't *good morning* me. Why didn't you wake me up? You
know I should've gotten up when my alarm went off the first
time." I shook my head as I pulled my skirt over my hips without
underwear.

"I did wake you up . . . then I put you back to sleep." She laughed. "What's the big deal?"

"The big deal is that I'm gonna get cussed out and maybe fired," I explained, reaching for my blouse.

"You're not gonna get fired over this. That's crazy."

"Okay, you keep thinking that," I snapped, searching the room one last time for my missing underwear. "Where the hell are my panties?"

"That sexy-ass thong you were wearing last night?"

"Yes."

"It's in here," Jerri replied, walking over to her night table. She opened it and pulled out my panties.

"What's it doing there?"

"I wanted a souvenir," she purred in a sultry voice.

I looked at the hands now holding my black Victoria's Secret thong and recalled the feeling of those same fingers as they trailed along my collarbone. I snatched my underwear, ignoring both the seductive smile and the sexual tension in the room.

"You're crazy," I said, more to myself than to her as I slipped on my panties. "I should've never come over here last night."

"Don't be like this. Fine, okay, I'm sorry I didn't wake you up. But you're not going to be fired. You work for your damn daddy, for Christ's sake."

"You just don't get it, do you? I'm a Hudson. I'm not supposed to miss meetings. This is unprofessional no matter who I work for. It may not seem important to you, but—"

"Des, calm the hell down. You're always so uptight. I thought I relaxed your ass last night and this morning." She let out a long, dramatic sigh, like she just couldn't handle me.

"Jerri, I'm serious." I slipped my foot into one of the heels.

"I am too. About you, about us."

Jerri took a step closer to me, and I stepped back, nearly stumbling because I had only one shoe on. She caught me just in time and gave me a smile that I couldn't resist returning. I stared at her as she stood in front of me wrapped in a towel, beads of water dripping from her short, curly hair onto her neck and shoulders. She was so damn sexy. That was one of the main reasons I was with her. I had never been attracted to a woman before, but Jerri was different. She was gorgeous even though she really didn't want to be, so she didn't flaunt it. There was something irresistible about the way she embraced her sexuality, which included her masculinity.

When we met, she'd had no problem letting me know what she wanted and how she wanted it. What she wanted was me, and she wanted me now. I tried explaining to her that I was a straight woman and happily single, but she persisted. As she pursued me, she made me laugh and think, and I began to enjoy her. It was then that I realized there was a mutual attraction, and before I knew it, I found myself doing something I thought I'd never do: date a woman.

"I'm not doing this. I'm getting ready to leave," I said, putting some distance between us before I allowed myself to give in to temptation.

"You're already late, Des. Being later won't matter." She touched my neck seductively.

"No, Jerri," I said, walking past her.

She grabbed me by the arm. "Des, wait."

I turned around to face her and glanced down at her hand. She released her grip as I asked, "What?"

"Are you coming back later?"

"I'll call and let you know once I see how my day goes," I told her.

"What time?"

"I don't know yet."

"I wanted to cook dinner for us. Netflix and chill, and maybe even if you're lucky . . ." She stuck her tongue out playfully.

"Dinner sounds nice, but no promises," I told her. Jerri was an executive chef and an amazing cook. They say that the way to a man's heart is through his stomach, but Jerri's cooking had definitely helped her find her way into mine, that was for sure.

"And you can provide dessert." She gave me a suggestive look. "Lord knows I enjoyed that tasty treat I had last night. Oh, and let's not forget this morning."

"I should've never let you go down on me this morning," I shot back, throwing cold water on her little fantasy. "That's why I'm late now. I'll call you in a little while." I headed out of the bedroom.

"Wait. Does that mean you're going to spend the night?" Jerri was right on my heels as I entered the living room.

"It means I have to go, Jerri, and I'll call you later."

"Can I at least get a good-bye kiss?" she asked.

I turned around, and the simple kiss I planned to give her turned into a minute-long exploration of tongues. That woman could kiss, and I enjoyed it, so much so that I found myself wanting to take off the clothes I had just put on. I ended the kiss, rushed out the door before she could stop me again, and made my way to my Benz that was parked in the visitor space of her parking garage.

In the car, I called my brother Lamont again.

"Yeah," he answered.

"I need you to cover for me. I'm running late for the meeting, but I'll be there in twenty minutes," I said.

"Don't worry about it. The meeting's over. Dad's headed back to the office, and I'm on my way to see a client."

"Dammit, is Daddy pissed?" I asked.

"What do you think? Of course he's pissed," he replied with no sympathy in his voice.

"Guess I'll go take my medicine from the High Bishop Hudson," I said sarcastically and hung up. My mind began working to figure out a lie believable enough for my genius of a father. I prayed for God to send a miracle that would get me out of the mess I would be facing when I arrived at the office.

A call came in from an unfamiliar number, interrupting my brainstorming session. Thinking it was probably one of the pro-bono clients I had taken on, I answered through the car's Bluetooth.

"Hello."

"Des." I recognized the voice but didn't have a clue why my little brother was calling me from some strange number.

"Lang?" I asked.

"Yeah." There was a lot of background noise, but I could still hear the distress in my brother's voice.

"What's wrong? Where are you?"

"I'm in Staten Island." There was an uncomfortable silence, during which I could hear my heart start pounding in my chest. "Des, I've been arrested, and I need your help."

# *Tony*

# 9

I'd been in this closet of an interrogation room in one of the police precincts in Staten Island for what seemed like forever by the time the two white detectives walked in and sat down. One of them was really skinny, and the other one was fat, but both of them were assholes as far as I was concerned. I had felt like I was in a nightmare from the moment I'd been tossed into the back seat of Officer Blake's car with Krush. Kwesi rode in the back of Lanier's car, and Langston rode in Collins' car. They'd probably separated us so we wouldn't coordinate our stories, and I'm not gonna lie; their tactics were intimidating the shit out of me.

"Anthony, is it, or do you prefer Tony?" the skinny cop asked. I'd heard enough stories from my brothers to understand that these two cops were about to try to play that good cop/bad cop shit on me.

"Tony," I said weakly.

"Okay, then, Tony it is. My name's Detective Cutter, and this is my partner, Detective O'Malley. Can we get you a soda? Something from the snack machine?" Cutter was obviously taking the good cop role today.

"Yeah, I'll take a Pepsi and some chips if they got 'em." My brothers always told me that if you get arrested and the cops offer you shit, always take it, because you never know when you might see it again.

"Sure, thing, Tony." Cutter got up and left the room.

"I see you're wearing your colors proudly. So, when did you get initiated?" Detective O'Malley asked. Maybe I was wrong; maybe he was the good cop. I mean, why else would ask me about my fraternity?

"Spring of 2016. Me and Lang went over the burning sands together," I told him with pride.

He looked a little puzzled as he sat back in his chair. "You and Langston, the kid driving the car?"

"Yeah, that's my LB," I said proudly.

"I'm kind of shocked. He doesn't look the type, I would have thought maybe the kid Krush, but not the other two."

"Please, me and Lang brought them in," I said definitively.

"I see," he replied as his partner walked in the room and took his seat. "I appreciate your honesty. It'll go a long way to get you boys outta here."

"They didn't have Pepsi, so I got you Coke," Cutter said, sliding the can of soda and a bag of Wise potato chips across the table. "So, what did I miss?" He glanced back and forth between his partner and me.

"Well, Tony here just verified that all four of them are members of the Bloods and that he and Langston brought the other two into the gang," O'Malley told his partner.

My mouth dropped open. What the fuck was this guy talking about?

"That true? All of you are Bloods?" Cutter asked.

"Hell, no, that's not true! This fucking guy is a liar. He's trying to entrap me. I ain't no damn Blood," I stood up and yelled.

"You little piece of shit! Don't you call me a liar," Detective O'Malley said, making it clear now he was, indeed, the bad cop. He stood up and pointed at the ceiling in the corner of the room. "You think we're not recording this interview? We got you throwing your little gangbanging buddies under the bus. Now, sit your ass down."

We glared at each other for a few seconds before I said, "I am not a gang member—and I'm definitely not a member of the Bloods. None of us are members of the Bloods."

"Yeah, and neither are your brothers Aaron and Adonis," Detective O'Malley retorted.

I have to admit he'd caught me off guard with that one. How the hell did he know that so fast?

"Man, that's my brothers, not me. I'm not a Blood."

"So, you admit your brothers are both Bloods?" Cutter asked.

"Yeah, it ain't no secret." I exhaled angrily. "But me and my friends aren't."

"What do we look, stupid?" O'Malley shouted as he slammed a file he'd been holding on the table. "Your brothers are two of the highest-ranking Bloods in New York City. They've been charged with drug trafficking and who knows what else. Meanwhile, you're wearing a bright red fucking shirt, driving around with two keys of heroin!" He laughed out loud. "I'm sorry, but that screams you're a fucking Blood to me. You're all fucking Bloods."

This guy was on another planet, so I turned my attention to Cutter. "We are not Bloods. We're members of a fraternity—at a *university*," I added for emphasis, "and crimson and cream just happen to be the fraternity colors. Check with the school."

"Oh, we will," O'Malley snarled.

The two detectives glanced at each other. I wasn't sure about O'Malley, but I think Cutter might have believed me. Damn, at least I hoped he believed me. I'd been trying to run from my brothers' gang affiliation since I was thirteen. If it hadn't been for my mom recognizing my potential and putting her foot down, I'd probably be down with them right now. But she had, and I was not, thank God. Now if I could just get these cops to believe me.

An hour went by, and I found myself nodding my head numbly for the millionth time. At this point, I didn't even know what question O'Malley was asking. The detectives had been drilling me with questions then leaving the room abruptly, during which time I would sweat with anxiety, only to return and drill me with more question. My brain was frazzled. I couldn't make sense of this entire situation.

"So, are your brothers the ones who gave you the heroin, or did you and your buddies get it all by yourselves?" This O'Malley son of a bitch was getting on my nerves even more than Sergeant Lanier, that black bastard.

I threw my hands up in exasperation. "I don't know anything 'bout no fucking heroin from my brothers or any fucking body else, a'ight?" My college vocabulary had gone to visit its cousin in the projects. Stringing my words together properly and using grammatically correct English just wasn't on my list of priorities anymore. "I done told you the drugs ain't mine."

"Okay, then, whose are they?" O'Malley asked.

"I'on't know."

"Yes, you do. Now, did your brothers give them to you? If so, maybe we can arrange for you to go home."

"How many times I gotta tell you? I don't know nothing about no dope, and my brothers ain't give me shit."

I knew what was going on here. They were trying to trip me up. I didn't have to be a rocket scientist to know the oldest trick in the book. I was sure he thought if he asked me the same thing over and over in different ways, it would wear me down. This technique had extracted many confessions from both the innocent and the guilty. I was sticking with my story, though, no matter how many times he asked. Tired, hungry, even if I had to take a piss, my answer would remain the same. My only question was, how many more times was I going to have to repeat my answer, and how many people would I have to repeat it to before someone actually believed me and let me go home?

# *Krush*

## 10

I guess the Staten Island police didn't pay their gas bills, because it was cold as shit in that little room they had me locked up in while I waited for someone to come tell me what the fuck was going on. I pulled my hoodie over my head and laid my arms on the table as a pillow, but before I could put my head down and get comfortable, I heard the door open. Two cops walked in and sat down.

"Hey, Kirby, my name's Detective Cutter, and this is my partner, Detective O'Malley. Can we get you a soda?"

"Man, fuck you and fuck a soda, my name is Krush. When the fuck do I get my phone call?" I asked as I sat back in my chair and crossed my arms over my chest. It was all an act. I was scared as fuck, but I wasn't gonna let these motherfuckers see me sweat.

"You can make a call in a few minutes, right after we have a little chat," Cutter said all nice and shit.

"What the fuck y'all want?" I huffed.

"We wanna know whose dope that was in the car," the fat cop snapped.

I shook my head. "I don't know, but it ain't mine."

"Look, Krush, Officer Blake already told us that you admitted to the pot. From where I stand, it seems like you're a standup guy. So, why play games? You might as well cop to the heroin and get it over with. Save us all a lot of time. That way we can go to the ADA and tell him you cooperated."

I leaned back in my chair again. "Look, I ain't copping to shit!" I regretted ever having opened my mouth about the weed being mine. Shit, I thought I was doing the right thing at the time, but who would have ever thought it would land me in this kind of trouble? If I had known that, I would have kept my big fucking mouth shut.

"You wanna get your frat brothers all caught up in your mess?" Detective Cutter asked. "Aren't you guys supposed to be tight, like real brothers?"

"We are brothers, and they're not caught in my mess, 'cause I ain't got shit to do with it!"

Who was this Cutter guy kidding? I had no doubt he'd been to each and every one of our interrogation rooms, trying to get us to talk. He'd probably fed the other guys the same bogus line about brothers. I hoped like hell they saw through his bullshit like I did.

He kept pushing. "Well, if it wasn't yours, then whose is it?

"I can't tell you what I don't know." I was trying to remain calm, but these motherfuckers were stressing me the fuck out. If they were getting to me like this, I wondered what they were doing to the other bros. Although Lang had a tendency to run his fucking mouth like he already had a law degree, I was pretty sure that he and Tony could maintain until Langston's pops got here and got us out. It was Kwesi who I was afraid would screw it up for everybody. I didn't know what crazy-ass Sergeant Lanier had said to him on the way over, but Kwesi looked petrified when I saw them bringing him inside. I wanted to tell him to stay strong and keep his mouth shut, but he never even raised his head to acknowledge me. Damn, I sure could've used a blunt right about now.

"Damn it, I swear to God, if you boys don't get to talking—" O'Malley slammed his fist on the table, unable to hide his frustration.

"You'll what?" I asked, fighting like hell to keep from grinning. His outburst told me he wasn't getting anywhere in this interrogation process, not only with me, but with the fellas either.

"I'll throw all your asses in Rikers, and then we'll see how tough you are," he threatened. "Sooner or later, one of you is gonna crack and wanna go home to Mama, and that's the one who's gonna get the deal." He leaned in until we were almost nose to nose. "And if not, all of you are going to prison for a long time."

When I swallowed, it felt like I was trying to force a whole boiled egg down my throat. I'd been trying not to lose my cool in front of these guys, but I didn't want to show them fear either. It sure was getting hard trying to hide it.

"Stay silent all you want," O'Malley said, "but somebody will talk first, and it's the one who talks first who's going to get out of here. Just remember that, kid." On that note, he stood and headed out the door. He was probably on his way to the next interrogation room to try to get the next fella to talk.

Hopefully, none of them would say a word.

# *Kwesi*

## 11

Never in my wildest dreams had I expected to ever be arrested for drugs. Guilty or not, with something like this on my record, getting accepted into medical school would be no more than a pipe dream. Even worse, what would my family think about the humiliation and embarrassment I was bringing to them? My mother and father had worked so hard to bring us all to this great country, and they wanted nothing more than for me and my brothers and sister to succeed. I could already see the shame on my father's face, and I had not even called him.

The two detectives that had come by earlier walked into the room again. They were nice men and had treated me kindly despite my accident.

"You all cleaned up?" Detective Cutter asked, taking a seat and placing a McDonald's double cheeseburger, fries, and a soda in front of me.

"Yes. Thank you very much for the sweatpants. That was very embarrassing."

"Eat up before it gets cold. These things happen. You're a college student, not a gangbanger," Detective O'Malley replied, taking a seat next to his partner. "Hell, if I was arrested for something I didn't do, I'd probably piss myself too."

I lowered my head in shame. "May I ask you gentlemen a favor, please?"

"Well, that depends on what it is, but we'll see what we can do," Detective O'Malley replied.

"Please, please, do not tell my friends that I relieved myself in such an embarrassing manner. I try to conduct myself around them with dignity and pride."

"Sure, sure," O'Malley replied kindly. "We weren't planning on telling anyone, and as long as you help us, we will definitely help you."

"Thank you," I said humbly. "What do you want from me, Detective?"

When the police took us into custody and were about to separate us, Langston announced that we should not talk to the police until his father arrived. But that was before I met Detectives O'Malley and Cutter. I was sure once Langston found out that they were trying to help us, he would not mind me explaining things.

"I wanna know the truth about those drugs and which one of your buddies they belong to. Because I'm sure they don't belong to you," Cutter said.

"I do not know, Detective. And to be honest with you, I do not think any of my friends would do this."

"You can stop trying to protect them, because when it boils down to it, if you think they are going to protect you, then you are sadly mistaken. I've seen it a million times."

He sounded sincere, but I had to disagree with his assessment of my frat brothers. "They are my friends. They are honest. You'll see. We do not advocate drugs. This is all one big mistake, and things will get figured out."

"They don't advocate drugs, huh? So, why did your friend Krush admit to the pot Officer Blake found in the car?"

He was making a point I could not refute, and what made it worse was that he began laughing like I'd just told a joke.

"I like you, Kwesi, but you really are naïve." He laughed for a while more before he managed to get himself under control. Then, he appeared deadly serious. "That heroin did not magically appear in the trunk of that car. Someone put it there, and you need to be honest with yourself. If you didn't put it there, who did?"

"I don't know."

"Then whoever did is playing you, because if you guys were such brothers, he would just come out and admit it so you wouldn't get in trouble. Isn't that what you would do?"

Once again, he was making a valid point, but where did that leave me? Here, stuck in jail, that's where. I didn't want to believe that Langston, Tony, or Krush would tell lies to save themselves; lies that would land me behind bars for God knows how long. My family would be so disgraced. I'd have nothing.

However, I was not going to give up on my friends, my brothers. "But there has to be another explanation," I said hopefully.

He rolled his eyes and sucked his teeth. "Forget it." He shooed his hand. "I can see right now you are going to be the first one they throw under the bus. I mean, technically, you're not one of them, because you're African and they're American. They are going to stick up for each other first. So, guess who, more than likely, is going to end up doing the time for everybody?" He walked over to me and pointed hard against my chest with each word he spoke. "You are, buddy. And it will be a damn shame because, like I said before, I like you."

The more I sat there and listened to Officer O'Malley, the more I began to question my friendship with my frat brothers, who I'd only known a little under four years. Were they really as loyal and steadfast as I'd convinced myself they were? After all, we'd never been in such dire straits before, so I'd never had to test their commitment. What if Detective O'Malley was right and they would react to the pressure being put upon them? Would my being African suddenly separate me from them, giving them a reason to accuse me? I had no way of knowing for sure. Maybe, just maybe, it was time to start thinking about myself.

# *James*

## 12

"Okay, what's so important that you dragged me down here?" I walked into the small corridor of rooms that peered into the interrogation rooms through one-way glass, stopping in front of Assistant District Attorney David Wilkins.

"Him." David pointed toward a young black man on the other side of the glass, sitting at a table and looking lost. I walked closer to the glass and studied the boy. He didn't look like much to me, but Dave Wilkins wasn't the type to call me down from the Staten Island DA's office, where I was the assistant district attorney in charge of all criminal cases, over something trivial.

"He doesn't look like a serial killer. What's he here for? Murder?"

"No, drugs," Dave said. "Highway patrol picked him and his three buddies up on the expressway with two kilos of heroin."

"That's some serious weight for a kid his age. Is he talking?"

"Not yet, but he's already pissed himself he's so scared. A day or two in Rikers and he'll crack like an egg," Detective Roger O'Malley replied. O'Malley was a lazy bastard about a year from his retirement. I'd always thought of him as a racist, although he was smart enough to keep his worst thoughts to himself when I was around. He knew I'd beat his ass if he ever pulled that bullshit on me.

I turned back to ADA Wilkins. "Okay, Dave, they found a couple keys of dope in the car of four kids. What's the big deal? This sounds like a no-brainer to me. You could have handled this yourself. Why am I here?"

"I thought it was a no-brainer too, until I found out one of the suspects is the son of Bradley Hudson," Wilkins replied, staring at me as he waited for my reaction to the name.

I could barely believe my ears. "What did you just say?"

"You heard me. One of the suspects is the son of Bradley Hudson." David smiled as if he'd given me a gift. "So, I think that's a good enough reason, don't you?"

"Hell fucking yeah," I said, turning back to the glass with enthusiasm. "It's like my birthday and Christmas all wrapped up into one. So, this kid's the weak link?"

"Pretty much," Dave replied.

"Okay, we have to move fast, 'cause we're not going to be up against some local yahoos from the island. Tell me everything you got on this kid."

O'Malley glanced at a file. "His name's Kwesi Adomako. His parents are college professors at Queens College and SUNY Stony Brook here on work visas. He, along with the other three, attends Howard University."

"So, whose dope is it?"

"We don't know. O'Malley and Cutter don't think it's this kid's, though."

"He's too weak," Cutter said.

"O'Malley, get this kid down to central booking ASAP. I want him in the system and in Rikers before we move the other three out of the building."

O'Malley got up and headed to the door.

"You did good, Dave, really good, and I ain't gonna forget it," I said.

"That's exactly what I was counting on, James," Dave replied with a smile.

David was a terrific prosecutor, probably second only to me in our office, but he had been relegated to the 121st Precinct as a case officer because of questionable relationships with some of the staff. That was no longer tolerated in this "Me Too" era by our liberal female boss who happened to be the district attorney. Dave was looking for a way out, and he knew currying favor by bringing me a case like this might just do it.

"So, what next?" Dave asked.

"I need you to ride over to the courthouse and make sure this kid gets moved through the system fast. Make sure the judge gives him a high bail. I don't want him on the street anytime soon," I explained.

"Piece of cake." Dave sounded confident.

"You sure about this?" Cutter asked. "They're just kids, and this kid especially isn't going to last very long in the system."

I looked through the window at the kid and O'Malley, who had gone back in there. I looked back at Cutter, who was tall and slim, wearing a dusty blue suit. It kind of reminded me of something one of the cops would wear on the old *Barney Miller* sitcom. "Well, then thank God he's not one of our kids."

"Damn, that's cold," Cutter said.

"No, that's life," I replied. "Oh, and Dave, on your way over to the courthouse, make a few off-the-record calls to the press and local networks. Make sure they know Bradley Hudson's son has been arrested for possession with the intent to distribute. Also let them know that it's one of the largest drug seizures in Staten Island history."

"But it's not."

"Well, I guess they'll have to print a redaction at some point." I laughed, and after a brief pause, Dave and Cutter joined in.

"Man, you really are a cold piece of work," Cutter said.

"Yeah, especially when I'm motivated," I whispered.

David slipped out the door while Cutter and I moved down the corridor to the next interrogation viewing room. I stared at the light-skinned young man handcuffed to the table in the adjoining interrogation room. If I didn't know better, I would have sworn he was staring back at me. "That's him, isn't it? That's Hudson's kid."

"Yep. How'd you know?"

"He looks just like his old man thirty years ago," I told him. "Anyone talk to him yet?'

"No, he lawyered up the minute we walked in the room."

"Smart kid." I headed for the exit.

"Where you going?" Cutter asked.

"I'm going to meet the son of the most famous black lawyer in the world and tell him he's going to jail for twenty years," I replied smugly. "Then I'm going to wait for his father to show up, and I'll tell him the same damn thing."

# *Langston*

## 13

I'd been sitting in that cramped-up, musty-ass room, staring at the one-way glass ever since we'd arrived at the police station. They'd taken my iPhone and my Apple watch, so I had no perception of time, but I knew it was no longer minutes. It had been at least a few hours. Once I told them I wanted my lawyer, no one had even come in the room to see if I was still breathing. So, I sat there anxiously, my knees bouncing up and down as I wondered when the hell my father would arrive and get me out of this mess. I didn't understand why the hell he wasn't there already.

I sure as hell hoped my sister Desiree believed me when I was able to make that quick call to her; otherwise, we were screwed. If the cops hadn't taken my phone, which contained all my contacts, I would have called my father directly. Like an idiot, though, I didn't have my family's numbers memorized. Desiree's was the only one I could dial from memory, so she was my only hope at the moment.

*Stay strong, Lang, The calvary is on the way. Stop being paranoid,* I told myself just as the door to the interrogation room opened. The sudden motion scared the shit out of me, but I tried to shake it off.

"Langston Hudson." A tall, well-built black man entered the room and announced my name with authority. He was wearing a much better suit than the two detectives I'd seen earlier, so I assumed he was their superior. I'd been hoping someone would eventually come and tell me what the hell was going on; I guessed that someone was him. I watched without saying a word as he crossed the room and sat down in a chair a couple feet away from me.

I nodded, sitting eagerly on the edge of my seat, although I still wasn't answering a damn question without my lawyer present. To my surprise, he wasn't talking either. He just sat there with a frown on his face, not even looking directly at me. After a few seconds, he came to life—not his body, but his eyes. He bent forward and rested his arms on his knees, hands clasped in front of him.

"I just wanted to introduce myself. My name is James Brown. I'm the assistant district attorney in charge of your case."

I couldn't help it; I laughed. I think it's just because I was so nervous. "Seriously, your name is James Brown? Do you sing and dance?" Then did my best James Brown impression. "Jump back and kiss myself! Heeeey!" I thought that was so funny, despite my current situation, that I was damn near crying—until I looked up and saw his agitated face.

"I see you have your father's sense of humor," he said. That shut me up real quick.

"So, you know my father?" I wiped my hand down my face nervously as ADA Brown jotted something in his notebook.

"Yes, we've met." He exhaled loudly. "I suppose you're going to tell me that the drugs aren't yours."

Shit, of course I was going to tell him they weren't mine—because they weren't. I didn't know how the hell those drugs got in my car. Unfortunately, no one in this police station was likely to believe that. Typical cops, they just wanted someone to pin the crime on so they could call it a win. That's why I was planning to stay quiet until my father showed up to help me out of this mess.

"No," I answered. "I'm not going to tell you anything. I'm simply going to ask for my right to counsel, just like I've been asking since I got here. I refuse to speak without my attorney present."

"Yep, you're your father's son all right." ADA Brown sat back in his chair. "But for the record, I wasn't asking you a question, young man. I was making a statement. Just like I'm about to make one now." He looked directly at me for the first time. "You're going to jail, and it's going to be my pleasure to put you there, because I hate drugs."

"They're not mine!" I snapped at him.

The door opened, and I was a little fearful I was about to get a beat down from the fat white detective who walked in.

"Kid's lawyer's here," he said.

"Finally," I stood with a sigh. Needless to say, I was more than ready to go home.

"Don't get too excited. You're not going anywhere," ADA Brown said forcefully. He then turned to the detective. "By all means, show him in, Detective."

# Kwesi

## 14

"Mister uh, Ad . . . Adam . . . Adamko?"

I stared at the man sitting across the table. "Ado*mako*," I corrected him.

"Oh, sorry. Mr. Adomako, I'm Glenn Morris, and I'll be representing you this afternoon when you go before the judge," the man said.

I was a bit confused by the presence of this scrawny white man who looked barely older than me. I'd known Langston for almost four years, and as far as I could recall, he'd never mentioned a white man working at his father's firm. The Hudsons prided themselves on being a black-owned, black-empowering law firm. Based on the cheap suit and the stained tie this man wore, I couldn't imagine Langston's father hiring him even if he were black. Something was very wrong.

"Are you with the Hudson firm?" I asked.

"Huh? Who? No, I'm with legal aid," he said with no further explanation. "Now, you say you don't know anything about the drugs found in the back of the car. Is that correct?"

"Yes, that's correct. I had no knowledge of it. I was just as surprised as everyone else when the police took it out," I said. "I explained that to the officers, and I'm sure my friends did as well."

I was confused about what was happening. I hadn't seen Lang, Tony, or Krush since being brought into the police station. I had been expecting Langston's father or brother to show up and get us out of there, but it had been hours. Now, this frantic stranger was in front of me, asking me questions that I'd already answered.

"Well, what's going to happen is you're going to be brought before the judge, and when he asks how you'd like to plead, then you simply say, 'Not guilty.' Understand?"

"Yes, I understand." I tried not to be offended by his tone. He was speaking to me as if I were a fifth grader about to be sent to the principal's office. I wanted to tell him that I was on the dean's list and a member of Phi Beta Kappa, along with several other academic organizations, in addition to pursuing a double major in biochemistry and physics. I was not dumb by a long shot.

"Where are my friends? Will you be representing them as well?" I asked.

"No, I will only be representing you," he said. "Your friends have their own representation."

"What?" I was now even more confused. Lang had assured all of us that he would make sure we were taken care of and that we would be fine as long as we stuck together. When did the plan change, and where did it leave me? I wondered if they had somehow been released and I hadn't.

"Don't worry about them," the lawyer said as if reading my mind. "Right now, you need to focus on yourself. Now, you've never been in any kind of trouble, so I'm thinking that the judge will be lenient on you. I don't see the district attorney being a problem."

There was a tap at the door, and he stood up. "Okay, I'll see you when we get in court."

"But, wait! I need to speak with my friends and—"

"That's not possible right now. The only thing you need to be worried about is telling the judge that you're not guilty so we can get you out of here." Glenn gathered the papers from the table and tossed them into his briefcase. Before I could say anything else, he was out the door.

I sat alone again in the holding room, just as I'd been doing for most of the past few hours. My mind was racing, and my stomach was in knots. I wondered if I should have just called my parents, instead of depending on Langston to help me. Why, all of a sudden, was I being represented by a legal aid attorney? I couldn't understand why I was even being brought before a judge. I had told the detectives over and over that I had no idea who the drugs belonged to or how they'd gotten into the trunk of the car. Despite their pressuring me to blame one of my boys, I'd refused. I remained loyal to all three of them, but now, I was wondering if they'd done the same thing for me.

About a half hour later, I was escorted into a small courtroom and led to the defense table, where Glenn was waiting for me. He gave me a reassuring nod, but it did nothing to ease the quivering in my stomach. I glanced over at the attorney sitting across the aisle. He looked stern and stoic as we waited for my case to be called.

"Kwesi Adomako." The court reporter read from the docket.

Glenn motioned for me to stand, and I did. My eyes widened and my jaw dropped as the stocky, older woman began reading off the charges like they were menu items at a fast food restaurant.

"Possession of a controlled substance, distribution of narcotics, intent to distribute narcotics . . ." The list went on and on. I couldn't believe how a simple ride home with my fraternity brothers had led to me being arrested and brought up on criminal charges. I felt like I was in the middle of a nightmare and couldn't wake up.

"Mr. Adomako, how would you like to plead?" the judge, a silver-haired white woman asked.

Glenn looked over at me.

"Not guilty," I said, my nervousness causing my voice to crack.

"Bail?" the judge asked the other attorney.

"Your Honor, these are very serious charges, and we're asking that there be no bail and the defendant be remanded. Mr. Adomako had a large amount of heroin in his possession, and we believe this crime is connected to a major drug ring," the district attorney told her.

"What?" I squeaked.

Glenn touched my arm and shook his head at me, then said, "Your Honor, my client is a college student with no criminal record. The drugs weren't even in his possession."

"They were found in the car that he was traveling in, Your Honor," the district attorney responded. Before Glenn could react, he added, "In addition, Mr. Adomako's passport shows that he has made several international trips over the past few months."

I looked at Glenn and rattled off an explanation. "I was visiting my father's family in Ghana and interviewing for internships."

"Shhhh." Glenn put a finger to his lips then addressed the court. "Your Honor, this is ridiculous."

"Bail is set at one million dollars," the judge said quickly without giving me a second look.

"A million dollars?" I began to feel faint.

"I'll speak with the DA and see if I can get him to request that it be lowered. But I'm telling you right now—if you know who that dope belongs to, you may wanna say something, because that may be the only way you're gonna get out of here." Glenn sighed like he was dismissing my concerns as trivial. My freedom was being taken from me, and the man appointed to represent me sounded bored. How the hell had this happened to me?

# Desiree

## 15

It took almost two hours for me to drive from Jerri's house in the Bronx to the 121st Precinct in Staten Island, where Langston had been arrested. I was still totally in the dark because he hadn't given me much information beyond saying he was in trouble and needed my help. I'd made a few calls and tried to pull a few strings on my way over to find out what he'd been charged with, but being out of law school only one year, I didn't have the contacts or the resources that my father, or even my brother Lamont, had. I was tempted to call Cathy, the firm's office manager/keeper of my father's secrets, but I was sure the moment I mentioned Langston's name, she'd be whispering in my father's ear. For a second, I also thought about calling my father directly, but decided against it. If I knew my goody-two-shoes brother, this was probably an arrest for something stupid like a suspended license or a DWI, but to my father, the seriousness of the offense wouldn't matter. He didn't tolerate any kind of screw-ups from his kids.

"I'm looking for my client, Langston Hudson," I said to the desk sergeant when I walked into the precinct. The young white woman dressed in a blue police uniform peered at me over the top of the thick black glasses she wore.

"Hudson?" she repeated and then began typing something into the computer in front of her.

"Yes, ma'am," I replied politely.

A few seconds later, she glanced back up at me and asked, "And you are?"

"I'm his attorney."

She looked unimpressed. "I'll let the detectives know that you're here. You can wait over there." She pointed to the row of hard plastic chairs lined against the wall near the door.

*Detectives?* I was starting to think this might be a little more serious than a DWI. My phone vibrated in my purse, so I glanced at the Apple Watch I wore on my arm. Seeing Jerri's name on the screen, I sent it to voicemail. *Not now, Jerri, not now.*

"What exactly is he being charged with?" I asked the desk sergeant.

She stopped typing and looked at me. I detected a bit of annoyance from her that I'd interrupted her bookkeeping or whatever.

"I'm sure Detective O'Malley will explain everything to you when he comes out, Miss," she responded. "Do you have some form of ID?"

I reached into my purse and handed her my license and credentials. She barely glanced at them before she handed them back without a word. I walked over to the chairs and took a seat. By the time I got comfortable, my phone was vibrating again, and I had to send it to voicemail again. Why did she not understand that I worked for a living?

After a few minutes, a heavyset white man in a suit walked over and introduced himself. "Ms. Hudson, I'm Detective O'Malley. You can come with me." He knew my name. I guess the sergeant at the desk had read my credentials after all.

He led me down a corridor to a closed door, where he raised his hand for me to wait while he entered the room. A minute later he came out and told me, "You can go in now."

Inside, I found my brother seated at a table with a bald black man in his fifties who did not look happy to see me. Langston, on the other hand, had never looked happier.

"Des!" he said, and I swear I could see the tension leaving his shoulders.

I looked to the man who sat across the table from my brother. "Why are you talking to my client? I'm sure he invoked."

I glanced over at Langston. The worried look on his face let me know that what I originally thought was a simple misdemeanor had to be much more serious. Fortunately, my brother and I grew up with parents in the legal profession. One thing we learned early on was our rights, and what *not* to do if we ever found ourselves in trouble. I was confident that whatever the detectives thought they would get from my brother, they wouldn't. He knew better than to say anything to them.

"Who are you?" the black man asked.

"I'm his attorney," I said forcefully, wishing my dad could see me now. "And I want to know exactly what my client is being charged with, Detective."

"I'm not a detective. I'm Assistant District Attorney Brown, and your client is being charged with possession of a controlled substance with the intent to distribute. He had two kilos of black tar heroin in his car."

"He had *what*?" I snapped, placing my hand on the wall for stability. *Shit*. I was sure the ADA had picked up on my moment of weakness. Suddenly, I knew I was in way over my head. What I really wanted to do was scream at my brother, "What the fuck is wrong with you?"

"It's not mine, Des. I swear to God it's not mine," Langston blurted out.

"Then whose is it?" the ADA asked calmly.

"Shut up, Langston!" Being in the interrogation room of the police precinct was not my forte, but this guy must have thought it was amateur hour. Caught off guard or not, I was still a Hudson, and we knew our shit. I had to get this situation under control in a hurry.

"I'd like to speak with my client," I said.

"Feel free," ADA Brown replied.

I tilted my head to the side but then quickly positioned it upright, straightening my shoulders to display strength and confidence. I was not about to go into sista-girl mode. Too many people in law enforcement already looked at black women in the legal profession as no more than bitter chicks with bad attitudes, so I was always conscious of how I presented myself. I'd worked too damn hard for people to mistake me for Cookie Lyon, when my aim was to be Olivia Pope.

"Privately," I said to both men.

I turned my attention to Langston.

"We can leave," the ADA said, eyeballing the detective, who stood behind me, to determine whether he was in agreement.

"Yeah, then you two can have all the privacy you'd like," the detective said.

"Yeah, right. I want the light turned on in that integration room." I nodded toward the two-way mirror that was taking up the wall behind the table. My asking for privacy was kind of a joke anyway. Langston knew the drill. Whether the officers were inside the room with us or outside of the room drinking coffee and eating donuts, big brother would be watching—and listening—whether they were supposed to or not. We would only be discussing so much while we were in that building, let alone that interrogation room.

"We won't be far," the ADA said as they walked out.

"Des, those aren't my drugs. I swear to God," Langston said when they were gone.

"First of all, are you okay?" I asked. As much as I hated seeing him there, I was glad that he was still alive and his name hadn't become a hashtag like so many other young black men who'd ended up shot and killed as a result of routine traffic stops.

"I'm fine." He nodded. "Where's Dad? Where's Lamont?"

"I didn't call them. I thought you called me because you didn't want them to know."

He dropped his head. "No! Hell no! We're going to need Dad to get us all off."

"What do you mean *all*? Are there other people involved?" I asked, pulling the chair out and sitting down. I made sure he noticed my quick glance toward the mirror behind him, reminding him of the eyes and ears that were on us before he started speaking.

He gave me a slight nod to indicate that he understood, and then he gave me a brief overview of how he and his frat brothers had ended up here.

"Damn it, Langston!" I said when he got to the part about the bricks found in his trunk.

"I swear I didn't know it was back there. You know me, Des. I don't get down like that." He shook his head, looking more like a preppy teenage nerd who should be headed to the library, not a twenty-year-old man who had just been arrested for drug possession. As bad as the circumstances seemed, there had to be some explanation that didn't include Langston's guilt. My brother was more into books than booze and had been on the dean's list consistently since his freshman year. This wasn't him at all.

"I know you don't. This is some bullshit. I'm gonna go to your arraignment and get you bail. Then we go home and tell Dad about this," I said.

"Des, you can't get just me out of here. You have to get all of us out," Langston said.

"What?" I frowned.

"I'm not gonna leave my boys. If I go, we all go," he explained. "We're in this together."

I stared at him, proud of him for his loyalty, but not exactly pleased that he was making my job a hell of a lot harder. "Langston, I know you and your boys are tight, but—"

"Naw, Des. You help one, then you help us all." He sat back and shrugged.

I exhaled loudly, knowing he was not going to change his mind. Standing, I said, "Let me go see what the deal is. You hold tight."

"Does it look like I'm going somewhere?" He tilted his head to the side with a smirk.

"The last thing you need to be giving me is a smart-ass comment," I warned, opening the door and stepping outside into the hallway. I looked from one end to the other, searching for the detective or the ADA. I knew they hadn't gone far.

My phone began ringing. I peeked at my watch and ignored Jerri's call again.

"Finished talking with your client?" ADA Brown strolled over to me. He was now with two more uniformed officers.

"I have. He told me what happened. Listen, I'm not trying to bullshit you by any means, but whatever you found in the back of that car did not belong to him. I can assure you of that. These are four educated young black men, all attending one of the most prestigious colleges in the nation, and they have bright futures ahead of them. Let's come up with a reasonable bail until we can figure this all out," I suggested. "I'm sure there is something we can work out."

"I don't think you're bullshitting me, and I understand everything you're telling me. Trust me, we've pulled the records of all the young men," he said.

"So, what's the problem?" I asked.

ADA Brown leaned his arm against the wall and looked me in the eye. "We're not talking about a simple marijuana charge, Miss Hudson. We're talking about possession with intent to distribute. You want your client out of there, then tell him to tell me which one of his buddies that dope belongs to, because until we find out, the only place any one of them is going is Rikers."

This was not good. On one side, I had a brother who was determined to save his friends; on the other side, I was facing an ADA who was determined to make my brother rat out one of his friends—and neither one looked willing to budge. For a moment, I felt frozen, standing there speechless as I stared at the ADA with the cocky smirk on his face. What the hell was I going to do to convince either one of them?

"Ms. Hudson?" he said when I failed to speak up.

"Yes?"

"When you finish with your client, we're taking him down to central booking to be processed."

I slowly took a step back, then returned to the interrogation room. Langston gave me a look of anticipation. When I shook my head at him, his body deflated.

"Langston, listen to me. This isn't the time for you to prove your loyalty to your friends, your fraternity, or anything else. You've heard Daddy say time and time again that self-preservation is the first law of nature, and this is one of those situations where you need to look out for self," I explained, hoping he would hear me. "That's the only way you're gonna have a chance in hell of getting out of here today."

"But the drugs don't belong to me," he said, his voice full of anger and frustration.

"I know that; you know that; shit, even the cops know that, I think. But they belong to somebody." I walked over and touched his shoulder, leaning down and whispering, "Langston, whose are they?"

Langston pulled away from me, shaking his head. "I swear, I don't know."

# *Lamont*

## 16

"Lamont Hudson for Felicia Cooper." I announced myself as I entered the reception area of Greene, Parker, and Cooper. The meeting at Klein's office had taken much less time than I expected, and I was actually early for my lunch appointment at the boutique law firm.

"I'll let her know you're here, Mr. Hudson. Can I get you some water or coffee while you wait?" The cute little Latin receptionist directed me to the waiting area.

"No, thank you." I was tempted to get my flirt on, but I was there on a more important mission, and I couldn't afford to get sidetracked.

I had taken a seat on the Italian leather sofa and was admiring the impressive skyline views when I heard the click-clacking of high heels, and then my name being called.

"Mr. Hudson."

I looked up to see some of the finest, shapeliest long legs I'd seen in a long time. Attached to those legs was Felicia Cooper, the beautiful light-eyed, biracial senior partner I was there to meet. Felicia was one of those smart, conservative sisters who was about her business but was so afraid to let down her hair that she came across as arrogant and bitter. But she always looked damn good, no matter how bad her attitude could be.

"Good morning, Ms. Cooper," I said.

"Mr. Hudson, why don't you come on back." Her footsteps clacked against the marble floor as she led me down the corridor into a large corner office. She closed the door behind us and motioned toward the large chairs in front of her mahogany desk. "Please, have a seat."

"Thank you." I waited for her to walk around her desk and sit first. And yes, I was being polite, but I was also checking out her impressive, J Lo–looking ass that could not be hidden by her business-appropriate skirt. Once she took her seat, I sat down, glancing around the room at her office, taking note of the educational accomplishments and various accolades from other organizations and civic leagues hanging on the walls. I was more impressed by her superhero figurine collection and martial arts trophies, along with the 90-inch television hanging on her wall. The damn thing was bigger than the one I had in my media room at my home. Her office would put even some of the best man caves to shame.

After a few moments of silence, I said, "I take it you're a comic book fan?"

"Yes, but I'm more of a super heroine fan. I like strong women. They motivate me," she said in a voice that suddenly made me imagine her as someone's dominatrix.

"I like a strong woman myself. They motivate me as well," I replied with a smile, which she returned. If I wasn't mistaken, we shared a moment, although it didn't last long. She opened the manila folder sitting in front of her and took out a piece of paper.

"I have to admit, I'm surprised. I didn't think you'd take me up on my offer," she said. It would appear she was getting right down to business.

Felicia and I had met about two years ago in a courtroom where I, quite honestly, whipped her ass. She didn't like that, but was impressed by my skills nonetheless, so two days later, she called and offered me a job. I declined, of course, but she'd been pursuing me ever since. We'd bumped into each other a few nights ago at a legal function, and she'd decided that she had to have me, so here we were.

"Well, I haven't decided yet, but I also don't see any harm in taking a meeting and hearing you out."

"You call it a meeting. I like to think of it as an interview." She stared at me as if we were playing poker and she was looking for tells.

"I guess that all depends on who's interviewing who?" I cracked a slight smile, leaning back comfortably in my chair.

"You're an interesting man, Mr. Hudson." She put down the paper, stood up, and slipped her blazer off her shoulders, placing it on the back of the chair. Underneath, she wore a silk camisole, and her lace bra was noticeable. Her eyes met mine, and she gave me a slight smile. "I've often wondered why you've stayed in your father's shadow for so long."

I stared at her intensely as I answered. "You're only in someone's shadow if you don't know your own self-worth, Ms. Cooper. My father's a great lawyer, and so am I, as you well know. He has his strengths, and so do I. Why should we compete with each other, when together we are damn near invincible?"

I think my reply shocked her a little bit. As good as she looked, she probably wasn't used to a man who could contain himself once she'd bared those beautiful, smooth shoulders.

"I can see you're the ultimate team player," she said, not giving up on her pitch just yet. "You definitely have a lot to offer that would be beneficial to me, and I have a lot to offer as well. I'm a strong believer in reciprocity."

She picked up the folder again, then walked to the front of the desk and leaned against it. Her shapely legs crossed at the ankles, and my gaze made its way up her incredible body. She was athletic and toned. I had no doubt she hit the gym on the regular.

"I'm really big on giving and receiving as well. Don't you feel that's important, Ms. Cooper?" I said suggestively as I let my gaze settle around her midsection, where I would have loved to bury my face.

"I do." She removed her glasses and asked, "So, what makes you feel as if you're qualified for the position I'm looking to fill?"

"You've seen my body of work, and I know that I not only have the qualifications needed, but I have the experience. If anything, I'm overqualified," I said with confidence. It might have come across as arrogant, but with a woman like Felicia, you don't back down if you want her to respect you as an equal.

"Well, Mr. Hudson, I would like to stress the importance of . . . flexibility in your job duties. Will that be a problem?" She placed the folder on the desk and then slid up so she was sitting on top of the desk. Her skirt slid up to reveal the sexy black garter that was holding up the sheer black stockings she wore. I allowed my eyes to linger there for a second before I looked back up into her eyes.

"No problem whatsoever, except you keep referring to this job as if it's a forgone conclusion that I'm taking it." I'm not sure if she realized I could see the rise and fall of her chest as she breathed. She could play it cool all she wanted, but I was getting a rise out of this sexy woman. "You have yet to put an offer on the table."

"Well then, Mr. Hudson, when you put it that way, I guess there is no reason to beat around the bush any longer." She raised her skirt all the way, showing off her freshly Brazilian-waxed kitty. "I'd like to officially offer you the position of fuck buddy with full benefits, but I must stress that you take it now, or I'll have to fill the job immediately with someone less qualified."

I admired the view for a second, enjoying the tension I created by making her wait for my answer. "You're rushing me, Ms. Cooper," I teased. "Under normal circumstances, I don't do anything under duress; however, I can see that you are in dire need of my expertise in this area. I accept your offer."

I swear I saw a ripple of anticipation pass over her body, and her thighs trembled ever so slightly. I leaned forward and lowered my head between Felicia's legs, running my tongue along her lips until I found her clit.

"Fuck! I knew you were the man for the job!" Felicia moaned, picking up the remote and turning on the TV so that the rest of her office wouldn't hear her moans.

I licked and sucked her clit until she couldn't take it anymore. She pushed me away after a very intense orgasm.

"Fuck me," she demanded, reaching for her purse to hand me a condom. "I've been waiting to feel you inside me for two years."

I dropped my pants and slipped on the condom. Felicia positioned herself over her desk, ass up. I couldn't wait to get up inside her—until I noticed the picture of my father on the television with the words *Breaking News* flashing beneath it. I stepped away from her, my eyes glued to the screen.

"What are you waiting for, Lamont? Put it in," Felicia snapped at me.

"Hold on a second." I reached for the remote lying on the desk and turned the volume up even higher.

"Are you serious?" She stood up, staring at me—not that I cared.

*"This just in: the youngest son of renowned attorney Bradley Hudson, best known for getting actor TJ Winter off for the murder of his wife and in-laws, was arrested today, along with three other men, in one of the largest drug seizures in Staten Island history."*

"Oh my God. Is that true, Lamont? Is that your brother?" Felicia came to stand next to me as we watched video of Langston being perp-walked out of a police precinct, handcuffed, for the world to see.

"Looks like him." I felt a giant knot developing in the pit of my stomach because I knew it was, in fact, my little brother. Then I felt my insides lurch, like I might throw up, when I saw my sister on the screen, standing to the side. Desiree was trying to stay in the shadows, but she couldn't hide from me. "Dammit!"

"Is there anything I can do?" Felicia asked.

"You can give me a rain check," I said, reaching for my pants to get my phone. I scrolled through my contacts and dialed.

"Hello," Desiree answered.

"What the fuck is going on? You and Langston are all over the news!" I shouted angrily.

"Oh God," she said. "I was just going to call you."

"Just going to call me? Our little brother just got perp-walked for all of New York to see. You should have called me when you first found out about this, Des! And you should have made them cover his hands to hide the handcuffs, and you should have made him wear his hoodie."

"I didn't think about that," she said. I could hear in her voice she was on the verge of hysteria, and I knew I needed to dial my anger back or she would lose it.

"I can imagine," I said calmly. "That's why you should have called me. Have you spoken to Dad?"

"No, I was hoping you would call him. He's already mad at me."

*He hasn't begun to be mad at you,* I thought as I stepped into my pants. Felicia zipped me up and buckled my belt.

"Okay, I'll deal with the old man, but you need to hustle down to the Staten Island Courthouse and slow things down until I get there."

"How do I do that?" she asked quietly.

I kept forgetting that she was only one year out of law school. Desiree had a good legal mind, but she was still green when it came to the inner workings of a criminal case. *Shit, a criminal case.* I couldn't believe I was even thinking those words in relation to my brother, the straight-laced college student. I had no idea what the details were, but this was a code red emergency, and Langston was going to need all the help he could get.

"Register with the clerk as Lang's counsel; then leave the courthouse until I get there. They can't arraign him without counsel being present. But whatever you do, Des, don't let him be arraigned. Okay? If you do, he'll get lost in the system for two days."

"Okay. Uh, Lamont?"

"Yeah, sis."

"Is Langston going to be all right?" she whispered.

"Langston is going to be fine. Me and Dad will figure this out. We always do." I said the words, but I wasn't quite sure I believed them myself.

# *Bradley*

## 17

I texted my driver to bring my car around to the front of the Manhattan Supreme Court the second I got off the phone with Lamont. My son was innocent. Langston might have been capable of many things, but distribution of drugs wasn't one of them. Of this, I was absolutely sure.

There was one thing I had to do before I left the courthouse and headed to Staten Island. It was something I had to do in person, face to face. Of course, I hated the idea of possibly missing Langston's arraignment, but Lamont was more than capable of handling it. Besides, the real lawyering wasn't going to begin until I found out who was prosecuting the case.

"Your Honor, my client had a non-disclosure agreement that forbade him from coming forward with any personal details observed while employed," Richard Engel, the counsel for the defense, stated as I walked into the courtroom of the Honorable Jacqueline Robinson. I'd known Richard for years. He wasn't a great lawyer, but he was a hell of a golfer.

"And your client's sexual harassment of my client makes that agreement null and void," argued Barry Engel, Richard's cousin and the attorney for the other side. I also knew Barry. He wasn't the greatest lawyer either, but he was an even better golfer.

These two particular lawyers had been in a continuous pissing contest ever since they split up their partnership five years ago and went out on their own. I guess Grandma had given more hugs and kisses to one of them. To this day, they acted like they were still competing for good ol' Granny's love.

Barry started, "Your Honor, according to Article—"

"Enough!" Judge Robinson slammed her gavel down.

"But, Your Honor." Richard insisted on getting the last word. "My client is a celebrity. This will have every money-grubbing sycophant filing a lawsuit."

"Especially the ones with three years of evidence," Barry said sarcastically.

"I don't know, gentlemen. This seems like a perfect time to settle," Judge Robinson said in a calm, authoritative voice. She made eye contact with me for the first time since I'd entered the back of her courtroom.

I watched as Barry and Richard shot daggers at one another. My courtroom sixth sense told me that Richard was considering her suggestion. Barry, on the other hand, wasn't convinced a settlement was the right way to go. Just when a flicker of hope sparkled in the Richards's eyes, Barry frowned at him and blew it out.

"We're not settling." Barry could hardly keep the wicked grin from lifting the corners of his mouth.

Richard just about sprang across the aisle, but he caught himself. He cleared his throat and then straightened his tie. I hate to admit it, but I would have loved to see that fight. He shook his head as if clearing it, then looked dead into Barry's eyes. "Then prepare for the first video to go viral on TMZ."

The judge slammed her gavel down again. "No, it won't, Mr. Engel. And if I hear that video is played at so much as a kid's birthday party, I'll lock you up for thirty days and hold you in contempt. Now, I'm sending this case to mediation."

Judge Robinson slammed her gavel down. With business before the court concluded, she locked her eyes on me. It was a cold, hard stare—one I was quite familiar with. She wasn't my biggest fan; but then again, I wasn't exactly in love with her either.

I walked down the center aisle toward the bench. Judge Robinson looked beautiful and youthful despite her fifty-plus years. She seemed ruffled by my appearance in her courtroom, but not intimidated. Unlike most people, she'd never been intimated by me. We continued our stare-down until court officers intercepted me at the little gate that separated her bench and the lawyers' tables from the public seating.

"Can I help you, Mr. Hudson?" she asked me in a no-nonsense tone.

I chuckled. "May I approach, Your Honor?"

She hesitated, releasing a sigh as she glanced at the small crowd of people sitting in her courtroom. Then, finally relenting, she waved me in. The court officer stepped aside, and I made my way to the judge's bench with him lurking behind me.

"Bradley," she whispered between clenched teeth while covering the microphone that sat in front of her. "What are you doing in my courtroom?"

"We need to talk, Jacqueline. It's important."

"You ever heard of a phone?" She could barely contain her disdain for me.

"Of course I have, but you take five days to return my calls. This isn't something that can wait," I replied sternly.

"You are a real piece of work, you know that? What do you want?" She sounded as irritated as she looked.

"Can we go to your chambers?"

"No, we can't go to my chambers. I have cases to try." She shot a quick glance at her court officer. "Now, what do you want to talk about?"

I stared at her for a brief moment, remembering in detail all the reasons we didn't get along. "Okay, I was trying to spare you the embarrassment of finding this out from a colleague, or even worse a reporter, but—"

"Finding out what?" she snapped.

"That your son has been arrested!" I didn't mean to say it so loud, but she had this way of getting under my skin that threw me off my game.

"Oh my God, what has Lamont done?"

"It's not Lamont. It's Langston," I told her.

Her mouth fell open, but my words had stunned her into silence.

# Langston

# 18

Although I had already been photographed and fingerprinted the moment I got out of the paddy wagon and was shuffled into central booking, I was still trying to digest the fact that we'd been arrested. All those reporters and television cameras waiting outside the police precinct when we walked out sure as hell hadn't helped things. My dad had always said that the media was like the opposite sex: you had to embrace them, and they'd fall in love with you. Well, maybe that was true, but so far, I was not feeling the love from those reporters.

Tony, Krush, and I were placed in a holding cell that housed about thirty men. Half of them stank of liquor and were probably there on DUIs, while the other half looked like drug addicts and dope boys. Krush seemed to get along just fine with them. I'd asked the cops several times about Kwesi, but none of them seemed to know where he was. I was worried about my little African buddy. I just hoped he was all right.

"What the fuck? Y'all just got here!" I heard someone yell as my frat brothers and I were summoned by a guard.

"That's what happens when you got a paid lawyer," Krush bragged, bopping over to the gate. "Come on, y'all. I'm ready to get the fuck up outta here," he said to me and Tony.

"Your friends over there hear anything about Kwesi?" I asked Krush as we were led out of the cell.

"Nah, ain't nobody seen him. He may have got his ass caught up in some ICE shit. You know how Trump's boys be fucking with immigrants," Krush said. The way he was talking, you'd think he'd been locked up a million times before, instead of being the suburban college boy he really was. Unfortunately, his comment about Kwesi's immigration status might have been accurate. The way things were going lately, there was a good possibility they were already working on Kwesi's deportation order.

We were escorted from the holding room to the courtroom and guided toward the defense podium, where Lamont and Desiree were standing.

"Wait. Why are your brother and sister here? Where is your dad?" Tony's voice cracked as he whispered to me. I peered back at the packed courtroom, looking for my dad, but he was nowhere to be found. *Jesus, I hope he's not mad.*

"Just chill. Don't worry. We're good. My brother ain't no joke either," I told him, but inside, I was more than a little nervous. I had to remind myself that the people standing next to me bore the Hudson name. We were a family of bad-ass attorneys, and I would one day be joining the ranks. In spite of my fear, I knew that my boys and I would be home in time for an episode of *Empire.*

"Lamont and Desiree Hudson for the defense, Your Honor," Lamont said.

"ADA David Wilkins for the State."

"Langston Hudson, Anthony Baker, and Kirby Wright," the silver-haired judge started in a stern voice after taking a moment to scrutinize each of us. "You are charged with felony possession of a controlled substance, possession with intent to distribute, as well as driving under the influence, in addition to use of a motor vehicle in the commission of a felony . . . the transportation of, and intent to distribute said controlled substance," the judge said all in one breath. "How do you plead?"

We all said, "Not guilty," at the same time.

"Bail recommendations, Mr. Wilkins?" the judge asked.

The ADA looked across the room. I turned to see if he was looking at anyone in particular. That's when I noticed a familiar face. It was ADA James Brown, that slick-ass Uncle Tom who'd been in the interrogation room. He was sitting quietly in the back of the courtroom, observing. Brown gave the other ADA a discreet nod, and Wilkins nodded back.

"Judge, we're going to ask that no bail be set at this time for any of these young men."

Lamont spoke up in protest. "Your Honor, my clients are three college students on the verge of graduating. They have no criminal records, not even a traffic citation outside of the ones received today. They pose no flight risk, and in all actuality, I should expect that they would be released on their own recognizance."

"Your Honor, this wasn't a simple traffic violation like Mr. Hudson is insinuating. The police confiscated several kilos of narcotics from the vehicle. In addition, Anthony Baker has ties to the Bloods street gang," the ADA said matter-of-factly, even though he was twisting the facts.

I was starting to get a bad feeling when the judge glanced at our crimson sweatshirts. I felt even worse when Tony started yelling, "This is some bullshit! I ain't in no gang! And I damn sure ain't no Blood!" Tony took a step toward the ADA.

"Control your clients," Judge Nichols warned Lamont.

"Let me handle this," Lamont whispered harshly to Tony.

"In addition, the young man who was in the vehicle with them during the stop has already been arraigned earlier and given key information." The ADA's announcement felt like a punch in the gut.

"What kind of information?" Lamont asked. That's exactly what I wanted to know. What the hell could Kwesi have said?

"What the fuck are they talking about? What did Kwesi say? This is crazy," Tony and Krush began mumbling simultaneously.

"Your clients, Mr. Hudson."

Lamont turned to me with gritted teeth, his eyes saying what his mouth wouldn't. "Will you keep these two quiet? They're not helping."

"Yo, Tony, chill. Let Lamont handle this," I said.

"Now, on the subject of bail," the judge said. "Bail is set at one million dollars."

"What the fuck!" Even I couldn't control myself this time. I stared at my brother, willing him to do something.

"Your Honor, this is a clear violation of my clients' Eighth Amendment rights!" Lamont interjected.

"Would you like me to take the DA's office recommendation, Mr. Hudson? I can always change it to no bail."

"But, Your Honor, they have no priors." Lamont made his tone more respectful as he tried to reason with the judge.

"No buts. Bail is set at one million dollars." Judge Nichols slammed the gavel down.

I wished I could slap the smirk off the ADA's face as he said, "Thank you, Your Honor."

"Can somebody tell me what the hell just happened?" Krush leaned over and asked. Tony, who always had something to say, just stood there in silent shock.

"You got bail. That's a start," Lamont said. "We're going to make a motion for a bail reduction hearing. We'll get it reduced."

"Easy for you to say," Krush spat, almost on the verge of tears. "You get to go home and sleep safe and sound in your bed and not have to worry about a four-hundred-pound Negro named Bubba crawling up in bed with you."

Desiree turned her attention to me. "Just hang in there, little brother." She looked to the others. "All of you just hang in there, please. I'm not sure what's going on. This is crazy, but I promise we are going to get you out of here. I promise. Daddy's on his way."

I could see the sincerity in Desiree's eyes and believed that she was going to do all that she could for us. For now, though, she could only offer encouragement as we were led back to the lockup.